Totally Bound Publishing books by Sierra Cartwright

Mastered
With This Collar
On His Terms
Over the Line
In His Cuffs
For the Sub
In the Den

The Donovan Dynasty
Bind
Brand
Boss

Mastered

WITH THIS COLLAR

THE 10TH ANNIVERSARY EDITION

SIERRA CARTWRIGHT

With This Collar: The 10th Anniversary Edition
ISBN # 978-1-80250-557-3

Interior text design by Claire Siemaszkiewicz
Totally Bound Publishing

Published in 2023 by Totally Bound Publishing, United Kingdom.

Totally Bound Publishing is an imprint of Totally Entwined Group Limited.

WITH THIS COLLAR

Dedication

For a great fan, Marie Hall!
And for the girls—Liz and Tiff
Always for BAB. I can't imagine trying to do this without you.
And for my own very special hero…

Chapter One

"And now, friends, Lana will offer her submission to her new husband," Damien Lowell said.

Julia scowled. *Submission?*

Lana and Julia had chatted on the phone earlier in the week to discuss the final wedding plans. Lana had warned that the union would be a bit untraditional. She'd been vague about the details, but she'd made Julia promise to say nothing during the ceremony.

They'd been friends since they were ten, and there was no way Julia would miss the festivities, even if they were a bit odd.

Until now, everything had been what she'd expected.

Lana and Ben were being married at their friend Damien's mountain home. Damien was also performing the ceremony.

About two dozen of the couple's closest friends had gathered in the great room and, at dusk, Lana had descended the stairs, carrying a single, beautiful, white rose to match her full-length gown.

The only gift requested had been a candle. In a romantic gesture, the pair had said they wanted all their friends to light their way into their future.

As Ben and Lana had joined hands and faced Damien, fat snowflakes had fallen from the cloudy sky. The vows had included the word obey, which was somewhat unusual among their circle of friends. But everything else had been normal. Lana had placed her rose on the mantel behind Damien before she and Ben had exchanged rings.

"Lana?" Damien prompted.

"Yes, Sir," Lana said.

'Sir'? Until tonight, Julia hadn't met Damien. She knew he was a friend of the groom's, and drop-dead, movie star handsome. The man had rakishly long, dark hair that curled at his nape, and he wore an indefinable air of command as easily as he filled out his charcoal-gray suit. But still, for her friend to call him 'Sir'…?

Lana cast her gaze at the floor and gracefully turned her back to her new husband.

Ben undid the row of tiny buttons that held her gown closed.

What the hell?

Ben drew the material from Lana's shoulders and let the dress float to the floor.

Lana, wearing stacked heels, a merry widow and stockings, stepped out of the dress, and another man scooped it up and laid it across a chair.

Like Damien, this man was also ridiculously tall. That was where the resemblance ended. This man had a sun-kissed complexion that hinted at a Mediterranean background. His head was shaved. He wore black jeans and a black T-shirt that revealed a number of tattoos. A thick, knotted silver bracelet adorned his left wrist, and a silver stud pierced his right earlobe. He could have been a pirate in a former life.

Suddenly *untraditional* took on a whole new meaning. Julia had never been more distressed. Part of her wanted to make an escape, and a bigger part of her wanted to shake some sense into her friend. But she was riveted in place by her promise to remain silent.

With a grace that spoke of practice, Lana kneeled.

Jesus. All through college, they'd each vowed to keep their independence. They'd pushed against the glass ceiling, and they'd fought for their positions in corporate America. And now her friend was kneeling in front of her husband, almost naked, for their guests to see?

Julia wondered if she was the only one who was frozen in shock.

Lana spread her legs a bit farther apart, and she leaned forward to kiss one of Ben's shoes.

Julia gasped.

From the front of the room, Damien looked at her, his eyebrows raised.

Firm, relentless hands landed on her shoulders. Her heart rate increased with her panic.

"Be quiet," a man whispered harshly into her ear.

"I—"

"I said be quiet."

She gritted her teeth. His tone was rough, graveled with command. And because he was so close, she inhaled the unmistakable—and sexy—scent of leather.

In that same rich and rough, for-her-ears-only voice, he went on. "Or else I'll haul your sweet ass out of here and turn you over my knee."

For the first time in her life, she was rendered speechless.

"This is Lana's choice."

She struggled against his grip, but he dug his fingers deeper into her flesh.

"Surely she told you to expect some unconventional things."

"But—"

"Trust her," he urged. "Like she trusted you."

When Julia had given her promise, she'd had no idea what that had meant or how difficult it would be to keep her word. Julia spent her entire life in control, and she hung out with women like herself. And now a powerful man had her imprisoned while her friend was on her knees in front of a roomful of people. The experience was surreal.

With unshakable force, the man pulled her back a few steps, so they were several feet away from the rest of the guests.

She still hadn't caught a glimpse of her assailant.

"Nothing you do or say will stop tonight's proceedings. So I recommend you behave yourself."

Julia struggled to escape him. In response, he imprisoned her against his hard, masculine body. "Let me go."

"Last warning."

His tone rang with an authority she didn't dare question. He was speaking quietly, but that made his words all the more terrifying. He'd threatened to turn her over his knee, and in that instant, she believed he'd do it. She stopped fighting. "Who the hell are you?" she demanded in a whisper.

"Marcus Cavendish. A Dominant, and friend of the groom's. I met Lana about six months ago. She's come a long way in the lifestyle. Ben's a lucky man to have earned the submission of such a lovely woman."

The floor lurched beneath her.

"If you promise to behave yourself, I'll explain what's happening."

She nodded.

At the front of the room, Lana stood and faced Ben.

"Would you like to offer your submission?" Ben asked.

Lana tipped back her head. "Yes, Sir, I would."

Damien picked up something from the mantel and offered it to Ben. Julia stood on her toes, trying to get a better look.

"To the vanilla world it looks like a silver necklace with a lock on it," Marcus said. "But those of us in the lifestyle recognize it for what it is. A collar."

"Collar?"

She wrapped her arms around her middle.

"In this case, it appears to be an ordinary piece of jewelry, but it likely has a hex screw so that she can't remove it."

Ben accepted the necklace from Damien and passed the chain through the flame of an enormous candle.

"He's purifying the metal," Marcus explained. "And then he'll ask her again if her submission is given freely."

Ben looked down at Lana and captured her chin, gazing deeply—maybe even adoringly— into her eyes. "I offer you this collar as a symbol of my love, and as a promise to be a kind, consistent and honorable Master. In return, I will demand your servitude. I will enforce the rules we have agreed to, and I will never touch you in anger."

Lana linked her hands at the small of her back, while she continued to look up at her new husband. Her voice soft, she spoke. "I accept your gift. In return, I offer you my humble devotion."

The words sounded just as practiced as their marriage vows had.

"We're here in front of our friends and mentors, and I want everyone to hear your assurance that you are willingly agreeing to be my slave."

The blood chilled in Julia's veins. As if Marcus sensed it, he tightened his grip on her. Oddly the touch grounded her rather than annoyed her.

"I am joyfully agreeing to be your slave, Sir."

Even from the distance and in the dim lighting, Julia saw Lana's smile.

"In fact, I'm begging for the honor. Sir, please collar me."

"Lift your hair, wife."

As Ben secured the lock in place, Lana gazed at him with an expression of surrendered bliss. Julia wondered what had happened to the woman she used to know. The two of them had sat on their dorm room couch eating popcorn, drinking wine and making fun of old 1950s television shows where the wife cooked dinner in high heels and a dress. And now a man was placing a collar around Lana's neck, and she'd asked him to do so.

Without being instructed, Lana kneeled again. She cast her gaze at the floor. Then Ben gently placed his hand in her hair and eased her head back. Dutifully Lana looked up once more. "Thank you, Master."

"Master?" Julia whispered, more disturbed than she ever remembered being.

"Not all couples use that term, but they have elected to do so."

"Ladies and gentlemen," Damien said, "may I present Master Ben and his slave wife, Lana."

"Jesus."

Once again, Marcus tightened his grip on Julia's shoulders, compelling her silence.

Ben pulled Lana to her feet and kissed her possessively. He had one hand on Lana's bare bottom, and the fingers of his other hand were spread wide across the middle of her back.

Lana shamelessly rose onto her tiptoes and pressed herself against Ben. Julia had never seen anything so sexy at any other wedding. Her friend was showing pure, unadulterated happiness, and no one seemed to care that she was only half-dressed.

Some people applauded, others hollered and gave catcalls, but Julia kept her hands wrapped tightly around her middle.

"A toast!" the man who'd picked up Lana's discarded gown called out.

On his cue, several servers moved into the room, bearing trays filled with glasses of sparkling wine. Their attire shocked her. The men wore bow ties around their necks, but no shirts. One had on a tight-fitting pair of shorts, the others wore slacks at least one size too small. The women wore aprons with thongs, stockings, and garters.

"What the hell is this?" She wrenched herself free from her nemesis and turned to face him. The first look at him sucked oxygen from her lungs and weakened her knees.

"A toast," Marcus said drily. He snagged two flutes from a passing server and offered one to her. "And you're going to continue to behave."

She shouldn't want to obey him, but a deep part of her yearned to.

Julia had never met anyone like him. Rugged and broad, he was at ease against the untamed Rocky Mountain backdrop. His hair was dark, cropped short, emphasizing his bright green eyes. He wore black boots and slacks, a crisp, white shirt and a soft, black leather blazer. His raw masculinity enveloped her.

"Everyone is half-undressed." *At a wedding.*

"Are they?"

She accepted the offered glass and wished it wouldn't be unladylike to gulp its contents.

"Face the happy couple." Command laced his soft suggestion.

When she opened her mouth, he raised his eyebrows. Having had a look at the size of his hands and their assorted nicks and abrasions, she wouldn't put it past him to follow through on his earlier threat to turn her over his knee.

Why did the unwelcome image rocket a delicious shiver through her?

His air of authority annoyed her as much as her instinctive response to him. She was a modern woman who ran an entire department at work. Julia didn't have a problem with a man being in charge. She had definite problems, however, with domineering men—like the one she was looking at.

"I will not tolerate your rudeness."

Rude? Her manners were impeccable. Or, rather, they had been until this evening.

Bristling, ready to make her escape as soon as possible, Julia turned toward the front of the room, the impossible Marcus Cavendish standing next to her. She couldn't help but inhale the scent of his leather blazer and, this close, she noticed other subtle undertones. He smelled cold, as crisp as the winter night. There was a layer of something spicy as well, maybe from his soap.

He was all man, with a capital M.

She tried not to let him overwhelm her. But something elemental in her responded to him.

Damien lifted his glass. He was standing next to the newlyweds, and all of them were facing their guests. "To a long future filled with happiness."

As the crowd responded with enthusiastic cheers, Lana and Ben clinked their glasses together then sipped.

After she'd taken one drink, Ben took Lana's glass and placed it on the hearth.

Julia clenched her teeth.

But no matter how much she might want to deny it, the truth was, she'd never seen Lana look more radiant. She didn't appear concerned by her lack of clothing, and she'd barely taken her adoring gaze from Ben's face.

For a moment, Julia stared before shaking her head. She'd never have suspected Lana would be a doormat for any man. When the three of them had met for dinner two weeks ago, Julia had not suspected he'd been hiding this kind of disturbing behavior. He'd been solicitous of Lana. In retrospect, Julia had found it a bit odd that he'd ordered Lana's meal for her, but he'd consulted her first, and the two had touched constantly. Julia had found their relationship endearing. Had it all been a polite act?

She couldn't make Lana's choices for her, but Julia knew a few things. No man would decide when she'd had enough to drink. She would never kneel for any man. And she would certainly never let anyone put a collar around her neck.

Once again, Damien's voice grabbed her attention. "Refreshments are available in the dining room. The bride and groom will join you shortly. In the meantime, please, make full use of the house." He flicked a glance in Marcus's direction before adding, "The dungeon is available should you need it."

Dungeon?

Was he serious?

Stunned, reeling from shock, and desperate to escape this whole, bizarre event, she decided to seek out her friend to say goodbye.

Before she could move, Marcus once again placed his large hand firmly on her shoulder. This time, she wiggled away.

Around them, the crowd dispersed. Some people moved toward the dining room and others headed for the stairs. "I need to go home."

"I thought you might be curious."

She shook her head. "I've seen enough."

"You don't want to understand your friend and her lifestyle better?"

Julia wasn't totally naïve. She'd seen movies, read books, been to adult bookstores. But witnessing a demonstration…? Nothing could have prepared her for that.

"Perhaps try out the dungeon?"

Clearly she'd entered an alternate universe. "That wasn't a joke?"

"In BDSM circles, his house is known as the Devil's Den."

"Seriously?"

"He didn't choose it. But since his name is Damien…" He shrugged. "But it was easier to agree to meet out at the Den—outside of Denver—than to keep saying Damien's place. Then somewhere along the line someone added Devil—the press, I believe, during an exposé—and it stuck. Some of us long-term guests still call it the Den. The basement has a punishment horse, a Saint Andrew's cross, stocks…"

"Medieval. Thumb screws as well?"

"You could call it fully equipped."

She blinked.

"Would you like to see it?"

"Good God, *no.*"

"Pity. I'd love to see you on the cross."

"That, Mr. Cavendish, will not happen."

"We'll see." He regarded her, and she did her best not to squirm. It was as if he saw through her words and into her darkest fantasies. "As Damien said, Ben and Lana will be back later. So you can't say your farewells until then. Their rose ceremony will be held in private."

Lana and Ben picked up the roses they'd placed on the mantel. Even from across the room, Julia noticed both stems still had thorns. Ben's was red, in full bloom. Lana's was white, and barely beginning to open.

Damien led the two from the room. Lana followed her husband, a step behind him.

Julia finished the rest of her drink, then placed the empty glass on a server's tray.

"Another, ma'am?"

"No, thank you." She needed to be clear-headed for the drive back to Denver.

"I know Lana would want to see you."

Was he trying to get her to stay?

"It was an honor that she trusted you enough to invite you to attend. Most collaring ceremonies are closed to the outside world."

"Are you telling me I'm the only one here who feels as if she's fallen down a rabbit hole?"

"Probably, yes."

Behind him, a woman in spiky heels and a short, short skirt put a hand on her companion's shoulder. Julia stared, wide-eyed, as the tall, broad man kneeled. The woman then pulled a long, thin strip of black leather from her pocket and affixed it to a collar around the man's neck.

"Is that...?" Stunned, words failed her.

"A leash." Marcus regarded her over the rim of his still-full champagne glass.

The woman walked from the room, and the man trailed, on all fours, keeping some slack in his lead.

Her knees wobbled. "That's..."

He waited.

"Appalling."

"Is it?"

This had to be a crazy dream. Had to be. Every time she thought she was understanding the evening's events, something even stranger occurred. "I would never allow myself to be treated like that!"

"Like what? Someone who is deeply cared for?"

"If that's how someone is treated when they're being deeply cared for, count me out."

"Things we don't understand are easy to judge."

She bristled. "Are you calling me judgmental?"

Rather than respond, he asked a question of his own. "Did you see him protesting?" He paused. "Do you suppose the woman with him, at least a hundred pounds lighter and inches shorter, could have done that to him if he objected?"

Julia scowled.

"And, furthermore, you'd look beautiful leashed."

"I'm not ever—"

"Don't say things you may have to take back."

"That's arrogant."

"Is it?" He shrugged, apparently unconcerned by her statement. "I'd like to know your name, if I may."

How could he have such beautiful manners while being so annoyingly confident? And the fact they were having this kind of conversation without polite societal constructs made the entire exchange even more surreal. "Julia Lyle."

"An absolute pleasure." He placed his drink on a nearby end table and extended his hand in greeting.

Shaking hands seemed so…normal, a polite societal construct that she could embrace and understand. It momentarily grounded her.

He held her too long, though, and when she would have pulled away, he raised her hand and kissed it. He looked at her, imprisoning her gaze.

Electricity lit up her nerve endings. Despite her reservations—and maybe because of them—she was attracted to Marcus. She'd dated her fair share of men, and she'd been in a couple of long-term relationships. Unfortunately the last man she'd been involved with—Jason—had been domineering. At first, he'd been charming and wonderful. Over time, after she'd allowed him to move in, he'd tried to control her, choose her friends, isolate her from her family.

The experience had left her determined not to let any man make decisions for her ever again.

So why was she so attracted to Marcus Cavendish? At his touch, untamed energy thumped through her. Power exuded from him, and its effect was intoxicating. He was dark and dangerous. In short, he was everything she shouldn't want, everything she'd vowed to avoid. Yet she wanted to continue talking, even though instinct urged her to run.

"I've been friends with Ben since college."

"Has he always been this way?"

"A Dominant? I suppose, yes. He was a natural leader, even in school. So that he would behave that way in a relationship makes perfect sense."

She extricated her hand. "I'm not sure what you mean by that."

"Has Lana told you nothing about her lifestyle?"

Julia shook her head. "I knew she and Ben were doing things she called kinky, but I think she probably should have told me more." She shrugged. "Or maybe she assumed I understood what she meant."

"At this point, everyone has heard about BDSM."

"Of course." Her agreement was instantaneous. "But it's different seeing it in person." More sensual. More *real.*

"Would you like to go somewhere quieter?"

She thought about it for a moment. If she were smart, she would already be driving back to her normal life, forgetting this event had ever happened, pretending she had never set eyes on the overwhelming and gorgeous Marcus Cavendish.

But she wasn't sure what had happened to the logical and linear part of her brain that made her good at her job as a statistician. She was behaving like a female to his larger, commanding male. Biology had her in its primal, inescapable grip. That knowledge, rationalization, didn't help her, though.

Around them, attendees were in various forms of dress, some in club attire—latex, PVC, figure-hugging dresses—while others wore nothing at all.

"Shall we?" Without waiting for her response, Marcus entered the sunroom. She could have protested, but a wayward, reckless part of her didn't want to.

Her pulse tripping over its beats, she followed him.

Except for him, the space was empty, and he took a place in front of a floor-to-ceiling window. Since it was dark, she could only make out vague shadows. Her legs barely supporting her, she joined him.

"I'm delighted."

Being here, alone with him, wrapped her in a cocoon of intimacy.

Because she needed to for her sanity, she pulled away from him and folded her arms across her middle, as if that futile act could save her.

He propped one foot on a windowsill, creating an intimate space for the two of them.

"The absolute first thing you have to know is that the primary foundation of BDSM is about consent. Here we practice what's known as SSC. Safe. Sane. Consensual. Nothing, absolutely nothing, happens without all parties agreeing to it."

She recalled Lana begging for Ben's collar.

"No relationship has the same rules or protocols, and there's no one true way of doing things. Some people use handcuffs in the bedroom, and perhaps a scarf or bandana as a blindfold. All that is well and good, if it works for the couple. Some of us prefer something more complex, something that's as emotional as it is physical. To many people here, BDSM is a much more serious construct, not just an occasional playtime in the bedroom. Some of us indulge twenty-four seven."

"I'm not sure I understand."

"Ben and Lana have entered a D/s relationship, meaning Dominant and submissive. They will have an agreed-upon power exchange. You heard Ben ask Lana if she willingly offered her submission. He didn't demand her servitude. He didn't threaten or compel her response. She gave it."

Julia waited.

"In return, you heard Ben promise to care for her. They have negotiated their agreement over time, then they asked trusted friends to witness their public vows. Lana gave him power. He didn't take it."

"And I'm sure she can revoke it at any time." She didn't try to keep the sarcasm from her tone.

"She can. Everything is negotiated and consensual. There are varying levels to a power exchange, everything from a single scene to a relationship that is ongoing, but for scenes only. Most subs and Doms have a safe word, or even a series of them. A sub will use an agreed-upon word or term if she or he is feeling scared or if something is too much to handle, either physically or emotionally. The most important thing is communication. Most relationships could benefit from having that kind of arrangement, something that's discussed ahead of time. No person can be a Dominant without the other agreeing to be the submissive."

"It sounds horrible."

"Does it?" He raised his eyebrows, and she squirmed beneath his scrutiny. "You've been friends with Lana for a long time, I assume. Since she met Ben, has she appeared unhappy? Has anything made you think she's lost her common sense?"

Actually, she'd been giddy. Julia, Lana and a few friends had been at a martini bar on Larimer Square celebrating Lana's last days as a single woman when talk had turned to sex. Lana had been grinning and giggling as she had told stories about Ben spanking her and binding her wrists to their headboard.

A couple of the other girls had admitted they'd done similar things, and that they'd enjoyed it. They'd encouraged Julia to loosen up and be a bit more adventurous. Honestly, she had been intrigued by the ideas. She just hadn't been with a man she trusted enough to experiment with. That night, though, with her supercharged vibrator, she'd had a few wicked fantasies...

"Julia?"

"I thought they just had an occasional wild evening. I didn't know they did *this*…"

He waited. "This?"

"Doing everything he tells her."

"Despite what you may be thinking, he doesn't just tell her what to do and have her jump to his bidding. Everything between them, everything, including punishment, has been talked about in advance, potentially over months, even years."

Who am I lying to? Myself? "It's still not for me."

"No? I'd be willing to bet your friend has more orgasms in one night than you've likely had in the last six months."

"Excuse me?" Pissed off, she scowled. "You don't know anything about me."

"A guess. Nothing more." His tone was light. "But with your reactions tonight, you seem like a woman who has repressed sexual needs. You jump when I touch you. And when I use this tone…" He lowered his tone, made it more commanding. "You come undone." The sound sent little skitters of awareness up her spine. "You need the right man to set you free."

The right man? She tilted her chin, hoping to project a confidence and disinterest she was nowhere close to feeling. "Are you always so overconfident and arrogant? Let me guess, that's why you're here alone."

Other than offering a quick smile, he didn't react.

"Come on, Julia. Admit it. You're protesting, but only because you think you should. Deep down, you're intrigued."

She curled her hands into fists at her side, more to keep him from seeing the way she was trembling than anything else.

"You're wondering what it might be like to surrender to a man. More specifically, you're wondering what it might be like to submit to me."

"Not in this lifetime."

"When Lana was talking about the things she and Ben do, you listened, maybe even fantasized about being spanked, feeling an unyielding palm on your ass cheeks, perhaps being tied up helplessly while you wondered what would happen next. And tonight, you pictured yourself in Lana's place, kneeling in front of a roomful of people."

Pretending her heart wasn't racing, she coolly met his gaze "Absolutely not."

"No? You don't want to have someone take charge so you can release your inhibitions and freely experience everything?"

His outrageous question sent ripples of awareness through her. She should protest, but she didn't, couldn't…

"How would you react if I dug my hand into your hair, dislodging those carefully placed pins, then tugged hard, forcing your head back and holding you tight for my kiss?"

Oh God. No. Yes… "You'll never know, Mr. Cavendish."

"Won't I?"

He dropped his foot from the window ledge and took a purposeful step toward her, then he captured her shoulders.

Even though mere inches separated them, she stood her ground. The massive breadth of him filled her vision. Everything about him tempted her, making lies of her earlier protests.

"Your mouth says one thing"—gently he traced the column of her throat—"but your pulse betrays you. The way you're biting your delicious lower lip betrays you. And the way you tremble, as if begging me to prove you wrong."

Desperately she shook her head.

"All of this is about consent. I'll release you if you want me to. Just say the word."

It wasn't just the scent of him that made her oh-so aware of being a woman. It was also the hoarse seduction in his voice. He was speaking softly, so no one but her could hear him, and the rough gentleness made shivers dance down her spine.

He moved his hand to stroke her cheekbone, ensnaring her gaze. "Tell me to stop."

Her pulse raced even as her thoughts fragmented.

"You're beautiful, Julia. I'd love to see you naked, helpless, writhing with the pleasure that only I can give you."

"Absolutely not." But... *God.* Her protests rang hollow. The truth was, she clearly saw the image he painted, and she yearned to experience exactly that, at his hands.

"It's your choice." He stopped stroking her cheek, but he placed a thumb beneath her chin, easing it up a little. "I'm giving you a chance to explore, not just yourself but your friend's lifestyle. You may discover untapped desires, passions. Your eyes are wide. You're intrigued. Nervous, apprehensive even. But what if you unleash a hidden part of yourself?"

"Isn't that an oxymoron? You're talking about submission. How does that equate to releasing passions?

"Admitting what you want is where true power lies. Asking for it is liberating. As I mentioned, D/s relationships are about power exchanges. I can't force you to turn yourself over to me. You give your submission freely, and I accept it, along with the responsibility to care for you."

As if she were a caged bird, her heart thumped madly.

"Shall I continue? Give you a small taste?"

She was tempted to look around, but he consumed her.

"Thirty seconds, perhaps?"

"I…" Half a minute. And then she'd know and could walk away.

With infinite patience, he waited.

"Yes."

His touch, confident and compelling, was everywhere at once. He ran his fingers across her nape, then pressed his palms against her back to draw her closer. He followed through on his earlier promise and dug his hand into her hair. A series of soft *clinks* echoed around her as pins dropped to the hardwood floor.

Now, unconfined, her long, thick locks fell over her shoulders.

Excitement flooded her. Then, with greater force, he gripped her hair. Shockingly, the sharp bite of pain added to the bombardment on her senses. She loved it.

"Ask me for it, Julia. Beg me to kiss you, to pleasure you, maybe to bring you off right here in the sunroom where anyone can see you surrender to me."

His words stunned her. Staring at him, she blinked. Everything he offered, she craved. Even though he shocked her.

It might be ridiculous, but she felt safe with him. Maybe because they weren't entirely alone, and Ben and Lana considered him a friend. The way he explained things reassured her and emboldened her.

"Or I'll release you this moment and send you on your way."

Chapter Two

Enchanted, Marcus watched the play of emotion through her revealing blue eyes. Arousal battled nerves. Fear warred with curiosity.

Her answer shouldn't matter to him.

So why did it?

The top of her head reached his shoulder, meaning she had to be at least five-foot-seven. That also meant she was the perfect size to fit under his chin, in his arms. A strange urge to protect her assailed him, as unexpected as it was unusual.

Then again, from the moment she had gasped at the collaring ceremony, Julia captured his interest.

Her feistiness, the way she fought her own reactions, intrigued him. Now that it had been released from its confines, her blonde hair fell in wild disarray, framing her face. Did it stay confined for long? Or was it like her inner nature, desperately trying to break free?

"I've never done anything like this before."

"Like...?"

"Asking for what I want."

"You've hoped that your partner would instinctively know?"

She sighed. "Put that way, it sounds ridiculous."

"We can start now. Tell me."

"I..." Julia curled her hands at her sides. "I want you to kiss me."

Fuck. He wanted nothing more.

He fisted her hair still tighter and eased back her head. Her eyes widened. "In this moment, you're mine."

She blew out a tiny, surrendered breath before parting her lips for him.

Ruthlessly he claimed her mouth, seeking her tongue. After a moment's hesitation, she leaned in a little closer to wrap her arms around his neck.

Marcus's cock had been hard from the moment he'd put his hands on her shoulders in the living room. Marcus preferred to play with experienced women who were eager to scene with him. Newbies didn't hold his interest. Until now.

This rush was heady, addictive. Seeing her trepidation yield to interest made him want to push further.

He brought her against his body, her soft curves against his hardened planes. He owned a construction company, most often making deals and working on the computer, but he often picked up a hammer or lent his muscle to a job, working alongside his men. He preferred the outdoors to being inside a gym, and he chose physical labor over a set of weights.

With his free hand, he stroked his fingers over the sweet curve of her ass and dug his fingers into her flesh.

The honesty and openness he found in BDSM negotiations was the first thing that had attracted him to the lifestyle. Even though there were rules and protocol, there was less pretense than he'd experienced in half a dozen years of dating.

That didn't mean relationships were easier. He'd learned the hard way, with the one woman he'd collared—Amber.

Though he'd loved her deeply, in the years they spent together, she'd given up who she was. She'd relied on him for all her emotional needs. As he'd been building his business, he'd been less and less available, and that had led to a corresponding increase in her meltdowns. Her calls had been hourly, and she even showed up at job sites dressed inappropriately. His rules had been meant for flaunting.

She'd interrupted a meeting with potential investors. As he'd punished her that night, he'd realized what was happening. Her actions had been meant to get his attention and goad him into a reaction. It had become an unbalanced, untenable situation that had exhausted them both.

The love he'd had for her drove him to support her financially while she tried to establish a new life, but the last he'd heard she was involved with an abusive Dom.

Determinedly shoving aside the memories, he deepened the kiss he was giving Julia, fucking her mouth, giving her a taste of what she was in for if she continued down this path.

Eventually he pulled back slightly. He bit her bottom lip then soothed the hurt with his tongue. She hadn't been kissed like that in the vanilla world, he was willing to bet on it.

"You okay?"

She looked up at him. Her eyes were wider than they'd been before, and the color more vibrant. "Yes."

"Scared?"

"Not at all." She unlinked her arms. "Not of you. Or your caveman demonstration."

"I assure you, that was anything but a caveman demonstration." In fact, it was as gentlemanly as he was capable of being.

"I see."

"If that's what you want…?"

She didn't protest. *Brave and so tempting.*

As he released the grip he had on her delectable rear, he captured her chin and tilted it back, to expose the vulnerable column of her throat. "Don't move." It was his first command. Would she follow it? "Understand?"

She swallowed hard.

Keeping her gaze captive, he touched her fluttering pulse in that vulnerable, exposed place. Then he leaned in and gently bit her collarbone.

Silently trusting him, she remained in place. Was there a more powerful aphrodisiac? "If this were a caveman demonstration, I'd begin by stripping you." He unfastened her top button.

A battle raged on her face. Wordlessly, she reached for him, gripping his wrist tight. Rather than stopping him, she hung on, as if seeking reassurance. He sucked one of her earlobes into his mouth then scraped his teeth against the tender flesh.

Despite the fact that she moaned, she didn't ask him to stop. Nor did she attempt to pull away. Her reaction pleased him. That she'd responded in such a way to that pain made him wonder if it might be possible to eventually send her into subspace. For him as a Dom there was no more satisfying experience than giving a sub such pleasure that she lost herself in the experience.

He wrapped his arms around her, and the position was more comfortable than it should have been. Natural. Inevitable.

Though there were dozens of people at the Den, this was their private, intimate cocoon. He opened a second button. "And then I'd force you to your knees with your hands behind your back. Then I'd demand you look up at me and offer your complete honesty. Are you capable of admitting what you want? Not just to me, but to yourself? That's the most important thing of all."

"I…" She exhaled. "This is harder than I thought."

Marcus waited.

"In that case…"

"Go on." She'd trailed off, bravado evidently failing her. "I promise you, nothing you say will surprise me. And if it's in my power, I will move heaven and earth to give you everything you desire."

"Everything."

"The kissing? Me pulling your hair? Me undressing you?"

"And more. I want to experience what you're talking about, but just for tonight. I'm a statistician. I like to understand how things relate to one another and I'd like to be a better friend to Lana. But tomorrow I'll resume my regular, scheduled life."

"You're asking for a single night with no strings attached?"

"Most men would jump at that chance."

Julia offered him a placating half-smile that unaccountably pissed him off. "I'm not most men."

In his arms, she shuddered. "Are you refusing?"

"Not at all. I mentioned earlier that your friend and her Dom would have negotiated their relationship, and that's what we'll do. I'll give you this evening."

She narrowed her eyes. "And in return?"

Clever girl. "I reserve the right to follow up with you, see how you are. You'll likely have questions, maybe things you want to talk through."

"How is that no strings attached?"

He couldn't help his small grin. "You don't have to answer my call. But, as a gentleman—"

"Gentleman?"

Ignoring her, he went on. "And a Dom who takes the well-being of his bottom into consideration—"

"I'm lost." She shook her head a little, making her hair flirt with her shoulders. "Bottom?"

"Sorry. I've explained a little about D/s. But other terms will be Top and bottom. People who don't have a committed relationship or some of the agreements around Dominance and submission may use those terms. In very simple terms, a Top will be in a more dominant role."

"The Top gives the spanking, and the bottom gets it?"

He nodded. "It can be more complex than that. But essentially, yes. Some people are switches, meaning they sometimes choose to Top, but enjoy the other position as well."

She tilted her head to one side. "That could be fun."

"Watch your step, brave"—*foolish*—"sweet submissive. I'm not a switch. For anyone."

"No." She shivered. "I don't imagine you are."

"So we're in agreement? If we continue, you'll give me your contact information so I can follow up with you tomorrow?"

"As you said, I don't have to answer."

If things went the way he planned, she wouldn't let the phone get past the first ring. "And now for my requirements."

Furiously she scowled. Her face was so expressive, charming him. "A negotiation means two parties make requests. Not just one."

"But I can counter."

She was a quick study. "Of course." Had he enjoyed a wedding more? "I want your honesty. To know all of your fantasies. You'll hide nothing from me, answering all my direct questions."

Though scarlet stained her cheeks, she continued to meet his gaze. "Like what?"

"Is your pussy damp now?"

Her lips parted.

He was willing to wager that no one had been this blunt with her before.

"Uhm..." She paused, then tried again. "That is direct, Marcus."

"When we're here, I prefer to be addressed as Master Marcus."

The scarlet on her cheeks darkened.

"It helps establish boundaries."

She twirled a finger into a lock of her hair. A nervous gesture?

"Is that open for negotiation?"

"Certainly. You can call me Sir."

"That's still ridiculous."

"Try it. It may be more natural than you think."

"I doubt that."

"Now repeat those words but add Sir to the end."

After stalling for a few more seconds, she complied. "I doubt that, *Sir.*"

The words were beautiful on her lips, like those of an angel. One he wanted to despoil. "We only have a few hours, so we don't have time to waste." He lowered his voice a bit, ensuring she heard seduction as well as command in his tone. "Answer my question. Is your pussy wet? Or shall I find out for myself?"

"I… You can take my word for it. I'm more turned on than I usually get even when I'm having sex."

The admission fed him, driving his determination to give her an experience she'd never forget.

"I liked the small amount of pain. I never thought I would. And…" She paused. "I think I'd like it if you squeezed my nipples. Sir."

God save me. Her boldness surprised him. He'd anticipated she might ask for a second kiss. This was considerably more than he'd hoped for. "And I'd like to. Unbutton your blouse the rest of the way, Julia."

Slowly she did, and he kept his hands on her shoulders because he liked touching her, keeping her close, inhaling the freshness of her innocence.

She looked up at him, and he was tempted to compromise by undressing her. But he remained resolved. "I told you there will be no doubt this will be consensual. I'd love to play with your nipples, to leave you breathless with desire. I want to hold your breasts and squeeze them. If you'd like that too, unbutton your blouse."

She knitted her eyebrows together in apparent indecision.

He released her to fold his arms. In silence, unwilling to push, he waited. More than a decade ago, Damien had mentored him in BDSM. Marcus had learned when to be patient and when to push his submissives. Julia might not be a sub, or his, but he needed to wait for her to take the next step. It was an internal battle he was unaccustomed to waging. Never had he been this tempted to rip the material from a woman, exposing her body to him.

She dropped her gaze to the floor. He sucked in a breath. Right this moment she was behaving with intuitive submissive tendencies.

God save me.

Finally, slowly, Julia untucked her blouse from her skirt and unfastened the bottom button. Her fingers shook. As she moved higher, the trembling became more pronounced.

He ached to sweep her hands aside and finish the job himself. Instead, he stood there, the sweetness of anticipation making his blood hum. By slow measures, she exposed her delicate collarbone. With her blonde hair hanging in wild abandon and her shirt open to reveal the stark white of her lacy bra, she was femininity and seduction in one beautiful package. *So beautiful.* "Look up at me."

Her mouth was parted slightly, and her chest rose and fell rapidly, but she did as he had instructed.

"You're absolutely lovely, Julia."

With a shrug, she slid the silk from her shoulders.

He extended a hand, and she obediently hung the blouse from his index finger. "I appreciate your trust." God, did he. "And I give you my promise nothing will happen unless you either ask for it or agree to it in advance. Understand? "Yes." The word was hardly a squeak.

"Are you doing okay?"

She gave a tiny frown. "A little nervous."

"I talked to you earlier about a safe word. Some subs like to use a code of red, yellow, and green. Green meaning everything is okay, yellow if you need to talk, take a break, maybe go a bit slower. Red means stop immediately. It's up to you. You can choose your own words, or we can go with the colors."

"What color would I be right now?"

"Your choice, depending on what you need from me. If you need to talk or some reassurance, then it would be yellow. You could still be apprehensive but want to proceed. It could be part of the scene for you, a type of excitement. In that case you'd say green. But please never try to hide any of your emotions. In fact, I want you to communicate with me every step of the way. That's the only way I can be sure you're enjoying the experience. Bottom line, that's what this is about."

"I'm not sure I follow."

"There's no reason, ever, to participate in anything to do with BDSM unless you like the experience. It should add to an already happy life. It shouldn't be a substitute for it."

He'd rarely had this kind of discussion, and never when an alluring woman had been standing in front of him with her blouse off. Then again, he'd never been with a statistician before. Maybe he should make her get dressed, for his sake if not hers.

"It encompasses many things. Some people are into bondage, including rope art, and take it no further. Some subs are into pain, and they'll do almost anything to feel their Dom's wrath. Conversely, some Doms are sadistic and just like to wield an implement of pain. Some subs prefer to live a life of service, much like a slave. Some couples are into spankings, others into more extreme eroticism or punishment. Still other people hook up for occasional scenes that may or may not include sex."

"Where do you fall on that spectrum?"

"I've had a couple of committed relationships that involved Dominance and submission. My most recent one was a twenty-four seven lifestyle arrangement. And no, I'm not still in it." He suspected she could find out a lot about him just from asking around the Den.

Even though privacy was paramount outside the club, inside was sometimes a different matter. Some participants had made gossip into an art form. "Right now, I have no emotional entanglements."

She licked her lower lip. "And no relationship outside the BDSM world?"

"None. That holds no interest for me."

"You like being in charge, in control."

She made it a statement, not a question. "You're correct. It's an essential part of who I am."

"And that complicates regular relationships," she surmised.

"By regular, I presume you mean vanilla?"

"If that's what you call it."

"I like the protocol in a D/s. There are rules, along with consequences if they're broken. I like tying a sub up and subjecting her to erotic beatings. While I'm not a sadist, I find a sub often has a more powerful experience because of a bit of pain, as you've already experienced. That said, I'd require you to use a safe word if there's anything you can't deal with it." He paused. "Would you still like to continue?"

Slowly she released a breath. "Yes."

"Have you selected a safe word?"

"I'd like to use colors."

Inordinately satisfied, he lowered his tone, filling it with Dominant authority as he spoke to her. "In that case, remove your bra."

Eyes wide, she glanced around. "We're in front of a window."

"Indeed we are. I'd prefer not to close the blinds since the house is surrounded by a dozen acres of wooded land. Only wedding guests are on the property. And anyone outside in this weather would be concentrating on staying warm. On the other hand, they would get a lovely eyeful if they saw you." He studied her expressive face. "If your modesty demands it, I will close the blinds."

"Are you always so accommodating and reasonable?"

"Not at all." He grinned. Would she comply? Or snatch her blouse from his fingertip?

She glanced from him to the window, then folded and unfolded her arms. Finally sucking in a deep breath, she met his eyes. As if drawing strength from his Dominance, she reached back and unhooked her bra.

"Nice." He laced his voice with approval as he accepted the delicate scrap of material from her. "You have lovely breasts and nipples." They were tight pink buds, and he couldn't wait to see them swollen and duskier from his handling.

Marcus placed her discarded garments over the back of a chair then faced her. "So perfectly obedient. Now, please pinch your nipples for me."

"Uhm..." She cleared her throat. "I... I thought you were going to do that."

"I enjoy your participation. As much as I like having my orders followed."

A beautiful red flooded her cheeks again. Clearly this woman hadn't had many sexual experiences of this nature.

Idiot men. What could possibly be better than taking a woman to the heights of sensuality, letting her explore, and savoring her discovery?

"Yes, Sir."

Were there any sweeter words?

Motions hesitant, she took hold of her nipples and squeezed gently.

Her soft sigh filled him with satisfaction. "Thank you. Now squeeze them again."

Drawing a deep breath, she did so.

"Harder."

She looked at him with her eyebrows raised. "Will you show me?"

Her breathless request startled him, filled him with pleasure. *Sexy little sub.* If she had any idea the lengths he'd go to in order to please her… "Like so…" He brushed aside her fingers. "Actually I'd like you to place your hands at the small of your back." It would thrust out her breasts more and grant him greater access to her delectable body.

After she'd complied, he nodded his satisfaction. "Please keep them there. I can bind them if it's easier for you?"

"No." Her response was as forceful as it was quick. "That's too much for me." Then a small spark passed through her eyes. "At least for now."

"You're free to change your mind if you find it difficult to follow my commands. It's better than earning a punishment."

"You're joking." Her mouth parted. "Right?"

"What do you think?"

She glanced toward the sunroom entrance, as if contemplating an escape. "You actually mean it."

"I do. You have safe words and are free to stop at any time."

"I understand."

"Good. When you're ready, pull back your shoulders and thrust your chest toward me, as if you're begging for your Master's touch."

Her movements slow and graceful, she offered herself to him.

Marcus cupped her breasts, closing his hands around her firm flesh. "It's tempting to hold your breath, but it's easier to manage emotionally, mentally, physically if you remember to breathe."

"I'll try."

He squeezed for a moment, then brushed his thumbs across her nipples, making them harden even more.

He released her, made sure she took a few breaths, then repeated what he'd done, this time holding a little longer, adding more pressure, then abrading her nipples.

Her knees sagged.

"Is that too much?"

She dragged in a breath. "Green." It was somewhere between a whisper and a plea.

"You fucking delight me." This time he grasped each nipple between his thumb and forefinger, studying her reactions as he inexorably tightened his grip.

Gently she swayed toward him.

Taking that as assent, he pinched harder, and she moaned in perfect response. Then he pulled on her nipples, distending them.

"Oh."

He hadn't thought she could take this much. Carefully he studied her features, watching carefully for a wince, anything to indicate real pain rather than exquisite pleasure. There was a line, and he wouldn't cross it. "More?"

"Yes."

When he complied, she cried out and grabbed his forearms, forgetting his rules.

Not disappointed, he continued on, then began to back off in tiny increments. Releasing his grip at once would have caused another layer of pain that he wasn't sure she was ready for. "How are you doing?"

"I... That was..." She blinked, then focused on him. "Amazing. I've never felt anything like that."

"And your pussy? Are you wetter than you were before?"

She glanced at the floor. He knew it wasn't from respect, but rather to cover her shyness.

"Show me."

"Show you? How?" There was no outrage in her voice—rather she appeared stunned by his request.

"I want you to remove your shoes and undergarments and I want you to lift your skirt and show me your pretty pussy. Prove how wet you are."

"That's... Wow."

"Now" He extended his hand to help with her balance. "If you please."

She hesitated for less time than he expected before accepting his assistance and slipping out of her high-heeled pumps.

"Keep going."

"I was hoping you'd changed your mind about my underwear."

Not a chance.

After easing herself from his grip, she reached beneath her skirt and removed her stockings and panties. He was looking forward to touching her bare skin. All of it.

Beautiful, lovely, trusting sub.

Her cotton briefs were plain, white to match her bra.

"I wasn't expecting to be showing anyone my underwear at a wedding."

Were her words an apology? But he liked that she hadn't been expecting a casual hook up. "Put them with the rest of your clothing."

Moment by moment, her breathing changed as she complied, each step bringing her more completely under his command. "Now hold up your skirt for as long as I say."

Her hands shook as she lifted her hem, revealing her thighs, then her pussy. Her pubic hair was neatly trimmed. "Nice."

If you were mine, I'd have you shave it completely.

Stunned by the thought, Marcus shook his head to clear it. *If you were mine*? Where the hell had that come from? He didn't want a relationship or a submissive. "Pull your skirt up higher."

Blushing furiously, she complied.

"That's right. Perfect. Now tuck the material into your waistband."

Her breaths were tiny, nervous pants. He liked it. Except for the scrunched material around her waist, beautiful Julia was nude, but he wasn't done with her. "Spread your legs a bit farther apart and tilt your pelvis a bit more forward. Show me that needy pussy."

She squeezed her eyes closed.

"You really are lovely, Julia. When we're playing in future, I may keep you completely naked all the time."

"I'm only experimenting for tonight."

If he treated her well, if he was worthy as a Dom, he'd make her introduction so memorable she'd want to seek him out. "Touch your pussy, then show me how wet you are."

"This is…"

"Yellow?"

"I… No. I don't think so. But… I'm not at green either." Though she kept herself bare for him, she wrapped her arms around her middle. "This is complicated."

"Let's talk. Tell me why you're hesitating."

"This is ridiculous."

"Not at all. It's all part of BDSM. Running up against unexpected mental or emotional walls is expected."

"I'm mortified. No one has ever asked me to do something like this."

He searched her eyes. "Are you torn between what you want to do—what you crave—and what society tells you to do?"

"Yes."

"You wanted an experience tonight. If you focused on that, what would you do?"

"I'd go for it."

"You have your safe words."

She nodded.

"In that case, I'll give you two options." *The time for patience has become the time to push.*

"Okay."

"You can touch yourself and show me your fingertips. Or I can find out for myself. Is that what you want? For me to slide my fingers between your folds, touch your clit, then enter you?"

"Oh. Jesus. God…"

"Your choice, sweet submissive." Damn, he liked how she hesitated. She was such a study in contradictions, as curious as she was hesitant.

"I'll do it myself."

He grinned. "Too bad." Marcus wanted nothing more than to explore her body.

Slowly she rubbed a finger between her legs before holding up her hand. Her cheeks still crimson, she glanced away to look out the window.

"Eyes on me."

After she complied, he ensnared her wrist "You are wet." Then deliberately, he tasted the juices on her fingertips. Musky. Sexy.

She gasped. "I can't believe you did that."

"Only the beginning." He dropped her hand. "I want you to play with your nipples again."

"Yes, Sir."

His temporary submissive drew her breasts together and squeezed the tips. Then she winced. "They're so tender. From you."

"That's hot."

"Is it?"

"Oh yes." Her nipples had hardened the moment she'd touched them. She was every bit as responsive as he'd hoped. "Sexy. Knowing you're sore from the way I used your body. Tell me, sweet sub, are you wetter than you were?"

"Why don't you find out? Sir."

Inordinately pleased with her sassiness, he regarded her. "Ask me to touch you. Tell me what you want. Be specific, without flowery language. Submissive to Dominant."

She frowned furiously and stopped fondling herself.

Eyes narrowed, he leaned toward her, stealing her personal space. "Did I tell you to stop playing with yourself?"

"Uh… No. No, Sir."

"This is the second punishment you've earned this evening, Julia. And it's going to be my absolute pleasure to make you pay for your transgressions."

"Wait." Frantically she shook her head. But she didn't argue with him. "Two?"

"Earlier, you didn't keep your hands behind your back. And now, you're still not tormenting your nipples." He tutted. "Which is adding to the number of spanks you'll be getting from me."

"That's not fair." But she determinedly followed his orders. "I'm still learning."

"And having a sore ass will reinforce my lessons." A safe word never crossed her lips. "Free yourself, Julia. Ask me to do what you're secretly hoping I will."

Would she?

Finally, whimpering, she did. "Touch me."

"Where? Be specific."

"My pussy. Finger my clit."

"That's it." He leaned even closer, inhaling her desire. He whispered his next words directly into her ear. "I'll do anything to satisfy you." Then he slid his index finger between her slick folds. "Is this what you want?"

She arched toward him, silently seeking more.

"What part turns you on the most? Is it the fact you're mostly naked where anyone can see you??" He made tiny circles on her clit. "Or perhaps it was from the tiny taste of pain when I pulled your hair or tugged on your nipples? Or maybe because my hand is between your legs while you're shamelessly moving against me?"

"I'm not!"

"Oh you most certainly are. And I appreciate it enough to reward you for it."

"Marcus! Please…"

"I love the way you beg, my sweet sub."

She wrapped a hand around his neck as she pumped her hips in time with his motions.

He loved her responsiveness so much that he didn't remind her of the position he'd requested earlier. "What do you want me to do next?"

"I want…"

Her body confessed her needs long before she did.

"I want to come." She feverishly increased her movements, all but grinding herself against his hand.

"I'll give you an orgasm. But not yet."

She cried out her protest.

"The wait will be worthwhile. Denial increases the ultimate reward." He pressed against that tender, sensitive nub. "Think about what I'm doing to you. In fact, look in the window. See your reflection. Your hair in disarray. Your eyes pleading. Your lips swollen from the way you worry them. And the way you're so shamelessly fucking my fingers." He shook his head. "Don't you dare be embarrassed. You're fucking gorgeous. So real. Honest. Uninhibited." Maybe more so than she'd ever been? "I mean it, Julia. Watch yourself."

Her struggles, her plaintive need, satisfied him.

After a deep swallow, she did as he'd said. "Perfect. Now think about how much I like to touch you. About anything except the powerful orgasm I'm going to give you."

Her eyes were wide, focused on him.

"I'm going to slide a finger into your hot pussy."

As if in invitation, she rose onto her tiptoes.

Slowly, drawing out his first possession of her, he did as he said while raining kisses down the column of her throat.

With a small moan, she opened herself to him.

Her response inflamed his passion. With control he hadn't needed for years, he restrained himself. Julia, this beautiful, trusting woman, was getting to him.

Focusing on her instead of his body's incessant demands, he eased out, then back in, adding a second finger as he did.

"So good." Her words floated on a breathless murmur.

Reading her needs, he turned up the dial on his actions, tormenting her with his kisses, touches, the way he played with her clit.

"I need..." She ground her toes into the hardwood floor.

"Tell me."

"I'm close."

"Mmm." The tremble in her voice appealed to him on a soul level, but the Dominant in him demanded more "Please give me an orgasm, Sir."

Julia, his Julia, was too far gone to protest.

"Please give me an orgasm, Sir," she repeated.

So dutiful. He moved his hand faster, working her into a sensual frenzy. He placed his free hand against the small of her back to bring her even closer to him. "Tell me again."

Desperately she wriggled, pleasing him with the scent and dampness of her arousal.

"Please? *Please, Sir*!"

He changed his angle slightly to find her G-spot. As he pressed against it, her breaths became ragged. "Come for me, sweet submissive."

"Oh God!" As she cried out, she grabbed hold of him.

"That's it," he murmured against her ear as she rode the raw carnality of her orgasm. "Take it. You've earned it."

Her body clenched around his finger as she shattered completely. Nothing could have delighted him more.

For several minutes, he soothed her with his touch, his kisses, rubbing her damp skin. When she'd stopped shuddering, he held her close, her head tucked beneath his chin. Protective feelings driving him, he moved her toward the couch. He sat, then eased her onto his lap, wrapping her in a fluffy blanket.

Snuggled against him, her cheek on his chest, she sighed, burrowing even deeper against him.

Soothing the long, wayward strands of her hair, he held her, savoring the intimacy. It had been a long time since he'd shared something like this with a woman. He'd missed it. The realization stunned him. How had this sassy woman worked her way past his defenses? When she started to pull away, looking around for her clothes, he tipped back her chin. "I'm not quite finished with you."

Her mouth formed a perfect O.

Damn, she was so appealing, wide-eyed, expectant, and at the same time a bit apprehensive.

"I thought... I mean..." She placed a hand on his chest and pushed herself a few inches away so she could look at him better. "We're not done?"

She'd been with some very selfish lovers. "There's the matter of our unresolved business. Your spankings. And because it's your first time, I'll allow you to choose the implement."

She blinked. "My...what?"

"Earlier, you were instructed to keep your hands behind your back."

"But—"

"I asked if you understood the rules. You said you did. I offered to bind you."

She licked her lower lip in that way that might drive him to madness.

"I even gave you a second chance to have me bind you. You didn't accept my kindness."

"Marcus... I... I couldn't help myself." The pulse in her throat beat like the wings of a frantic butterfly.

"I tried, but I almost lost my balance when you started playing with my nipples so hard."

"I see." He struggled to suppress his grin. Her floundering charmed him. "I'm understanding it's my fault you didn't follow directions?"

"Well..." Her eyelashes fluttered. "I've never felt anything like it before. The room spun. So I had to hold on to you."

"You could have said so. You could have said the word yellow and asked me to slow down. You could have asked me to tie you."

"But you're such an excellent Dominant that I couldn't think straight."

This time, he did smile. "Your flattery and excuses should get you out of a discipline?"

She blew out a breath.

They'd reached a turning point. What happened next was completely up to her. She could get dressed and go on her way. Or she could offer her trust and see where the path took her.

Though he wouldn't admit it aloud, her answer mattered a great deal. "Well, sweet Julia, what will it be?"

Chapter Three

Julia's thoughts collided.

Everything they'd shared, including his nurturing, rocked her world, made her question everything she thought she knew about sex and pleasure. In her experience, men took their own pleasure, then moved on to video games or the television. But Marcus snuggled her, keeping her warm and safe. In that moment, nothing seemed more natural.

Yet if she went further, would that conflict with vows she'd made to herself?

After her last relationship with Jason, an overbearing blowhard, she'd sworn she'd only get involved with nice, uncomplicated men. Yet here she was, sitting in the lap of a tall, broad, rugged man who claimed to be a Dominant. *Claimed?* What was she thinking? Silently she scoffed. There was no claimed about it. This man *was* a Dominant. It resonated in his every word and action. He expected to be obeyed and he'd already pushed her outside her comfort zone.

From the moment Lana had removed her wedding dress and kneeled in front of her groom, Julia had stepped into an alternate reality. She was in a stranger's sunroom, nearly naked, while Marcus Cavendish cradled her, still dressed, leather blazer included, and insisting she'd earned a punishment.

Damn it. He had a point. His warning had been explicit. And the truth was, all she had to do was utter a safe word and he'd immediately release her. In under five minutes, she could be in her vehicle, on the way back to Denver, putting miles and memories between her and Marcus.

But a secret part of her yearned to surrender to him. Already she'd had experiences that she'd remember for a lifetime. *Could it get better?* And if she didn't seize the moment, would she regret it?

She pushed away a bit farther and angled her head to study him.

Patiently he regarded her, waiting.

Before she could voice a decision, Lana and Ben entered the sunroom. Julia wanted the floor to swallow her. With her pile of discarded clothes over the back of a chair, her state of undress was obvious.

Marcus gently moved her onto the couch, ensuring the blanket was tucked around her, while he stood and moved to greet Ben.

"Jules! I'm so glad you came." Lana smiled as she glanced from her friend to Marcus. "And doubly glad you stayed."

Her smile was broad, and Julia recognized Marcus had been right. Lana had taken a risk in sending her a wedding invitation. She'd trusted Julia in a way she'd trusted none of their other friends.

"I see you've met Master Marcus." Lana sat on the couch next to Julia.

"I—"

Saving her from the embarrassment of the admission, Marcus replied on her behalf. "I've been giving Julia an introduction into our lifestyle."

Lana smiled. "Thank you for taking her under your wing."

When the men began speaking, Lana swept her gaze over Julia. "Are you doing okay?"

She took a moment to sort through her reactions. "Yes. It's been..." What was the right word? "Instructive." Then she went on. "I was a little surprised by the whole event."

"I'm sorry about that. Honestly, I didn't know what to say. I figured you might want to save me or rescue me, or at least feel obligated to try to talk me out of it. At best, I figured you'd be worried. At worst, I was afraid you wouldn't come at all."

A little hurt, Julia blinked. "Am I really that judgmental?" She hoped she was the kind of person who'd always be there for her friends.

Lana sighed. "If you were, I wouldn't have invited you. It's just hard for outsiders to comprehend the complexity of this lifestyle. If the situation had been reversed, I'm not sure I would have understood. I know we've talked about kink, but in general terms, so I thought you might understand. And really, I'm selfish. You mean so much to me that I wanted you here. Forgive me?"

She hugged her friend. "Of course. As long as this is what you want, I'm happy for you." If she hadn't stayed and talked with Marcus, would she have understood? "I'm glad you invited me."

Lana smiled then hazarded a glance toward the men. "I'm glad you and Master Marcus have hit it off."

That was a bit of an understatement. "I am a bit overwhelmed, honestly."

"I'm sure you are. I was, too, when I first met Ben. I had no idea he was into BDSM, and it took me a long time to accept it, and then embrace it."

"You obviously have."

"Ben has been understanding and wonderful. This"—she swept her arm wide—"completes me. I'm happier than I ever knew possible. Ben is my partner in all ways. I found things in this relationship that I didn't know had been missing."

"Like what?"

"The sense of security that comes from talking about the most personal things. Ben doesn't let me off the hook for anything."

"Does he punish you?"

Lana tipped her head to the side. "I call it funishment."

Julia raised her eyebrows.

"It's not really part of our relationship, except when we're in a scene. We've had a lot of discussions, and we've both agreed to the rules in our relationship. Everything we do is negotiated and discussed." She glanced at her husband, then looked back with a quick grin. "I've been known to break the rules on purpose."

"Seriously?"

"It's called being a brat. Ben will sometimes indulge me, but occasionally I have to listen to a lecture about asking for what I want." She rolled her eyes. "And those times, I get sent to bed without an orgasm."

How would she have coped if Marcus had withheld her pleasure earlier?

"It really is worse than being spanked and getting it over with." She sighed. "There are many aspects to a physical relationship with a Dominant. Maybe Master

Marcus has already told you that all lifestyle relationships are different?"

"Yes. He has."

"A lot have punishments, others don't. Others incorporate servitude. Some are more about masochism and sadism. Impact play. Many get their kicks from using blindfolds or being tied up, like rope bondage. There's a whole art to it, and it's beautiful. I even have a stained-glass piece depicting a woman who is surrendered in suspension. But frankly I don't have the patience for that." After a quick shrug, she continued. "I know people who confine their activities to the bedroom. Then there are people like Annie and Sam who like to come to the Den on occasion or to another club in Denver."

Annie was one of their friends who shared kinky stories at happy hour. Maybe at the next gathering, Julia would have stuff to share. On the other hand, she might prefer to keep it secret. "What kind of relationship do you have?" Although maybe she had enough information to guess.

"Ben and I share a twenty-four seven relationship. It *is* the relationship, meaning it's part of who we are rather than being something we indulge in on the side. We have some sort of physical interaction every day. I love getting spankings—I get off on them. Since I met Ben, I have dozens of orgasms a day." She glanced in his direction.

As if sensing his new wife's gaze, he glanced over his shoulder at her. His expression softened as he swept his adoring gaze down her body.

Julia's heart panged. She'd never been looked at in that way, even in the mad-rush early days of a relationship. If only for an evening, she'd like to be that happy. She'd spent her life working hard, setting goals and feverishly focusing on them. Her entire life was a giant to-do list. She was restless and dissatisfied. Or had been, until Marcus placed his hands on her shoulders for the first time.

Moments later, Lana refocused on Julia. "If you want, we can talk more when I get back from my honeymoon."

"I'd like that." She might need to discuss her emotions.

"Are you going to continue to play with Master Marcus? He seems interested in you. And I haven't seen that for a while." Quickly she clamped her hand over her mouth. "Oops. I'm not supposed to gossip."

Julia lowered her voice. "You've got my interest. That means you can't stop."

She shot a covert glance at the two men. "He had a relationship that ended badly. And he generally only scenes with the Den's submissives. No strings attached."

"Oh?"

"You're the first woman I've seen him show an interest in."

Since they seemed to have another few moments to talk, she clutched her blanket a little tighter. Whispering, she confessed what was on her mind, seeking her friend's input. "He believes in having his orders followed and enforcing his rules if they're not."

"Oh." Lana studied her. "You've learned that already?"

When Julia didn't answer, Lana continued. "I trust Master Marcus implicitly. He and Ben have been friends for years. But, more than that, I scened with him a few months ago."

"You…?" Speechless, Julia couldn't finish.

"With my husband's permission, of course. And he was standing there the entire time. Master Marcus wields a mean tawse."

Obviously noting the way she narrowed her eyes in confusion, Lana explained. "It's not unusual for some Doms to have a particular implement they prefer to use. Master Marcus makes his own tawses. He told me you have to be very deliberate with how you use it. I'll be honest, I wasn't really listening at that point. I just wanted to feel it, not hear about it." Lana made a show of rolling her eyes, after first checking that neither man could see her. "It's something to do with how you hold it and how you swing it. All I know is he's very strong, and he pays a lot of attention to where he stands and how long he takes. He's… I don't know the best word. Maybe controlled."

"Ben was really okay with it?"

"Oh yes." Lana fanned herself. "He provided the aftercare. And the sex we had that night…? Holy hell, was it hot. So what do you think? I can tell you from personal experience that he's considerate. Thoughtful. Kept checking with me and with Ben."

"I'm…" She had to be honest with herself. "A little tempted."

"If you're interested, he'd be perfect for an introductory experience. And you have to admit, he's handsome."

"If you like rugged and rough."

"Do you?"

She hadn't. Until now.

"Look, Jules… Master Marcus is nothing like Jason the Jackass. He came across as this confident professional, but he was just a control freak. That's totally different from"—Lana waved a hand around—"this. If you're tempted, give it a try. You're at a party, having fun. It's totally safe." She lowered her voice a little more. "I've never seen Master Marcus with the same woman twice. So he's apparently not looking for a relationship, either. What's the harm? Don't judge yourself." She exhaled with great drama. "We both know you're your own worst critic."

They both laughed, but there was a lot of truth in that statement.

"You might learn that you're not cut out for this, but you'll never know if you don't try."

That had been their college motto. That was how they'd talked each other into rock climbing, sky diving, riding dizzying rollercoasters, even renting snowmobiles and building a makeshift igloo to protect themselves from the elements while drinking Irish coffee.

"Quit pouting about Jason the Jackass."

Julia straightened her shoulders. "I'm over him, remember? I'm back out in the world. I went on a date last month."

"That's right. With what's his name? Harvey the Hairball?"

"That's terrible!"

"You went from one extreme to the other."

"He's okay." In a boring, talk about mechanical engineering projects all night type of way.

"Why settle for rice pudding when you could have chocolate cake?" She glanced at the man in question.

So did Julia. "Chocolate cake can be too rich."

Lana, with the knowledge gleaned over years of friendship, laughed. "Uh-huh. Nice try. Can't wait to hear what you have to say when I get back from my honeymoon!"

Further conversation was interrupted when the men joined them.

Ben gently touched Lana's shoulder. "Shall we say hello to the rest of our guests? I'm ready to get you out of here so we can enjoy our first night as a married couple."

"Yes, Sir!" Lana looked up at him with a contented smile.

Have I ever been that serene?

"Congratulations on your wedding." Julia glanced from one to the other. "I hope you're very happy together."

"And on Lana's collaring," Marcus added.

Lana traced her fingers across the small heart that dangled from the D-ring. "I still can't believe it's real."

Ben helped his bride from the couch then placed his hand against the small of her back and guided her from the room.

Once they were alone, Marcus spoke, sending now-familiar excitement down her spine. "Did she reassure you?"

"She said you two had played together."

"We did, a few months ago." Marcus dropped on the couch next to her. "She was curious about other Doms, and Ben had never used a tawse, so he arranged for the scene. We did it here at the Den. Damien and Ben both supervised."

"I don't think I'd want to play with anyone but you."

He sucked in a sharp breath as he regarded her. "If you had a Dom and that was on your limits list, your wishes would be honored. But if you wanted to scene with someone else, that decision would ultimately fall to your Dominant."

You?

Even though the house was warm, she shivered as she studied the heat in his eyes. "She also said she's never seen you with the same woman twice."

"Did she tell you my grade point average in college? I'll have to talk to Ben about his wife's proclivity for gossip."

Julia grabbed his forearm and was taken aback by his strong and unyielding body. "It's my fault. Please don't blame Lana."

"I'm not serious. She was trying to reassure you, and I appreciate that. To set your mind at ease, I'm single, and I intend to stay that way. Is that a problem for you?"

"I prefer it." Marcus was a thousand times more overwhelming than Jason had been. And he'd been too much for her to deal with.

"And you? Entanglements of any kind?"

"No." She started to pull her hand away, but he placed his over hers.

"There's the matter of your punishment from earlier. Would you like to see the dungeon?"

In an instant, he was her unrelenting Dominant again. As if he'd ever forget. Now he invited her to take the next step on the journey. She yearned to be as self-assured as Lana was. Instead, frantic anticipation crashed through her.

"You're welcome to have a look around and see if anything appeals to you. If not, we can leave any time you want."

"What about my clothes?"

"They can stay here. I told you I want you naked."

She dragged the blanket more tightly around her shoulders.

"That stays too."

"Do you show no mercy?"

He studied her intently, studying her reactions, seeing not just into her, but through her. "Do you really want me to?"

Do I? Or do I want the new experience?

"Tell me about your hesitation."

This admission was more painful than any she'd made. "I'm not very comfortable walking around in the nude, even in my bedroom."

"Is there a reason for that?"

Embarrassment flooded her, and she retreated as far into the corner as she could.

In quiet, reassuring tones, he spoke again. "BDSM is about dropping pretenses. About honesty. Especially when it's difficult."

"I need to lose some weight. My previous boyfriend pointed it out all the time. Bought me a gym membership for my birthday. For Christmas I got exercise equipment."

"He was a fucking idiot."

She blinked.

"You look like a woman, Julia. Delectable curves."

That wasn't what she'd repeatedly been told.

"You're beautiful. Every part of you. Even the ones you want to hide. If I hadn't found you gorgeous, I wouldn't have pursued playing with you."

The damage Jason had inflicted went deep.

"You should be proud of your form. If you were my submissive, I'd want you completely exposed."

As she waged an internal debate, he remained silent, even though he kept a hand on top of hers—a connection, reassurance. That was the thing that struck her the most about him. He seemed to know when to wait for her to work through her doubts and fears. "I can't." She brought up her chin.

"Yellow?"

"Yes. I want to see the dungeon, but I can't do it naked."

"What would make it possible for you?" Before she could answer, he held up a hand. "Something that I could agree to?"

"Uhm..." This kind of negotiation was foreign to her. But his questions thrilled her. Maybe she could even be bolder in her future relationships. "I could wear a bra and panties." *No worse than being at the beach.*

"With your heels?"

"Is that a little bit of a kink, Sir?"

"What they do for your calves, and the way they change your body posture? Most definitely." Raw heat blazed in his eyes. His approval filled her with courage.

"Will you...? Will you stay near me?"

"Of course."

When she'd gone to work parties with Jason, he'd wandered off, leaving her to fend for herself for hours. Whatever was in the basement here promised to be much more unnerving than that.

"Unless you decide you want to explore a little on your own. In that case, let me know."

"That definitely won't happen." More confident than she had been five minutes ago, she blew out a determined breath. "I want to try."

His smile was instantaneous. "Brave, brave, sweet sub."

His terms of affection were like a drug, and she couldn't get enough of them.

Slowly she lowered the blanket. "Would you...uhm get my clothes for me?"

He grinned. "Absolutely not."

"You're frustrating."

"Hmm." His response told her nothing.

What had she expected? Though he'd been accommodating, he obviously had limits.

Aware of his heated gaze on her, she stood.

"Your nipples are gorgeous. Hard. Begging for clamps, potentially?"

Arousal crashed through her. She enjoyed stimulation, but she'd never experimented with anything like that. "I don't know."

"Interested?"

"I might want to try it." Still, since they weren't in the middle of a scene—and she wasn't caught up in momentary passion—she smoothed her skirt over her hips and down her thighs. "You mentioned a limits list?"

"That's correct. Things that you refuse to do, and they're not open to negotiation."

"I wouldn't know what to put on it."

"Being shared, for instance."

"But..." She frowned. "I don't know enough to have many things on it."

"Many subs, bottoms, have implements they ban. Broken skin. Body modifications."

She shuddered. "Okay. I get it. The last two are a definite no from me."

"We'll discuss everything tonight. If we were to scene in future, I'll remember what you've said."

In future?

They'd agreed they weren't looking for relationships. And yet...the idea of never seeing him again made her heart ache.

What is wrong with me?

Wanting—*needing*—to put distance between them, she hurried to the chair where he'd draped her discarded undergarments.

Saying nothing, the man dominating her turned slightly to watch her movements.

She donned her bra and panties before wiggling out of her skirt.

Movements slow and deliberate, he stood and walked toward her. "You are remarkable."

His gruff tone resonated with sincerity, but his nearness, how big he was, and his crisp, masculine scent overwhelmed her.

"Before we go downstairs, I want you to be aware of some things."

Grateful, she paid attention. "The Den is a low-protocol club which means we're informal. You're not expected to walk behind me. You're permitted to speak to anyone you'd like, and you're not required to address anyone—other than me—with total respect."

"But you still want me to call you Master Marcus or Sir?"

"While we're here, yes."

"I'll do my best to remember."

His grin was as quick as it was lethal.

"And if I don't, I'll be punished."

"Quick study."

Once again, nerves pummeled her.

"You'll have questions. And I'll do my best to answer them. For now, we'll check out the space. Then we'll discuss how you'd like to proceed."

"I can do this." *Who am I trying to reassure? You? Or myself?*

"You can. We'll start by having you stand up straight. I want you to show off your body. Be proud."

When he studied her in that way, green eyes smoky with desire, she could refuse him nothing.

She tossed her head so that her hair spilled down her back as she did what he said.

"Stay where you are."

It took all of her will to remain in place as he slowly walked around her.

"Place your hands behind your neck. And keep your eyes open. That's another way you have of hiding from me."

Do you miss anything?

Being with a man who saw her—and through her—was unnerving.

He circled her. Trying to keep her breathing under control, she looked straight ahead. Gently he drew a finger across her skin, inflaming nerve endings as he went.

Then he stopped in front of her and cupped her breasts in his palms. Confounding her, she ached for him to toy with her nipples, making her regret that she'd insisted on covering up. Was that also part of his diabolical ways?

Leaving her wanting, he stepped back. "Good girl. So well-behaved."

Before coming here, she might have found his words patronizing and objected to his use of them. Tonight, though, they fed her with an illicit thrill.

Now she was starting to understand Lana's dilemma better.

Julia would never be able to tell her friends what he said. No way would they understand. How could they when even she was confused?

"Ready?"

"As I ever will be."

"You can leave your skirt and blouse here. We'll come back for them later."

"Okay."

He raised an eyebrow, as if waiting for her response.

"Yes, Sir." The formality of her response gave her some comfort. More self-conscious and nervous than she had ever been, she followed him from the room. A few people greeted him as they made their way through the house but no one paid much attention to her.

They descended the staircase and emerged into a dimly lit space with guests standing around talking.

The dungeon was nothing like she'd imagined. She had expected a large, cold, barren room, with shackles attached to stone walls.

Instead, the space could have been photographed for a luxury magazine. The floor was an expensive tile, and a few thick rugs were scattered around. A bar stood in the far corner, tended by two servers, one male, one female, each wearing a bow tie and not much else.

There were several couches, lots of pillows, and a number of blankets. Lana, Ben, and Damien chatted in a semicircle.

And no one was chained to the wall. At least as far as she could see.

Marcus regarded her. "Well?"

"I thought it would be scarier."

"Can I get you something to drink?"

"Merlot?"

"Sorry. No alcohol is permitted while sceneing. It can cloud judgment, for Tops as well as bottoms."

"But there's a bar." She scowled. A little liquid courage would have been appreciated.

"Mocktails only. Juice. Energy drinks. Water."

"In that case, sparkling water? With lime."

"You got it." He hesitated. "Are you okay by yourself for a moment? I promised not to leave you alone."

She nodded. In fact, she relished the chance to take it all in by herself.

"I'd prefer to hear your response."

"I'm fine." She met his gaze. "Sir." That he'd asked reassured her. There were differences between the men she'd dated and Marcus. Was he always this solicitous? Or was it because they were engaged in a BDSM scene? "Thank you."

Without another word, he strode to the bar where Damien joined him. The two exchanged a few words. Then they glanced over at her. It took all of her resolve not to cover up. Instead, she looked away.

The bald man she'd seen upstairs at the wedding ceremony was talking to a Dom with another man a respectful distance behind him, head lowered. As she watched, the bald man took the sub's wrists in one hand and seemed to apply pressure to the man's shoulder. The bottom slowly lowered to his knees.

Nothing surprised her any longer.

Momentarily Marcus rejoined her, and she gratefully accepted the beverage.

"You might have noticed I chatted with Master Damien. I arranged for a private room, but only if you want to scene, and only if you want to do so in private. I'm happy to use the public areas if it suits you."

"Is it okay if I think about it?"

"Of course."

The interaction she'd been watching recaptured her interest. "Can you explain what's going on there?"

He followed the direction of her gaze. "That's Gregorio. For lack of a better term, he's the property's caretaker. He lives here full-time and keeps the dungeon ready for entertaining. Damien allows others to lease the space, and a production company films here from time to time. He's also the Dungeon Monitor who ensures house rules are enforced. At times, he scenes with people."

"He forced that man onto his knees."

"It doesn't take a lot of pressure. And I understand his background makes him an expert at controlling recalcitrant submissives."

Whatever that meant…

Across the room, Gregorio helped the sub to his feet. The Top moved into the place where Gregorio had stood. The Dom placed his hand on the man's shoulder, and Gregorio repositioned his touch.

Moments later, the sub was on his knees again.

"As you see everything that happens is consensual."

Though she was overwhelmed, what he said made sense.

Still close to her, his voice quiet, he spoke in a tone meant only for her. "Gregorio is a switch."

From earlier, she remembered. He could be both a Top and a bottom.

Her observation led to new concerns. "Does he participate when we're playing?"

"No. And he won't intervene unless you're in trouble in some way or he sees something that's not quite right."

Gregorio supervised the Dom one more time before moving away.

"There are a few private rooms down here. But mostly there are screens to divide the space."

So maybe there are subs chained to the walls elsewhere.

"Shall we watch a scene before you decide whether or not we should use the room?"

Her heart thundered from dread as much as anticipation. She was saved from answering when Damien joined them.

"I like to meet my guests." He offered his hand. "Damien Lowell."

She blinked. Though Marcus had coached her earlier, she was unsure how to respond while she was half naked, especially since he was striking in a well-tailored gray suit and a tie.

Under normal circumstances, she would find him disarming.

Instinctively she looked to Marcus for guidance. He was grinning, as if delighted by her confusion.

"Shake Master Damien's hand."

"Master Marcus and Lana tell me this is your first exposure to our lifestyle."

His grip was firm, but not overbearing. This man wore authority as easily as he did his bespoke clothing. "Uh... Yes, Sir."

"Welcome. I hope you'll find us hospitable." He unclasped her hand, and she had that same odd feeling that she'd had when Marcus had touched her for the first time. These men were powerful, as untamed as the Rocky Mountains surrounding them.

"Thank you." Aware of Marcus's gaze on her, she resisted the temptation to cover up.

"Master Marcus tells me you may use one of the private rooms? There's a matter of your punishment?"

Mortified, she looked at Marcus again.

"I..." She willed the floor to open and swallow her whole. "Yes."

"And you've been made aware of safe words?"

"Yes. Red and yellow, Sir. Green means everything is okay."

"And you've been informed that you can use those words at any point? Say red and the scene stops immediately. Gregorio or myself will enforce the rule, if necessary."

The last part she hadn't been aware of, but she appreciated the information.

"And you're choosing to go through with this?" Damien asked.

She looked at Marcus. The man who wanted her to call him *Master.* His hands were big, and they were capable of giving her so much pleasure. He radiated vitality and it affected her on a deeply feminine level. She didn't question her attraction or desire. After tonight, she might never be this brave—or foolish—again. "Yes, Sir."

"Very well. The Den also has a safe word. *Halt.* Gregorio or I will immediately put a stop to any scene if you utter that word. No questions asked. No repercussions from any Dom or Top. Enjoy your experience." He bowed rather formally before moving off.

"Are you ready to continue exploring?"

She took a sip of her sparkling water. "I think so. Sir."

For the next half hour, they watched others playing. A bottom was being flogged on an X-shaped structure—a Saint Andrew's cross, according to Marcus. Across the room, a man was being paddled on a bench. A third was flailing desperately, a short skirt around her waist, as she was receiving an over-the-knee spanking.

The first bothered her a little. But—like earlier—Marcus kept his hands on her shoulders and held her close, explaining what was going on.

The second scene made her curious. The final one turned her on. "Her ass is red."

"The color is beautiful, isn't it?"

The woman was as curvy as Julia, and she did indeed look gorgeous as she kicked and cried out her protests.

"Does she seem to be suffering?"

"No." In fact, the sub's protests seemed like an act to elicit a greater punishment. Her body heated, and she squirmed beneath his touch.

"Are you intrigued?"

He feathered the word into her ear, sending fresh skitters of awareness down her spine. "Yes." The admission startled her.

"So am I. I want to know how you respond to my touch. I'm looking forward to discovering all your secrets."

So am I. No way was she brave enough to admit that out loud.

Gently, still behind her, he stroked the back of his hand up the side of her neck.

The man was a master of seduction.

"Are you ready, my sweet sub?"

Am I?

Marcus took the empty glass from her and offered it to a passing server before capturing her hand. His grip was both reassuring and commanding. He lit a fire of response in her that she'd never experienced with any other man.

They walked down the hallway, and he released her momentarily. "Wait here." He stepped past a room divider.

Moans and whimpers reached her, wrapping around her. Despite her trepidation, she was intrigued. Moments later, shaking his head, he rejoined her. "The couple is open to being watched, but we're going to pass."

"Why?"

"They have been together for several years, and there is a lot of trust between them. It may be a bit much for you."

Her heart jammed its next two beats together. "I want to try."

After a moment's hesitation, he spoke quietly "Please remain silent and do not disturb their scene. If it's too much, squeeze my hand."

"I promise."

He led the way behind the partition. He indicated she should stand next to him, then he once again took her hand in his.

The back wall was exposed brick, and the floor a polished, gleaming wood.

In the middle of the space, facing them, a woman was strapped to a Saint Andrew's cross, her wrists parted above her head, her legs spread wide while a spotlight illuminated her in all her naked, submissive glory.

A man dressed only in black leather pants stood with his back to them.

The sub was focused on her Dominant, and neither acknowledged Julia or Marcus. "Fuck you, Sir." The woman's voice trembled. "Fucking get on with it! Give me what I want."

"Pain slut." Though he picked up a wicked-looking whip, he didn't approach her.

"I need it." The sub looked at him, raw need in her eyes.

Will I ever get to that place? She wrapped her arms around herself. Not that she wanted to.

"Be a man and whip my breasts."

The Dominant flicked his wrist, and the leather jumped in response. The sub fixated on his motion, but the Top didn't respond to her goading.

"Bastard. Don't tease. Give me the whip. Do it."

Steps deliberate, he moved toward her to force back her head. "Is this what you want, Lindsey?" He dangled the implement in front of her.

"*Yes.* You goddamn well know it!"

"Then fucking use your manners, slut."

Even from across the space, it was obvious he was squeezing her jaw tighter, making her response difficult. Still, Lindsey managed a whimpered plea.

"Better." He released her. "Now keep your mouth shut, unless you're screaming or begging. Otherwise, I will end the scene and take your ass home."

He was threatening to withhold her beating as a way to make her comply?

Julia shifted. Why was this so appealing to her?

"Do you need to leave?" Marcus whispered.

She shook her head.

"This may be unsettling."

The two appeared connected, physically as well as emotionally. The scene was riveting, making it impossible for Julia to walk away. "I'm fine."

The Dom grabbed Lindsey between the legs and squeezed. A combination of pain and ecstasy crossed the sub's features, making. Julia wondered if she had looked like that when Marcus had been torturing her nipples.

"Is that the best you've got, Sir?"

As the moments passed, Lindsey's breathing became ragged. She squeezed her eyes shut, then, yanking feverishly against her bonds, she screamed.

"You drenched my hand, bitch."

Lindsey's body sagged but she smiled.

"I ought to take you home right now."

"Whip me." This time, it was a plea, rather than a demand. "Or fuck me."

"Didn't I tell you to keep your mouth shut unless you were screaming? Don't you ever learn?"

Julia's breaths threatened to strangle her. Marcus had been right. This whole thing was intense. But there was no doubt Lindsey wanted everything her Dom meted out. As Marcus had said, things were consensual.

"I'm ready to have you to myself." Marcus offered his hand.

With some reluctance, she accepted.

Together they left the small space.

Behind them, Lindsey sobbed. Had Julia ever heard anything more haunting, more enticing?

Marcus drew her into a private alcove. Julia's breaths stuttered, and she could hardly string two cohesive thoughts together.

"I'd like to hear your impressions."

"It was…interesting."

"In what way?"

"I get what you mean about certain things working for different people." She had a difficult time verbalizing her thoughts. "Like the way she seemed to provoke him, for example. As if she wanted to increase the stakes."

"Exactly."

"And… He denied her."

When she fell into silence, he encouraged her. "Go on."

She reminded herself she never had to see him again after tonight. For once, she could be as honest as she wanted. "The way you made me come in the sunroom… What we did… It wasn't like the scene we just watched. You did what I wanted."

"You're a quick study."

The approval in his tone made her weak.

"And you're right. I watched every one of your reactions. As I was telling you earlier, Lindsey and Nate have been together for years. She's a masochist, craves pain. Nate is an excellent match for her. He ensures she gets what she needs without things getting out of hand. The provocation is part of her ploy, but Master Nate always stays in control. He's been known to walk away from a scene. And if she pushes too hard, he will take her home immediately."

"This is more complicated than I imagined."

"It's about knowing your bottom. Nate can't give her a spanking for bad behavior."

Julia tried to take it all in. "Because that's what she wants."

"Exactly."

"You need to know what to expect from your punishment."

"I'm pretty sure I'm not a masochist."

"Shall we find out what it is you want?"

Slowly, nervously, excitedly, she agreed.

He guided her behind another partition.

"This is the spanking room," he told her. "It's set up slightly different from some of the other spaces."

Paddles, some with holes drilled in them, and all sorts of implements she didn't recognize hung from hooks on a wall.

One corner had a shelf and a pedestal sink with a few hand towels arranged on top.

A plain chair sat against the wall, and a type of vaulting horse was off to one side. Although it looked similar to ones she'd seen in gymnasiums, this one had all sorts of straps and ties affixed to it.

Now that they were away from the Den's other activities, all other sounds in the background and her pulse filling her ears, the situation was very, very real.

"Since it's your first time, I want you to know what to expect and offer you a chance to negotiate anything you need to. We'll start with a simple over-the-knee spanking. In my opinion, a hand is the most intimate way of punishing a sub. I can feel how you respond. The heat of your skin will keep us connected. I will learn how much pressure you want or need."

Her mouth dried, as if it had been stuffed with a gag. "But I also want to introduce you to my tawse."

The implement Lana had mentioned earlier.

"I'll administer that while you're attached to the punishment horse."

"I don't know what one looks like or how it works."

"It's one of the most perfect implements." He pressed a button on the side wall. "I'll have one of the club submissives fetch it for me."

Less than a minute later, a woman appeared.

"Master Marcus. How can I help?"

"My bag, please, Brandy." He opened his jacket and pulled out a small piece of paper that appeared to be a claim check.

"Of course, Sir." She accepted the small piece of paper. "Anything else?"

"That will be fine. Thank you." Marcus dragged the chair to the middle of the area, and adrenaline zipped through her, imagining the way his palm would connect with her skin.

Before long, Brandy returned.

After placing the bag on the shelf, he unzipped the duffel and extracted a wicked-looking implement.

In horrid fascination, she stared. The thing was about a foot long. The handle was also leather, and the outside was stitched with a lighter shade of thread. Just below the handle she saw a design, a brand of sorts that seemed to resemble an eagle. About a third of the way down, the leather forked into two distinct strands.

"It won't bite."

She looked at him, trying to decide whether or not he was serious.

With a grin, he amended his statement. "Until later."

"You're not reassuring me."

"Get acquainted with it." He offered her the horridly fascinating implement.

The heft was greater than expected, and the leather was both rigid and supple at the same time.

"Smack it on your palm, on the outside of your leg. Get a feel for it."

She flicked her wrist, and he shook his head.

"With a tawse, you keep your wrist straight. It's a whole different action than wielding a flogger or whip. Flicking your wrist allows the leather to wrap, perhaps catching flesh where it's not intended."

"Does that matter?"

"My pain is deliberately inflicted. I want my stroke to land with precision." He nodded. "Try it again."

She kept her wrist locked and smacked her calf. The leather stung, but not in a terrible way.

"Are you ready?"

Am I? With courage she was nowhere close to feeling, she whispered her agreement.

He extended his hand for the tawse, and she turned it over.

"Face me." When she did, he continued. "Remember to breathe."

"Okay."

"I'm sorry?" From the time they'd entered the dungeon, he'd been kind and solicitous. And now when he spoke, his voice held a terrible, uncompromising tone.

"Yes, Sir." Her response had been automatic, something unthinkable earlier.

"I take your safety seriously. You may have some red spots on your buttocks tomorrow, perhaps even an outline of my handprint. A small bruise or two is unlikely, though possible."

"I understand."

"If I suspend the scene and ask if you want to proceed, the only answers I will accept are yes, Sir and green, Sir. Yeah or uh-huh will not work. Anything less than yes is equivocation, and we'll need to stop.".

"Are you always so formal?"

"We'll go through this every time we play."

But since we'll never play again...

"Tell me what color you are on."

"Green, Sir."

"You wanted to keep your panties and bra on while we were in the more public areas. Now that we're alone, are you willing to be naked for me?"

After gulping, she quietly responded, "Yes, Sir."

Without further prompting, she stripped.

"Thank you. I love the sight of your gorgeous curves."

She quickly glanced away, then back at him again.

"When you're ready to proceed, please kneel and place your hands at the small of your back."

His instruction was unexpected. She'd thought he might sit and draw her over his knees. But this... He wanted her completely submissive.

"Still green?"

She managed a half nod. Then remembering herself, she answered. "Yes, Sir."

"That little trick you saw Gregorio perform? He taught me. The choice is yours. Would you like to kneel for me, Julia? Or shall I force you to?"

In the silence that dragged between them, she regarded him for any sign that he was joking.

"Five seconds."

Deciding she wanted to be in control as much as possible, she lowered herself to the floor in front of him.

Being on her knees while her Dominant claimed the space above her was a bigger mindfuck than anything she'd ever experienced.

He fisted his hand into her hair, his grip forceful, yet not painful. As he regarded her, adrenaline hummed through her. She wanted, hungered, for an intimate connection with him.

"Good girl. Such a natural."

It seemed that way for her as well. Maybe not ever with anyone else. But with Marcus, in this moment?

Slowly he released her then shrugged from his leather blazer. Leaving her on her knees, he hung the garment on a hook near the wall that held the spanking instruments.

Mesmerized, she watched while he faced her to unfasten the top two buttons on his shirt then the ones at the cuffs. He rolled the material to his elbows, exposing the sinews of his strong forearms that were covered with an appealing scattering of dark hair.

He returned to his previous position, and she moved in closer until he stood inches in front of her. She had to tip her head back to see his eyes.

"I'm going to sit in the chair." He paused.

For effect?

"Then I'm going to ask you to stand, walk over to me, and drape yourself across my lap."

Her pulse accelerated again. "How many spanks do you think you deserve?"

Having no idea how to answer that, she frowned. "Uhm, how many is customary, Sir?"

"Excellent response."

He was so masculine, so powerful standing above her. She had never been more aware of her femininity. "Maybe I should ask how many you think I deserve, Sir?"

"You *are* a natural." With addictive power, he smiled. "If you were more experienced, I'd suggest twelve over-the-knee spanks and another dozen on the horse. And in a punishment spanking, I generally deny my submissive an orgasm. But tonight..."

Tonight?

"I think eight and eight. And if you take them appropriately and ask nicely for each, I'll consider allowing you to climax when we're finished."

Damn you. He'd done it again, scrambled her brains so that her only thought was of pleasing him.

"The first eight will be with my hand. The second will be with my tawse, if you are willing?"

"I can use my safe word if it's too much?"

"Always, Julia. Of course." He crossed to the horse and placed the strap on top of it.

Then, as he'd said he would, he sat in the chair. Fear collided with nerves and excitement. He looked so imposing, so threatening.

"When I say so, rise slowly and make your way to me. Drape yourself over my lap."

At her sides, her hands shook.

"*Now,* sweet submissive."

In order not to flee, she concentrated on him.

As she stood, her motions were jerky and awkward, unlike what she'd seen from other submissives at the Den.

Would she get better with time?

Not that she'd find out. She had the courage to do this because it was a one-time thing.

As she neared, he extended his hand. In this moment, it was a lifeline, one she greedily accepted. Another mindfuck. He intended to punish her, and at the same time, she sought comfort from him.

"You're welcome to hold on to the chair leg and me for balance. Since you're new, I will trap your legs with one of mine to prevent you from kicking and struggling. In the future, I'll require you to control your own motions.

"The spanking will begin when you ask for it. Count each stroke aloud and then ask for the next. A little gratitude will go a long way to ensuring my good nature when we're finished. Any questions?"

A million or more.

But she couldn't find her voice. Goose bumps chased up her arms. *Now or never.*

Chapter Four

Everything about her enchanted Marcus.

Pleasing her, making sure she had an experience she'd never forget, mattered a great deal to him.

She met his gaze. Her lips were slightly parted, and she was in no hurry to release his hand. Truthfully neither was he. "Whenever you're ready."

He remained silent and watched her dig deep for courage. Waiting was easy when you knew you were going to win.

Finally she accepted his help as she assumed the position he'd requested.

With a soft sigh, she braced her fingers on the floor as she settled. Her hair fell in wild disarray and the scent of arousal inflamed his senses. Her perfectly round little ass begged for his touch.

Her trust was complete—her surrender sublime.

Holy fuck.

What had he been thinking? That she was an ordinary sub, and this was a regular scene?

He shook his head.

She was new to the lifestyle, curious, and perfect in every way. He wasn't sure how he'd let her go. This was the first time since Amber that he'd been tempted by that kind of thought. And it unnerved him.

To distract himself from the unwanted realization, he stroked the backs of her thighs. "Relax for me?"

"I wish it were that easy."

He curled a hand around her waist. But it wasn't to ensure she remained in place.

Eventually, with a deep exhalation, she released the tension from her body.

"That's right." He loved the way she responded,

As he'd promised, he captured her legs between his.

Having her trapped, helpless, hardened his cock.

He'd keep her like this for hours, but he wasn't certain he could endure the torture.

Ever since he'd reached beneath her skirt to pleasure her, he'd wanted to sink into her welcoming heat.

All other sounds receded until the only thing filling the space were her soft, gentle breaths.

A few seconds later, she shifted, trying to look at him. "I'm ready, Sir."

Am I?

Stalling, savoring, he ran his fingers up her thighs, caressing her soft skin. Julia—with her combination of beauty, innocence, and sass— made it difficult to focus. "I'll want you to keep still." *So you don't rub against my aching dick.* "Remember to breathe. I'm going to warm you up a bit to get the blood flowing to the area. That will ensure you enjoy the experience more." Because he intended to thoroughly turn her on.

"Yes, Sir."

Her responses already flowed so much easier than they had half an hour ago.

He stroked her beautiful rear with slow strokes.

When she sighed, no longer holding herself rigid, he rubbed harder.

"How are you doing?"

"This is so unusual."

"In what way? The way I'm touching you?"

"And the amount of time you're taking."

Maybe she'd been with some selfish lovers in the past.

He'd happily spend the rest of the night pleasuring her.

When her skin glowed, he reminded her of his expectations. "I'll begin when you ask me to."

She shuddered. "Now. The anticipation is making me nervous."

"It can be part of the pleasure as well."

"Right now, it's not."

Marcus delivered his first smack on that tender place where her thighs and buttocks met.

Gasping, she struggled to escape.

He held her still. "Easy." To take away the small ache, he pressed his fingertips against the reddened spot.

"Damn, Sir!"

"Not what you expected?"

Julia settled again. "It stung."

"More than you can bear?"

"No." She shook her head. "I'm ready."

Fuck. She was fantastic. "How many was that?"

"One, Sir." She settled herself back into position. "I'm ready for the next one."

"This will be easier if we find a rhythm, which happens if you release your inner struggle."

"Spoken like someone who has never been spanked."

"I wouldn't put a sub through something I wasn't familiar with. Breathe, my sweet submissive." He caught her right cheek with another spank.

She yelped as she kicked her legs.

The door opened, and Damien entered the room.

"We have company."

"Oh God, no."

As he met his friend's gaze, Marcus placed his palm on her back, keeping them connected physically as well as emotionally. "You can stay where you are, my sweet. Or you can get up. I'm sure Master Damien is here to check on you."

"I was afraid you were using a cattle prod on her." Damien grinned.

"I'll try to be quieter."

"How many spanks have you had, Julia?" Damien asked.

"Two, Sir."

"What color are you on?"

"Mortification," she mumbled.

"I'm afraid that answer won't suffice."

Her grip tightened on Marcus's leg, as if she were seeking reassurance from him. In response, he trailed his fingertips down her spine.

After a steadying breath, she spoke. "Green. I'm green, Sir."

"Are you under duress?"

"It just hurts more than I thought it would."

Marcus prompted her. "Master Damien needs a yes or a no answer."

"No, Sir. I'm not under duress, Sir."

"Might I suggest you use a gag, Master Marcus?" With that, Damien left.

"We're alone again."

She released a soft sigh. "Thank goodness."

The interruption seemed to have solidified the intimacy between them. "Relax." To reestablish their intimacy, he trailed his fingertips across her warm, silky skin.

As the seconds ticked by, she relaxed her muscles, all but melting beneath his touch. Her trust made him want to hold her and cherish her.

"I don't suppose we can do this all evening, Sir?"

Had he ever wanted anything more? "We can."

"Mmm."

"Now breathe. Accept. Enjoy."

"May I have the third, Sir?"

This woman… Beautiful submissive.

After rubbing the area he intended to spank, he smacked his open palm on her ass.

This time, she cut her gasp short and swayed her hips, resuming the correct position without being prompted.

"Please, Sir. I'm ready for number four."

He complied, and her tiny cry was much softer this time. "You're doing so well."

She gripped his leg tighter, establishing a deeper connection. "I'm ready for the fifth."

Her voice had lost its edge of tension. Instead, her words were breathless. With need? Anticipation? Longing? *Dare he fucking hope…?* "My sweet…" With a tenderness that surprised him, he caught her once more beneath her butt cheeks.

Her body went still, but she didn't protest.

"Don't hold your breath."

"I'll try."

"Inhale for me."

He waited until she did, then he rained a smack on her left buttock. "Now exhale."

"Oh, Sir! That was..." She released his leg and allowed her fingers to brush the floor. She'd taken six, and she seemed too far gone to remember to count.

"That was...?"

"Amazing."

Blood rushed to his groin. There was nothing more exquisite than her trusting surrender.

He gave them both a moment to absorb her realization. He'd been a Dominant long enough to recognize this moment for the gift it was.

"Can we keep going?"

"You have two more."

"Is that all?"

If she wanted, he would take her deeper, giving her experiences she'd never dreamed possible.

He waited until her breaths were steady and rhythmic before spanking her twice in quick succession.

When he'd finished, she whispered her gratitude.

"Such beautiful words."

He helped her up, then tugged her into his lap. She blinked as she focused her wide, blue eyes on him. "How did you enjoy that?"

With her squirming in his lap, nestling into his chest, his cock throbbed hard. He ached to bury himself in her, so hard, so deep that she screamed his name in submission. What the hell had he been thinking in promising her just one night? He wanted her with every beat of his heart.

"That was..."

Arms around her, he waited while she sorted through her words, her thoughts.

"Not what I expected."

"In what way?"

"At first, it hurt like hell. That made my fear even worse. Then..."

Maddeningly she adjusted herself, making him all the more aware of his insistent dick.

"Well... It didn't hurt. Toward the end, it felt less intense." She splayed her hand on his chest and pushed back a little, making eye contact. "Did you use less force? I mean, did you go easier on me?"

"Not at all."

"It was as if I could handle more than I could have in the beginning."

He nodded. "Endorphins, maybe?"

"And..." She wrinkled her nose as she hesitated. "It became about trust. Just you and me. I was able to move past my fears." She lowered her head a little and her hair fell forward to shadow her expression. "I don't begin to understand it. But it was sexy."

"Was it?"

"It... You... Turned me on."

Fuck.

Now he vowed to never let her go. He caught her chin so she could no longer hide. "I'm glad it did." *How hard – how far – to push?* "Part your legs so I can see how turned on you are."

Crimson painted her cheeks as she wrapped her arm around his neck for balance and spread her thighs.

He skimmed his fingertips across her clit. "Your pussy *is* wet."

"Oh God." She moved against his hand, seeking, silently asking. "Yes. It is, Sir."

"It wouldn't take much for you to come, would it?"

Closing her eyes, she lifted her hips.

"You already know that I'm strict about my subs not coming unless they ask. Which also means you need my permission." Relentlessly he continued to tease her.

"But you're doing your…" She swore as she tried to pull back from him. "Your…best to make sure I…I…"

"Exactly. I want you focused on coming, obsessing about it. You'll need it more than your next breath." With exquisite tenderness, he abraded her clit. "You'd sell your soul to receive the pleasure that is mine to give or withhold. I want you sobbing and begging." He parted her labia to plump her clit, then he gently began to spank her slickened pussy.

In a broken, desperate plea, she cried out.

"Do *not* come, my sweet."

As she panted and gasped, she dug her fingernails into his shoulder. *"Please."*

"Fight a little longer." He was relentless, pressing a thumb against her clit, then sliding his fingers inside her warmth to find her G-spot. "For me. Because you want to please me."

Thrashing her head, she arched her back. "Sir!"

Earlier she'd given him everything—her trust. He rewarded her with an orgasm that made her scream.

In her ecstasy, she was even more stunning.

When she'd finished riding the waves of pleasure, she collapsed against him. There was no place more perfect for her than in his arms.

Outside their space, conversation hummed, broken by yelps of pleasure and the crack of a single tail. But here, completion wrapped them in quiet peace.

"Oh. *Oh.* That was incredible."

He grinned. "And there's more."

She swept back strands of her hair to look up at him. "How can there be?"

"I allowed you to come before I should have."

"Honestly? I was coming apart from the inside out."

"And yet I could have kept you on the edge longer."

A disbelieving scowl settled between her eyebrows.

"It might have been uncomfortable, but not impossible. Let's find out, shall we?" Before she could respond, he moved, scooping her up as he stood, then lowered her to the floor. "I want you on your knees."

Eyes wide and luminous, she gulped. He was tempted to capitulate and gather her against him once more. "There are greater heights, if you dare reach for them." He intended to make her ache for his touch, and when she came again, the emotional release would swamp her.

Then, pressing her lips together, she did as he asked.

Marcus pressed his hand to his thigh. Was there anything sexier than having a lovely, trusting submissive at his feet? "Fucking lovely."

She lowered her gaze in a beautiful, respectful way.

"Spread your knees as far as you can without discomfort, and place your hands behind your neck, then thrust out your breasts."

When she had, he continued. "When I ask you to kneel in future, this is my preferred position. It will make your body available for my pleasure and heighten your awareness." He waited. When she remained silent, he prompted her. "Any questions?"

"No, Sir." Finally she looked up at him.

A dozen emotions filled her radiant blue eyes.

"Are you getting aroused again?" He'd know if she lied. The truth would be in her gaze, and her body would betray her.

"Yes, Sir."

Satisfied, he grinned. But there was so, so much more still in front of them.

He crouched in front of her to place a finger beneath her chin and tip back her head. "I'm going to find out for myself."

She gulped.

He slid a finger between her slick folds. "You were honest." *Of course she was.* With ruthless determination, he swept his touch back and forth. "Stay still, my sweet."

But she didn't. With a sharp inhalation, she gyrated her hips.

"Julia." He said it with a growl, issuing a warning. But mostly, his tone signified his triumph. For him, her responses were sexy. "You're moving, even though I commanded you not to."

"I'm...*trying* to do what you want." She pulled back, as if that were following his wishes.

"Are you trying not to come?"

"I... *God.* This is unfair!"

His fingers grew damper. "Is it?"

"You don't care? No mercy?"

Looking at her, reading her grimace, her desperation, he grinned. "None at all." Then he gave her pussy half a dozen gentle slaps. Though she flinched and gasped, she didn't try to escape. "That's it."

When he was finished, he held his hand in front of her face. "Lick your juices from my fingers. Taste your hunger and need—what I'm doing to you, and the way your body responds to me."

Dutifully, never severing their connection, she dutifully sucked them dry.

An image, as visceral as it was powerful, plowed through his mind, one of her doing that to his cock.

"It's time for the other half of your punishment." His voice was gruffer than intended, and he cleared his throat.

Needing distraction before he grabbed her head and lowered his zipper, he stood.

When she started to follow suit, he shook his head. "Wait for instructions."

"This is confusing."

"Frustrating?"

"Yes." She exhaled a shaky breath.

"Wait for my direction. Allow yourself the experience. It's only one night," he reminded her. *Reminded her?* Reminded himself.

After silent deliberation, she whispered, "Yes, Sir."

"Unless you object, I'm going to remove my shirt."

"Should I object? Do you look like an ogre beneath your clothes?"

"Keep it up, my sweet." Despite his veiled warning, he grinned, enjoying her gentle tease.

As he released his buttons, she stared. And when he shrugged the material from his shoulders, her lips parted.

"Oh!"

"Oh?"

"You're sexier than I imagined."

"I'm not an ogre?"

"Not that I've seen." She tipped her head to one side. "Yet."

Ridiculously pleased, he regarded her. "You enjoy living dangerously?"

"Until tonight, I hadn't thought so."

He walked to the horse and stood next to it. "Crawl to me."

Blinking, she remained in place.

"Is it uncomfortable for you?"

She hesitated for a moment. "Terribly."

"Good. Thrills lie at the edge of our comfort zone." Tension grew and stretched. "I want you across the top of the horse, lengthwise."

Her breaths ragged, she lowered herself to all fours. He moved the tawse to the left side of the horse, leaving it close to where her body would be.

Julia took her time coming toward him, and he savored every moment as her breasts swayed and her hair cascaded around her.

When she reached him, she hesitated, and he offered his hand to help her up. "You can't possibly know how beautiful you look."

"I…" She blinked. "Thank you."

"Perfect. Now raise up onto your tiptoes. And drape yourself across the top of the apparatus." When she did, he added, "There are straps on the far side for your hands. You may choose to hold on to them, or I can secure you."

She turned her head to the right so she could see him. "Will I get more spanks depending on my decision?"

"Good question." She was catching on fast. "Not this time."

"I'm supposed to say thank you?"

"Always your choice, but gratitude is appreciated and may be rewarded."

"In that case, I think I'd like to be tied so I don't have to be thinking about staying in place."

"You're learning." He smiled his approval. "Is your pussy still wet, Julia?"

"Honestly? No, Sir. I think I'm a bit scared."

"Nerves can heighten anticipation, if you don't fight against them." He moved away a little to secure her wrist in place.

She tilted her head back so she could watch him.

"I need you to be a bit higher. Stay where you are." He moved behind her and adjusted her slightly.

She gasped. "My feet can hardly touch the floor."

He could lower the horse, but the combination of this angle and her helplessness would drive him mad.

Then he secured her left wrist.

Satisfied, he swept her hair to one side. "Make yourself as comfortable as possible."

Her choices left her even more vulnerable to him. "You have no idea how beautiful you are."

Her breaths shallow, she continued to look at him, as if he were a lifeline.

Slowly he walked to stand behind her. "Your ass cheeks are still red." Marcus wasn't sure he'd ever seen anything more appealing than the evidence of his hand on her curvy derrière. "And they'll be more so when I'm finished."

Crouching, he drew her right ankle toward the outer edge of the apparatus and tightened a buckle around it. "How does that feel?"

"As if I'm being pulled apart, Sir."

"I want to be certain you don't move. The position will make you even more aware of your submission to me."

She shivered.

He fastened her left leg in place, then looked at her for a moment. Her blonde tresses tumbled around her.

The scent of her, citrus and feminine determination, intoxicated him.

After picking up the tawse, he brushed it across her back, continuing down her right side.

She flinched.

"Ticklish?"

"A little."

Using a firmer touch, he brought it up her left side. This time, she moaned, and he relished the sensual sound.

Next, he eased the leather up the inside of her thighs.

"Oh, Sir!" Her legs quivered.

Once he'd taken a slight step back, he pressed the edge against her clit.

As much as she was able to, she thrust her hips toward him.

"Greedy sub." He pulled the implement away.

She moaned her protest.

"Tell me why you're spread like this on the punishment horse."

It took her a few seconds to answer. "Because I didn't keep my arms behind my back when we were upstairs, Sir."

"And how many strokes will you be taking from my tawse?"

Her body shook. "You said eight, Sir. But I can assure you I've learned my lesson. I asked to be tied for this one so that I can follow your orders perfectly."

"Good. That will spare you another spanking before the night's out."

She lifted her head. "Does anything influence you?"

"A safe word. If you simply can't do this, we can negotiate a different punishment. Like me bringing you to the edge of a climax eight times and refusing to grant you relief."

"Like I wouldn't get to orgasm at all?"

"That's correct."

"Lana told me that's worse than a spanking."

"It most definitely can be." Marcus struggled to suppress a grin at the thought of edging her. "What will it be?"

"Get it over with."

"More Lana wisdom?"

Julia didn't respond, and he spent a few minutes warming her up, trying to help her return to the right headspace, where fear was in the background rather than being something that consumed her.

When her skin glowed and she relaxed some of the tension from her body, he calculated the correct distance to stand from her. When using a tawse, he never reached. He delivered each stroke with deliberate, blunt force. "Let me know when you're ready."

"I think I am."

He gave her the first one.

With a gasp, she strained against the bindings, but she didn't raise her head, and she didn't cry out.

A glorious shade of red blazed across her buttocks. "Perfect." This tawse was one of his favorites. The leather was well-conditioned, and it was perfect for someone new to his type of play. He crafted some with three or four strands, and he'd use them if he were asked to scene with a more experienced player, or with a recalcitrant male sub.

He repositioned himself so he could catch her on her upper thigh.

"Damn." She expelled a breath. "When do we get to the fun part?"

"Aren't you glad you're restrained?"

She nodded, but then evidently remembered his rule. "Yes, Sir."

Still, he pressed his fingers against the stripe, soothing the hurt.

When her breathing returned to normal, he placed the third, and she barely pulled against her bonds. "That's excellent. You're no longer fighting. The more you surrender, the easier it becomes."

The fourth spank landed just as precisely as the others, this time on her left thigh. Her leg flexed, but she inhaled. "Any guesses on the next one?"

"Above that one, Sir?" She didn't reflexively tighten her muscles.

He gave her what she was expecting, and she gifted him with a small smile. *Fuck.*

"That..." Her eyelids drifted shut. "Was nice."

He stepped back to trace the outline of each red mark.

She'd moved past surrender to serenity.

"I'm going to finish you off. One more on your thigh. The rest on your buttocks."

"Yes, Sir," she murmured.

"You're doing okay?"

"It's... *Yes.*"

A hazy sleepiness laced her tone. If they played again, there was no doubt he could take her to subspace. That was a rare treat with most bottoms, all but unheard of with neophytes.

"I'm ready for more. Please."

He moved to stand near her left hip, then he gave her the remaining lashes in a rhythmic symphony of his leather and her sighs.

When he set aside the tawse, a fine sheen of perspiration dotted her back. Her skin bore the marks of his fierce possession. The sight aroused him.

He knelt in front of her and smoothed back her hair, then he gently kissed her forehead.

Affection didn't come easily to him, and it hadn't in any scene since his breakup with Amber. Yet with her curiosity and trust, the skeptical Julia had chipped away at the chains he'd placed around his heart. "How was that?"

As much as she was able, she tipped back her head so she could look at him. "You want me to be honest, right, Sir?"

"I expect nothing less."

"I need to come. Please, will you bring me off?"

He hadn't been prepared for that question.

"I'm so needy. And my whole body is on fire."

"Beautiful, sweet sub."

Rather than arguing, she agreed. "Thank you, Sir."

"In all ways, you've earned a release." Keeping her gaze as captive as her body, he reached between her legs. "So wet."

With all of her muscles straining she jerked against his hand "I've never felt this way."

He slipped two fingers deep inside of her while simultaneously pressing his thumb pad against her clit.

"Oh, oh…"

Her pussy tightened around him, and he slid his digits in and out rapidly, penetrating deeper and deeper, stretching her wide.

She pressed her tiptoes into the floor, lifting herself up as much as possible, granting him access, wordlessly seeking more.

"Beg for it."

"This… You… I'm unraveling. Please, Sir, give me an orgasm."

Whether she'd followed instructions or not, in this moment, he'd give her anything she desired.

Changing his angle, he found her G-spot. "Now, Julia. Take it."

She cried out as the climax engulfed her. As he continued to please her, she shuddered. Then, rather than withdrawing, he continued to play with her hot pussy.

"I… There's no way. I've never been able to come more than once in a row." Even as her lovely mouth formed the protest, she closed her eyes and thrust her hips toward him.

With each second, she was getting wetter. She possessed untapped depths, and he wanted to be the one to discover her secrets.

When he added a third finger, she screamed.

"So sexy."

She rode each of his strokes.

"That's it." He continued to play with her clit.

"I… Sir… I'm getting close. May I?"

He loved that she remembered to ask. "Come for me, my sweet." He applied pressure to her G-spot. *"Now."*

As she yelled his name, her pussy clenched his hand. He whispered nonsensical words to her as she rode the climax, then continued to encourage her as the tremors receded. Grinning ridiculously, he traced the outline of her jawbone.

"That's never been possible."

"And now you know it is."

"Most times I don't orgasm at all."

"Then I'm a lucky man." He meant it. That she'd trust him to take her there was a gift.

She opened her eyes. "Thank you, Sir."

"I was wondering if you'd mind your manners."

"Or I'd earn another spanking?"

"No doubt."

"In that case, I should have kept my mouth closed."

Oh? He raised his eyebrows. Another unexpected delight from her.

As he reached to unfasten her left wrist, he had only one thought. How the hell was he going to keep her?

After she was free, he rubbed her shoulder and arm. "Move slow. You were in an unnatural position."

"Is this what Lana was talking about earlier…? Aftercare?"

"That's more like what we did upstairs, on the couch. But I believe in taking care of my submissives."

"Is it usual? I mean, does everyone do it?"

Grateful for the distraction of the conversation, he released her other wrist, and took care to rub her skin to help with circulation. "Not all subs want or need it."

"And all relationships are different."

He met her eyes to discover a dreamy, faraway look in their depths. "Exactly."

"So why do you do it?"

"There's a transition between a scene and the ordinary world. Think of it like a movie. Have you ever remained in the theater after a film ends?"

"All the time. I like to watch the credits because I want to linger in the moment a little longer. Not ready to go outside and get in my car and return to the reality of laundry or getting ready for work the next day."

"Exactly."

"Sir's cock is hard."

"You're observant." It would take him less than half a dozen strokes to spill his load inside her sweet pussy.

"Will you fuck me?"

"It's not an expectation." He dropped his hand and looked at her. "Ever."

"That's not why I'm asking. I want you inside of me."

"We never discussed having sex."

"Do we have to talk about it? Surely someone here has a condom?"

He stroked her upper lip. "I refuse to take advantage of you."

"I know my mind, Sir. I want you to fuck me. Now."

"You probably have questions, maybe something you need to say to me—"

"You can't have it both ways, Sir. Either I'm a woman capable of asking for what I want, or I'm not. You said each person has different aftercare needs. I want you to make love to me."

He set his jaw. He wasn't strictly against having sex with a sub after a scene, but with Julia, he was in unexplored territory.

"If you don't want to, I could ask someone else—"

"Don't." Primal possession beat through him.

"Take me or let me go."

He didn't blister women's behinds in anger. He prided himself on control. Tonight was the first time he'd ever been tempted. Though she was goading him, that didn't make her threat more palatable.

He stood and took two steps back.

"Do you want me to beg for that as well?" Her voice trembled with emotion. "I will, but I wish you wouldn't make me."

"This is about you. Being certain you know what you're doing."

She tipped back her head, revealing the glossiness of unshed tears in her eyes. "I want you, Marcus."

Fuck this. Even in this short amount of time, she'd worked herself inside him. "Your safe word still applies."

"Of course."

"I'll untie you."

"No. Let me stay like this. I want to be bound and helpless."

Jesus. He ran a hand through his hair. He'd never been with a sub like her.

When he didn't immediately respond, she strained against the leather straps.

"Tell me your safe words again."

"Yellow and red. And I am so green right now it's like being in a forest."

Enough said. He took his wallet from his back pocket and fished out a condom and placed it on top of the horse.

After toeing off his boots, he hastily removed the rest of his clothes.

His cock jutted out, and urgent need made him throb. Wanting to remind them both who was in charge, he moved in front of her to capture her hair with his left hand, then he used his right hand to guide his cockhead across her lips.

With a small smile and without being asked, she opened her mouth.

Tentatively she licked him. "Keep going."

Even though the angle was awkward, she took him inside her mouth. "That's a girl." He thrust his hips shallowly.

She gagged a little but didn't try to pull away. Instead, she doubled her efforts to suck him.

Her efforts to please him had him on the verge of ejaculating much sooner than he'd have ever imagined. Gritting his teeth, he stilled her. "Stop."

Ignoring him, she continued. In future—if there was a future—he wouldn't tolerate this kind of behavior. But right now, her enthusiasm pleased him. "It's customary to thank a Dom for allowing you the privilege of sucking his cock."

"Is it?" She licked precum from her upper lip. "In that case, thank you, Sir."

"Are you sure you don't want me to release you before I take you from behind?"

"Just get on with it. Sir."

Her muscles had to be tired and achy. Yet the idea of taking her—owning her—while she was helpless fed an ancient need in him.

Marcus didn't need to stroke his cock before rolling the condom down his length. Even if she hadn't taken him in her mouth, the sight of her punished skin would have made him instantly hard. "Your ass is still red. And so are the backs of your legs. It might be difficult to sit tomorrow." If they were at his place, he would make her soak in the hot tub before he rubbed her with arnica and put her to bed.

Using both of his hands, he parted her buttocks, and he teased her pussy with his cock, sliding back and forth. She was wet, slick and inviting.

"I'm so ready. Fill me, Sir!"

He had to angle his body to take her the way she wanted.

Then, unable to hold back any longer, he surged into her. "Take all of me."

"Yes!"

"Your cunt is so hot, my sweet. Is this what you need?"

"Yes!"

She squeezed him tight, and he dug his fingers into her waist to control his responses. "Tell me what you want."

"More. Harder."

He changed the angle, gripping one of her hip bones, and reached between their bodies to stroke her.

She shook and shuddered. "Please, please, please!"

"Come whenever you want."

Screaming and convulsing, she strained against the straps.

Her passion was as honest as it was unbridled.

Finally, after breathing his name, she stilled, sagging against the horse.

"I'm not finished with you yet, Julia."

Chapter Five

Detached from time and reality, Julia floated on a cloud of bliss.

Until this evening, she'd had no idea anything like this really existed. It was one thing to listen to stories over cocktails or to watch movies, but to be a participant, to have had delicious pain sear her skin followed by orgasms that had left her shattered… It was the magic of dreams, something she'd never imagined she'd experience.

And then to end it with mind-blowing sex?

It was a good thing she was secured to the horse. She wasn't sure her legs would support her otherwise.

"I've got you, Julia." As if from a great distance, his deep, rich voice reached her.

Since her breaths came in short bursts, she couldn't respond. And being stretched wide and having her head hanging down left her slightly disoriented.

The backs of her legs ached from his tawse. Her nipples throbbed, and her pussy had been tormented, then stretched wide by her temporary Dominant's enormous dick. Every place he'd touched had become an erogenous zone.

She was glad she'd promised herself only one night. It would take forever to sort through the implications of everything they'd shared.

This evening, she'd surrendered to the desire swirling inside her. For the first time in her life, she was aware of herself as a sensual being filled with needs, and she'd shocked herself by craving his domination.

Though she wasn't the type who slept with a man she barely knew, the feelings he'd caused had overwhelmed her. She'd craved the joining and completion with an urgency she never had before. At some point, she might regret her impulsivity, but she hadn't wanted to drive back to Denver after that spanking. A vibrator would have been cold comfort when she wanted his strength and heat.

"How are you doing?"

"I'm…" With a sigh, she closed her eyes. "Sated."

"I'm going to unfasten you." He said the words softly, near her ear.

He used his voice masterfully, controlling his tone and changing the volume, depending on the situation. He could be uncompromising and comforting, all in the space of a few seconds.

"Please stay in place and follow my directions."

"Yes, Sir." That would be easy. At this moment, she didn't think she *could* move.

He loosened her wrists then released her ankles. Then he took a few minutes to rub every part of her body, paying special attention to her shoulders. Their time together was winding down, and she wanted to savor every remaining moment.

"Ready?"

Suddenly the world swam. "To be honest I'm not sure."

"We'll go slow."

With a grip that was both gentle and firm, Marcus wrapped his arms around her from behind. She expected him to help her stand. Instead, he turned her, then swept her from the floor and into his arms where he held her against his chest.

In a few strides, he crossed to the chair then he sat, still cradling her.

Her senses reeled. No man had ever cared for her like this, making her feel safe and treasured. Earlier, upstairs, he'd wrapped her in a blanket. This time, he used his arms to keep her warm.

She had no idea how much time elapsed as she surrendered to the moment, enjoying the thump of his heart beneath her ear and the masculine scent of him surrounding her. Seemingly content to remain as they were for as long as she wanted, he made no attempt to move.

"Thank you." Julia prided herself on her independence, but after that experience—and the entire evening—she appreciated this.

"Take your time."

A couple of minutes later, she became aware of his dick beneath her bottom. He was still hard and had made zero attempt to seek his own pleasure. His self-control, and the way he thought of her first made her dizzy.

"You didn't come."

"Contrary to what most men would have you think, I will survive the experience."

"But..." She looked up at him. "I want you to..."

"To?"

"Be satisfied."

"I am. You came. That's all that matters."

"That's gentlemanly of you, Sir. But it's not fair."

"Things don't always have to be fair." A smile toyed with his lips, making him even more appealing. "

She shook her head. "I want this. I want you."

For several seconds that dragged, she waited for his answer. She'd never had to ask a man for sex, well, unless it was several months into a relationship and monotony had set in.

"You're sure?"

More than she'd ever been. "Yes. I am."

With his hands on her waist, he helped her to stand. "Let me take care of this." He discarded the condom before rolling another into place. Eyes narrowed purposefully, he reclaimed his seat. "In that case, my sweet, straddle me."

Keeping her steady, he helped her into position, and she lifted onto her tiptoes as he guided his cockhead toward her pussy.

When he'd taken off his shirt, she'd noticed a smattering of dark hair arrowing down to his waist.

"You're a goddamn goddess, Julia. Wrap your arms around my neck."

She slowly lowered herself onto his shaft. Even though he'd already been inside her, this angle was slightly different, allowing him to penetrate deeper. "*Oh!* God…"

"Take me." He reached behind her to spread her buttocks, then he thrust up in a single, harsh movement.

He filled her, possessed her.

"Much better."

When she was fully seated on his enormous cock, she sucked in a steadying breath.

"You've got this. Now arch your back a little."

The angle tilted her pelvis and allowed him to cup her breasts. "Yes…"

"Hard?"

"Please, Sir." How was it that in her submission, she was freer than she'd ever been before—able to ask for what she wanted?

Pain simultaneously consumed and thrilled her. Closing her eyes, she moaned.

Relentlessly he trapped her nipples between his thumbs and forefingers. He pulled on the swollen tips, then tightened his grip and rolled them back and forth.

It was as if there were a direct line from her tortured nipples to her clit. She began to rock, digging her toes into the flooring as her orgasm built.

She'd been honest with him earlier. Until now, she'd never been able to come more than once. With him, she'd already had multiple climaxes.

All of a sudden, need swamped her. "Sir!" She wasn't sure she could hold it back. "I can't stop myself."

"Ask for it."

He lessened the pressure on her nipples. Then, as blood rushed to the tips once more, he squeezed again.

She teetered on the edge of sanity.

"Ask."

"Sir, Sir, Sir! Please, may I?"

"That's what I needed. Yes, my sweet. You may come."

Her resolve splintering, she pitched forward, and he caught her as she cried out her orgasm.

"That's it." He stroked the length of her spine.

Long moments later, she became aware of the easy intimacy between them.

Tonight had changed her forever.

She remained where she was, supporting herself on the strength of his shoulders. He was lean, without any excess fat. He either spent time at the gym or did some type of physical labor. Either way, she had never felt more protected than she did with him.

"You're very pleasing, Julia."

With a grin, she eased back to look at him. "So are you, Sir."

"Reaffirming that I'm not an ogre?"

"How would I know? I've yet to see you completely naked."

"I'll rectify that."

A thrill spiraled through her.

When her breathing returned to normal, he held her around the hips and guided her motions, up and down on his thick, swollen cock.

Though her energy waned, sex with him completed her.

"That's it."

Gruffness edged his tone, and he dug his fingertips into her buttocks. The muscles in his neck tightened. Her Dominant was less controlled than he'd been all night, filling her with a feminine sense of power.

She threaded her fingers into his hair and pulled firmly, like he had done to her.

In response, he growled, grabbing her shoulders to hold her in place as he drove up into her. She responded to his surges by squeezing her internal muscles.

"Damn!"

His cock throbbed as he ejaculated. Then, with a primal growl, he thrust a few more times, emptying himself inside her.

Leaning against his shoulder, she smiled. This experience had been magnificent.

He continued to stroke her, and she held him. Eventually she became aware of the sounds around them, soft cries, the tinkle of laughter. Her body chilled as perspiration dried on her skin. *Odd.* How far away the real world had become since she'd entered this private space with Marcus.

Eventually he eased her up so that their gazes met. "I've enjoyed sceneing with you. You're a very sexy sub."

Before she could protest, he placed a finger against her mouth.

"You are. Deny facts all you want, refuse to ever play again, but that won't change the way you reacted to me and my commands."

She shuddered because he was right.

With her still straddling him, he stood. Then he placed her on the chair. "Stay there for a moment." He crossed to the side of the room to run water in the sink, and she unashamedly took in his glorious, naked body.

She hadn't really had the opportunity to look at his naked body. His shoulders were impossibly wide, and his legs were big and muscular, his ass gorgeously sculpted. No doubt he'd fill out a pair of jeans.

A pang of regret ricocheted through her. Their first time would also be their last.

He disposed of the condom, then, when he faced her, the full-frontal view of him took her breath away.

His cock was still semi-hard, with a tiny drip of cum on the tip. She remembered the salty, masculine taste of him as he'd filled her mouth while she was hanging over the horse. Each thrust had been a reminder of her helplessness, but the rawness of their union made something unknown flare to life inside of her. With determination, she shook her head to dislodge the vivid memory.

"Not an ogre?" he teased.

With as much praise as he'd given her, how could she be anything less than honest? "Definitely not."

He turned away to dampen a washcloth.

"Thank you." She reached for it.

He shook his head. "Stand up and spread your legs."

With a sigh, she did. Arguing would get her nowhere, or a spanking. And her bottom was still smarting from his tawse.

The water was warm, and he soothed and cleansed her. She could get used to this. The entire experience with him had been a dichotomy, from scalding pain to delicious tenderness.

"You did well." He wadded the cloth and tossed it back toward the sink.

"I…uhm…" *What now?* "I'm not sure of the protocol. Do I say thank you and shake your hand?"

"Whatever is comfortable. If you'd like I'd enjoy spending some more time together."

"Thank you. No." Now that the scene was over, she needed to think things through. "I think I'll head back to Denver before it gets any later."

"I'll walk you to your car."

"There's no need. I can find my own way, but thanks."

His eyes narrowed. "Don't try my patience."

The terrible Dom tone was back in his voice.

She swallowed.

He might be naked, but he commanded the space.

He pulled on his trousers. As he fastened his belt, she wildly wondered what it might feel like on her skin. Shaking her head, she mentally urged him to hurry.

"Problem?"

"No. No, Sir."

A sense of self-preservation urged her to flee…before she surrendered to the temptation to stay.

He finished dressing.

Since she was still naked, she was once more aware of the power dynamic between them. God help her, but the feeling thrilled her as much as it terrified her.

Quickly, now more uncertain than ever, she slipped back into her undergarments.

"Would you hand me the tawse?"

With him waiting—watching—expectantly, she crossed to the horse and picked up the sturdy strip of leather.

"Keep your gaze focused on the floor as you bring it to me."

He wasn't done with scene yet? Or was this the way he always behaved—with Dominance being a part of who he was?

Still, she was helpless to refuse him.

When she reached him, she extended her hand.

"Kneel and offer it to me."

Hypnotized by his roughened tone, she did as he commanded.

"Not like that." He shook his head. "Across your palms."

His words seemed calculated to give her the deepest submissive experience possible. Even though she complied, he didn't move or speak.

As she waited, she recalled the heat of the leather as it caressed her skin. It had burned, but that sensation had paled next to the ache of desire it left in its wake.

"Beautifully executed, my sweet. Thank you."

He took the implement, and she bit her lower lip to prevent herself from asking him to use it on her again.

"You may stand."

He offered his help, and she accepted it. So strange how his touch could sear, yet comfort, and even support.

"Come here, Julia."

He continued to hold her. Instead of pulling away, she stayed there, inhaling his fresh woodsy scent.

He seemed no more interested in ending their evening than she did, but he didn't protest when she stepped back from him.

"Let's get the rest of your clothes." He paused long enough to clean and sanitize their space and repack his bag. Then he draped his leather blazer around her shoulders. "Ready?"

"Yes." *A thousand times no.* How would she go back to the real world after this?

As she followed him down the hall, sounds reached her—whips snapping, subs crying out, harsh commands, and soothing words of approval.

How much better she understood now than she had several hours ago.

In the main area, servers continued to offer drinks. Doms chatted among themselves or intimately with their partners. Some subs were on their knees, others were leashed. Nothing had changed.

Yet everything had.

"Stay here." As he regarded her, Marcus pointed to a spot on the floor.

Shocking herself, she didn't argue. She didn't move, but she kept her gaze on him. She jumped a little when someone touched her elbow.

"I didn't mean to scare you."

She turned and met the deeply dark brown eyes of Gregorio. Up close, he was more handsome than she'd imagined. His skin was a beautiful bronze, maybe from the sun. He had on a black T-shirt with the arms shorn off. His trousers looked as if they'd been tailored. No doubt he could appear in the videos filmed at the house.

"You're new here." Without waiting for her agreement, he went on. "According to Master Damien, it's also your first experience."

Marcus had told her Gregorio was a switch but, to her, he had the same air of authority as the other Doms she'd seen. "Yes." She hesitated, unsure how to proceed. "Sir."

"I watched for a few minutes."

"Did you?" She hadn't been aware of anything or anyone other than what was happening inside her own head.

"While you were tied to the horse." He paused. "You appeared serene."

She would have never used that word, but in a strange way it fit. "I suppose."

"How was your experience?"

Gregorio asked the question as if there were an easy answer. "Mind-blowing." She pushed her mussed hair back from her face. "At first it was too much, and it stung like hell. And then..." Julia shrugged. "It was amazing."

"Confusing?"

"Maybe a little."

"I'd be surprised if it wasn't. Do you have anyone you can speak with?"

"Lana. After she's back from Mexico."

"I'll have Master Marcus give you my contact information. If you need someone to talk to, feel free to get in touch."

"Thank you." She closed her mouth, refusing to tell him she had no intention of giving Master Marcus her contact information. Even if it was difficult, she'd sort through this on her own.

A few seconds later, Marcus returned with a bottle of water from the bar.

The two men greeted each other, and her temporary Dominant clamped a possessive hand on her shoulder.

"Drink this." He loosened the cap and offered her the beverage. He didn't check to see if she obeyed. Perhaps he assumed she would.

The two men talked, and neither of them addressed her. She sipped the cool water, more because it gave her something to do than anything else.

Under normal circumstances, being ignored might offend her. Right now, it didn't. She needed time to think, to process the events.

"I told Julia you would give her my contact information in case she needs someone to talk to."

Danger darkened Marcus's eyes. "I'll be the one handling that."

"Nonnegotiable." Though Gregorio hadn't changed the pitch of his voice, his tone was implacable.

Then he bowed toward her. "Enjoy your evening. I'll look forward to hearing from you."

After wishing them both a good evening, Gregorio excused himself.

"Ready?"

"Yes, Sir."

Possessively, Marcus pressed his fingers to the small of her back.

They headed upstairs and found the sunroom empty, and her clothes were where he'd left them.

"Thank you for the evening." She gave him a small, awkward smile as she removed his jacket and offered it back to him. "I can see myself out."

"I'm sure you can." He made no move to leave.

With a resigned sigh, she slipped on her stockings, then she wiggled into her skirt. Her fingers shook as she tried to slide the buttons of her blouse through the suddenly too-small holes.

"Let me." He brushed her hands aside.

Rather than starting at the top, he fastened the bottom one first. As he touched her, tiny tremors rocked through her. "Thank you." Julia had never been cared for like this before. It would be far too easy to grow accustomed to it.

He adjusted her collar before stepping back.

After straightening her shoulders, she slipped into her shoes. She told herself that she was once again in control, but that was a lie. Having a man who'd so thoroughly dominated her stand so close undid her completely.

They moved to the foyer where she found her purse and coat.

"Your keys, please?" He extended his hand.

"I—"

"Don't argue, Julia."

Gritting her teeth, she fished out her keys from the cavernous depths of her purse.

He opened the large oak doors, and a brutal, swirling wind nipped at her nose and ears.

"Which car is yours?"

"It's that one." She pointed to the street. "It's that small, black SUV."

"Stay here. I'll bring it around."

"Marcus—"

"Master Marcus." Fury sizzled in his eyes. "Question my authority one more time, and I'll have you back over that spanking horse so fast you won't remember your name."

Her knees weakened.

"Clear?"

"Yes, Sir." The idea of getting into a warm car that had the windshield cleared would be pure luxury. "Thank you."

"I wondered when you'd remember to use some manners."

Without another word, he sealed her inside the warm house while he braved the cold.

She didn't relish the drive back over Berthoud Pass. The gentle dusting of snow during the ceremony had been beautiful, but the whipping wind could make the roads treacherous.

A few minutes later, he re-entered the house. Snowflakes clung to his hair, and his hands were red. Her heart melted. He'd gone outside *for her*.

"Your chariot awaits, madam."

"Thank you."

"I'd prefer that you let me drive you home."

While appealing, it wasn't practical. Getting back up here would take hours.

He took hold of her elbow, ensuring she didn't slip as he guided her to the car. Like a gentleman, he opened the driver's door and handed her inside.

"Contact me any time." He offered his business card. "My cell phone number is on there, and so is Gregorio's."

She dropped it on the console beside her.

The air hung silent and still. He was apparently waiting for her to reciprocate. "I appreciate your bringing the car around." Heat whispered from the vents, and ice was already melted from the back window. But she knew the cold had to be stinging him. "You'd better get back inside." Her forced smile felt as brittle as the icicles hanging from the nearby ponderosa pine trees.

He closed the door and gave her a mock salute. As she drove away, she resisted the impulse to look at him in the rearview mirror.

* * * *

Safely at home after a surprisingly easy drive home, Julia dropped her purse and keys on a small table just inside of the door. Then she took Marcus's business card from her coat pocket. His name was embossed, along with the name of a company, Silver Eagle Construction.

Did he own the business? Or was it simply a place he worked? The fact that he did physical labor explained a lot about the bronze color of his skin and the muscles that had rippled his forearms and biceps.

She stared at the card for a full minute before dropping it in the wicker trash can she kept handy to dispose of unwanted mail.

Julia was looking for a nice guy. And he definitely wasn't.

After the awful experience with Jason, she'd vowed not to spend time with any man who was demanding, dictatorial, or domineering.

So why couldn't she get thoughts of Marcus—*Master Marcus*—from her mind?

She sighed.

After hanging up her coat, she went into the bedroom and changed into her coziest pajamas.

Sleep eluded her, and she tossed and turned for over an hour, consumed with thoughts of him. In frustration, she punched the pillow into several different shapes, but, no matter what she did, she couldn't banish the memories that flashed through her mind. She saw him in his leather blazer, then wearing his shirt with the sleeves rolled up. And then, heavens, completely naked.

For a moment, she wondered if his cock really was as big as she remembered.

Finally, exhausted from the battle, she climbed back out of bed. The scent of him lingered on her skin, a vivid reminder of the way he'd held her in his arms as she'd snuggled against his chest. She needed a shower. Or, better yet, a hot bath. Her legs hadn't been spread that far apart since her high school gymnastics class. Her calves felt as if she'd run a marathon, and even her arm muscles ached.

She drizzled a relaxing blend of salts into the water then sank up to her chin.

Lying back on the inflatable cushion with her eyes closed and steam wafting around her didn't help relax her as she hoped.

Stubbornly, though, she stayed in until the water chilled before pulling the plug.

As she wrapped a towel around her body, she caught sight of her reflection in the mirror. She dropped the towel and moved closer.

Though they were faint, there were small marks on the backs of her thighs, along with the outline of a handprint on her right butt cheek.

She waited for a rush of mortification, but it didn't come. Instead, arousal rocked through her.

Since she couldn't relax or vanquish images of her time with Marcus, Julia surrendered to the inevitable.

After grabbing her vibrator, she climbed on top of her bed, then selected the toy's slowest speed and placed the pulsing head against her pussy. A snapshot flashed through her mind—that of his hand beneath her skirt and the determined set of his features as he had brought her off in front of the window in the Den's sunroom. She'd never done anything as scandalous as that.

But that had barely been the beginning…

She lifted her hips, as she remembered the sound of his voice, sandpaper on velvet, as he had ordered her to lie across his lap. Her whole body jerked as she flashed back to the shock of raw energy exploding across her skin when his palm had connected with her buttocks.

An orgasm built deep inside as she recalled the way he'd efficiently and effectively tied her to the horse.

The climax drew closer, and memories moved at warp speed—the harsh explosion of leather on her helpless body, kneeling for him, and, God help her, the way he had held her head while forcing her to suck his thick cock.

With her free hand, she pinched her sore nipples, tugging on them.

In desperation, she moved against the vibrator, then, needing more, pulled back the hood of her clit. The tiny bit of flesh already felt abused. The reminder of the way Marcus had used her, smacking her pussy hard, drove her.

Panting, she turned the switch to high. She moved the quivering vibrator across her swollen clitoris.

Her body jerked and convulsed as if wired by electricity.

Within a few seconds, the sensations overtook her. Screaming his name, she came *hard.*

She dropped the still-running bullet next to her and gulped for air. Never had she had an orgasm like this before at her own hand.

Julia wasn't sure how long she lay there, shaking and shivering as she tried to remember how to breathe normally.

The orgasm alleviated some of the restlessness clawing at her. But no sooner had she got her heart rate under control than frustration replaced it.

She'd endured so much at Master Marcus's hands. How could she go back to normal, boring sex?

Marcus Cavendish—who had a bag filled with spanking implements—was many things, but he definitely wasn't the nice guy she was looking for.

The vibrator continued to shake, and she finally found the energy to turn it off.

Then, worn out, she snuggled under the covers, curled into a tiny ball, and eventually fell asleep.

* * * *

Far too early the next morning, the alarm jolted her awake. *Of course.* It seemed like the minute she'd actually drifted off, it was time to get up.

She hit the snooze button twice before realizing she was supposed to meet Harvey for breakfast.

Harvey. He fit her definition of nice guy to a tee.

They'd met online, and the first date had been pleasant. He'd insisted on paying for the coffee and scones, and they'd strolled Boulder's Pearl Street Mall. He'd been solicitous and he was passably good-looking.

He was exactly the type of man she was looking for. He'd said he hoped he wasn't being too forward in noticing she was cute. She'd tried to keep the wince off her face. That was a description that best fit bunnies and kittens.

She'd hoped the man she would end up with would find her wildly attractive. She yearned to hear she was sexy and responsive and that her ass was made for a tawse. But a solid, predictable partner wouldn't say that. And, really, there was nothing wrong with being cute. That Harvey had already hinted that he'd like to take her home to meet his family was a bonus.

With a deep sigh, she threw back the blankets and padded to the kitchen to turn on the coffee maker, then glared impatiently as the machine delivered miserly drips into the glass carafe. She didn't wait for a full pot before pouring a cup and adding a more than generous splash of cream. Then, after deciding that if a little was good, more was better, she topped off the cup.

Leaning against the counter, she downed the contents of the mug in several long gulps. Once she was semi-awake, she refilled the cup then headed into the bathroom. No matter what she tried, she was unable to tame her hair. After failing, she opted for a ponytail before opening the makeup drawer. A layer of foundation made no noticeable difference. The first coat of mascara did little to help her look more awake.

She all but troweled on the eye cream then applied a second coat of mascara. It, too, was a remarkable failure. Her eyes looked extra small, and they were slightly puffy. Despite being on her second cup of coffee, she could barely keep her eyes open.

And it was all Marcus's fault.

Until last night, until she'd screamed as she'd come, she'd been looking forward to meeting Harvey in downtown Denver for breakfast.

For all the good it would do her, she selected a matching bra and panty set from her dresser drawer. Since he hadn't tried to kiss her after their first date, she doubted he'd be seeing her lingerie.

She stepped into a pair of jeans and avoided looking at her backside in the mirror. It didn't matter whether or not her skin was bruised or if the outline of Marcus's massive hand could still be seen.

She pulled on a too-tight sweater and wondered if Harvey would even notice the low-plunging neckline. Regardless, Marcus wouldn't pay attention, either. He'd have the cotton off her body and folded in a pile so fast, it would make no difference what she wore.

Pictures of Marcus and Harvey collided in her mind. Since there really was no comparison, she pulled back her shoulders and decided to forget she'd ever met the delicious Dominant.

* * * *

She arrived at the restaurant a few minutes late. Harvey was waiting inside of the door, and he made a show of checking his watch.

"Did I have the time wrong?"

"No. Sorry." With a smile, she unbuttoned her coat and flicked off the snowflakes from her shoulders.

He didn't help her remove the garment or place it on the empty chair. He just stood there, looking at her.

"The roads were a bit slick. So it took a few minutes longer to get here than I thought it would."

"Are you always late for events? Or are you just not a morning person?"

She blinked but was saved from a reply by the arrival of the hostess.

The restaurant was already crowded, and loud. Once they had been seated, a harried-looking server slowed down long enough to ask, "Coffee?"

"Yes." Harvey spoke for both of them.

Why that annoyed her, she had no idea. "I'd actually like a chai."

The woman gave a thumbs-up and kept moving.

"I'm just curious." Harvey moved the condiments to the exact center of the table. He picked up his menu and looked at her over the top. "Are you often tardy?"

She laid her coat next to her. "Do you often continue to grind on things after someone has already apologized?" she countered.

He sat back carefully, still holding the menu. "You're being a little defensive, Julia. I was simply making conversation."

"You're right." Last night had made her edgy. "Sorry." *Why the hell am I apologizing? Again?*

"Because I'm always early for events and meetings."

"I have dozens of faults." Her patience snapped. There was a huge difference between a Dominant and an asshole. "Maybe hundreds."

"I'm trying to be serious here."

"So am I."

The server arrived with their drinks. "Ready to order?"

"We are," Harvey said.

Julia shook her head. "I haven't looked at the menu."

Harvey sighed. "I looked at it before you arrived."

"On second thought, I have decided." She unzipped her purse and fished a ten-dollar bill from her wallet. She dropped the money on the table and smiled, suddenly feeling lighter. "I want a man who is sunny-side up, with a large sausage, and two hot buns."

"Girl, same." The server winked at her.

Harvey gasped. "Now just a minute." The menu still clutched in his hand, he glanced around. "Be reasonable, Julia. I insist you behave yourself. You're making a scene."

She grabbed her coat, slung her purse over her shoulder and strode toward the door.

Outside, the gust of wind that smacked her in the face didn't slow her down. Instead, it invigorated her. As she'd learned last night, there was something exhilarating about being honest with herself and with others.

The cold, the wind, the icy streets didn't bother her.

She entered her condo and dug Marcus's business card from the trash. She stared at the eagle emblazoned on the paper, and she recognized it as the same symbol that had been stamped into his tawse.

Her hand trembled. She knew why she hadn't slept last night. It was because she hadn't been willing to face the truth—she'd liked the time she'd spent with Marcus. She'd enjoyed the way he'd spanked her, made her question her beliefs and the way he'd cared for her afterward.

Slowly, reluctantly, she admitted the truth to herself. She wanted to see him again.

So what am I going to do about it?

Chapter Six

Well, well. Marcus looked at his cell phone. *Julia.*

The night of the wedding, he'd given her his contact information. Although she hadn't reciprocated, he'd believed he'd hear from her.

During their time together, he'd done everything possible to give her a memorable experience. It sure as hell had been hot for him, more intense than most scenes he'd recently participated in.

After more than a month of silence, he'd forced the thoughts of her from his mind.

Despite his resolve, he'd had random flashbacks to the sight of her buttocks, upturned over his lap, exposed for his punishment. They'd had a taste of playing together, and every one of her reactions had been honest. She'd been upfront in telling him she wanted nothing more than a one-night stand. Obviously she didn't need him to complete her life.

And now, when he'd given up hope, his phone was ringing. He waited a full five seconds before answering. "Cavendish."

"Hello…" She paused for a moment.

The word *Sir* hung between them, unspoken.

He waited, wanting to see where she was going.

"It's Julia. I met you at Ben and Lana's wedding."

"I haven't forgotten."

She forced out a gentle sigh. "I've been thinking about you."

"Have you?"

"I was wondering…" For long moments, she hesitated. "That is awkward."

"It doesn't need to be. I've got as long as you need."

"You said it was okay to contact you."

Nerves layered her voice, stretching it tight. It had clearly taken some courage for her to contact him. "I'm glad you did." He reached for the fine Bonds whiskey that was on his desk then leaned back in his chair.

"I was wondering…" She blew out her breath. "Damn it. For the past few days—okay, weeks—I've been rehearsing what to say. I was hoping to reach your voicemail, honestly."

"You've got me, live and in the flesh."

"I'm not doing very well, am I?"

"You're doing fine." He took a sip. "If you had left a message, what would you have said?"

"Do you mind if I'm blunt?"

"I prefer that to games."

"I'd like to see you again."

Fuck. The words he'd been hoping for. "When?"

"Whenever it's convenient for you."

"Whenever it's convenient for you, *Sir.*" He gave her a moment to process his correction. "I do hold to some

BDSM proprieties. I expect you to comply with them, as well. Unless you're looking for a vanilla friendship. In which case, I'm wondering why you called."

He could almost imagine her worrying her lower lip before she responded. "I understand, Sir."

His cock hardened. It wasn't just the use of the honorific—it was the respect and inflection in the word and the fact she'd respected his request.

"Whenever it's convenient for you, Sir. And no, I'm not looking for someone to take me to the opera. I'd like to scene with you again, Sir."

"How many times have you masturbated since we were together?"

She gasped. "Excuse me?"

He didn't answer. Instead, he looked out of the window of his Highlands loft. He loved the view from this vantage, skyscrapers, the amusement park, the events center. Denver seemed to pulse energy, fed by the Platte River.

He was proud of his place. It had taken six months to remodel the space to his specifications. He'd taken out walls to create a massive great room, opened up the staircase, even enclosed part of the outdoor space so that he had a deck and sunroom. Glass and metal defined the three thousand square foot piece of urban heaven.

He'd hosted several parties for clients since he'd moved in, but he'd never entertained a sub here. Until now, he hadn't wanted to. "I'm waiting, Julia. For an honest answer."

"I don't know." She exhaled. "Almost every day. Twenty or thirty times in total, I suppose, Sir."

A sex drive to equal his. "Do you fantasize when you play with yourself?"

"Oh God. This so isn't the conversation I'd been thinking we'd have."

"We've established that you didn't call me because you needed an escort to the opera. So answer the question. Do you fantasize when you play with your pussy?"

"Yes. I do, Sir."

"Tell me about some." She was quiet for so long that he checked the phone to be sure they were still connected.

"A belt. Coming when you say. And…the sub we saw that day at Master Damien's house…"

"Yes."

"I imagined what it might be like to be her. I've been curious about the Saint Andrew's cross. And I thought I might want to try a flogger."

At the Den, she hadn't known what either one of them were. "You've obviously been doing some research."

"Voraciously. I've watched a lot of videos and I've done some reading. I talked to Lana more after she got back from her honeymoon." She spoke slowly as if confessing a sin. "She offered to let Ben scene with me, and I was tempted to agree. But I thought I'd ask if you were interested first. I liked what we did. I trust you. And, well, you've seen me naked."

The idea of any man but him introducing her to the sexual delights of a flogging pissed him off. Reminding himself he had no right to be angry, he refocused on her and the fact she'd called. "Tell me why it appeals to you."

"When we watched that scene… The woman's expression was so intense. And when he struck her, she looked peaceful. I have been imagining what it might feel like to have all those strands fall at the same time. And I want to see your expression as you're doing it."

A lot of Doms preferred to have their partner face the cross so their back and buttocks were exposed, and he was among them. But he liked the idea of flogging her breasts so they could look at each other.

"I understand if you don't want to. I mean—"

"I'd be happy to make your dreams a reality."

Once more, she was quiet.

"How does Saturday work for you?"

"That's..." She drew a breath. "*Really*? Thank you. Saturday is fine, Sir."

Since it was only Monday, that would give him time to prepare. His playroom currently had very little equipment in it, but he would certainly change that before her arrival. He had a carpenter who was currently between projects, and Marcus's ideas would keep the man busy for the remainder of the week. "Would you like me to send a car?"

For a moment, she hesitated. "I prefer to drive myself."

So she could escape when she wanted? Like she had at the Den, despite his objections. "I'll text you my address and the code for the parking garage. Follow the signs for the guest spots. I'll meet you there. I'll expect you at six, promptly. Is being on time a problem for you?"

"No, Sir. It's not."

"Wear the highest heels you can manage comfortably. I want you dressed in only lingerie beneath your coat. Is that clear?"

"What kind of lingerie?"

"I'll leave that to you."

"No guidance or suggestions?"

"Surprise me. Any other questions?"

She was silent for so long that he wondered if she'd answer. "None, Sir."

He swirled the drink around the inside of the crystal glass. "Where are you now?"

"At home."

"What are you wearing?"

"Workout clothes." Her voice was quiet. "I just got back from the fitness center."

"Put the phone on speaker, then set it down and undress."

"Are you serious?"

He arched an eyebrow. "Tell me what my tone said."

"That you meant it, Sir."

"In future, don't ask that question. You have safe words. Use them if needed."

"I understand."

"Now, Julia, be a good sub and do as you're told."

How would she respond? Part of him expected her to refuse. She'd insisted that she wanted nothing to do with domineering men, and he was a Dom to his marrow.

It might be easier for her to follow orders when they were sceneing, but different when they weren't together. But that was a part of the mindfuck he loved.

"All my clothes?"

"That's typically what I mean by getting undressed."

"Yes, Sir."

"Talk me through it."

Silence echoed between them.

"Unless you'd rather turn on video so I can watch?"

A thump told him she'd slammed the phone onto some surface. He grinned.

"I'm removing my shoes and socks."

At the Den, her toenails had been peek-a-boo pink. Were they still?

"Now my shirt."

"Sports bra?"

"Yes, Sir."

As he sipped, he pictured each step.

"Leggings and panties are off."

"So you're nude?" He should have insisted on video.

"And cold. Yes, Sir."

His mind supplied a vivid image of her generous rear and pouty breasts.

"Do you have a vibrator?"

"Yes, Sir."

"Is it handy?"

"No, Sir."

Her answer was quick. Too quick.

"It's in the bedroom. I'm in the living room."

He liked the sound of her voice. When she was being compliant, there was a slight huskiness in her tone. Each word, every pause revealed her emotional state. He knew if she was aroused, apprehensive, nervous, all without seeing her. She could protest that she wasn't submissive, but he knew different. "Not a problem. You can crawl there."

"Crawl, Sir?"

"When we're together, Julia, you may repeat an order if you don't understand it. But if you are stalling, you'll earn a punishment." He leaned back even farther in his chair and crossed his feet on top of the desk. Images of her continued to assail his senses. He was looking forward to seeing her sexy body sway as he had her move toward him on all fours. "Is the vibrator electric or battery?"

"Battery."

Allowing the silence to drag, he said nothing.

"I mean, it's battery operated, *Sir.*"

"I'll get you one with a little more power. Are you crawling?"

"It's difficult while holding a phone."

"You can always place it on your back if that's a problem."

She laughed. "You have an answer for everything, Sir."

"It's a Dominant trait. I have a solution for any submissive objection."

The tiny sounds in the background as she made her way through her space pleased him.

"I'm in the bedroom."

"Good. Now turn on your vibrator and let it run for a few seconds so I can hear it." The hum was satisfactory. "Is that as high as it will go?"

"Uhm..."

Ah. She thought she could stay one step ahead of him?

A moment later, a louder sound filled the distance between them. "Better."

"You may temporarily turn it off." After she'd complied, he gave his next command. "Kneel, please."

"I am, Sir."

"Describe the position to me."

"My knees are wide apart, and both of my hands are behind my head."

"And your breasts?"

"I just thrust them out, Sir."

"Where is your gaze?"

She hesitated. "I'm looking at the floor."

"Where were you looking before I asked?"

After softly swearing, she confessed. "At a picture on the wall."

"I want honest answers at all times. If you want to play games, find another Dom. You knew what I was asking."

"I apologize, Sir. I just..." She remained silent for a few seconds before sighing.

He wouldn't let her off that easy. "Finish your sentence."

"Don't want to be in trouble. And I want to do things right. But I'm not very good yet."

"As long as you're honest with me, you're doing fine. Even if the truth earns you a spanking, it's better that than damaging the trust between us."

"You're right, Sir. I apologize."

"Discussed and forgotten. Now please masturbate with the vibrator until I tell you to stop." First the delicate hum reached him, then came her little sounds of pleasure. He waited until her first groan, and then spoke. "Stop."

The background fell silent.

"That's my good girl. Was that on the highest setting?"

"Lowest, Sir."

"I have a rule about when a sub may orgasm. Do you remember?"

"I may only come with your permission, Sir."

"That applies anytime we're in contact. Now turn the vibrator all the way up. This time, I want you grinding your hips against it like you did with my hand."

"Anything you say, Sir."

He hadn't heard any sarcasm in her tone, just a desire to please. *Damn.* His cock had been hard, but now it throbbed incessantly.

This time, her moans were louder.

Perhaps a full two minutes later, she whimpered a desperate, "Sir!"

"Off. Turn it off, Julia."

She made an adorable sound like a growl.

"Do you remember the first time we played? You told me one of your fantasies."

"No."

"You wanted to come when commanded."

"But—" Her breaths were short and ragged. "I didn't know how powerful your hold over me was."

Her confession rocked him to his soul.

Does she have any idea how powerful her hold is over me?

Since they'd been together, he'd only masturbated a few times, all quick sessions in the shower.

Now, his cock throbbed, and his balls were heavy with the need that crawled through him.

With determination, wanting all of his focus on her, he shoved away the feeling. "Silently count to thirty and then turn your vibrator back on."

"Sir…" She sighed. "Yes, Sir."

God above, she's fucking delightful.

Exactly half a minute later, the familiar hum filled the distance between them.

He imagined her squeezing her buttocks, pictured her body straining and squirming. Was she gritting her teeth, determined to follow his orders? "Keep going for twenty seconds, then turn it off again."

"I'm not sure I can last that long."

"You will, though, won't you?" He made sure his voice was sensual and husky. "For me?"

"You do know what you're doing to my insides?"

"Of course."

Whimpers became pleas.

"You may turn it off."

For a moment, silence echoed around him. Then she exhaled raggedly.

"My pussy is tingling, Sir."

"Not nearly enough, my sweet. Now do it again, and do it right. Really work your cunt. Quit making this easy on yourself."

"Easy?"

"Get back to it, Julia."

He half-expected her to protest, but she didn't. There were a couple of seconds of silence before she complied.

Within moments, she moaned. Less than a minute later, she whispered a soft curse.

"Fuck, fuck, *fuck!* I want to come."

Delighting him immensely, she was much more verbal.

"Please, Sir. Oh, oh!"

"Stop this instant."

She cried out.

Her aggravation all but thundered across the distance. He'd bet his company that she'd never been more aroused. "Did you come?"

"No. No, Sir."

"How close are you?"

"My whole body is shaking. I… Oh, God. Please?"

"Breathe. Focus on how you're pleasing me. I like you to suffer for me, Julia. I'll ask you to do it often."

"Damn."

"Problem?"

"It's just… I'm frustrated."

"You're enjoying suffering for me?" When she didn't answer, he prompted her.

"It's... Spectacular."

Fuck me.

Dropping his legs to the floor, he reached for the whiskey and took a sip of the exquisite distillate. Anything to stretch the tension. "I want you thinking so much about what will happen Saturday night that you're obsessed."

"If that's your intent, you've already been successful. What if I say please, very nicely?"

She could try. But he wasn't easily persuaded. "You've never been with a man who subjected you to this kind of denial."

"Like I told you before, they were glad or at least relieved if they could get me to come before they gave up."

"Interesting."

"How?"

"I've found you very responsive, my sweet." Her climaxes were nectar on his tongue. "Deliciously so."

"I'm not sure what to say."

He grinned. "If you recall, sub, manners and gratitude are always appreciated."

"Yes. Of course, Sir. Thank you for saying so."

"You're getting better." He adjusted his jeans in a vain attempt to give his throbbing cock some room. "A hard spanking will reinforce my lessons."

"Sir! All this denial is hot. I really need to come now."

"Mmm." He ignored her request. "After all this, you'd still like to play this weekend? Knowing how much of a hardass I can be?"

"Even more so. In fact, I'm not sure I can wait that long." She gave a shaky laugh.

"If you scene with me, you follow my rules. You'll put away your vibrator, and further, you will not orgasm between now and then."

"What?"

A long silence followed, and he did nothing to break it. He waited for his edict to sink in, giving her time to realize how unbearable the demand was.

"That's not fair. I'm already so turned on I'm going to explode."

"Good."

"You're really mean this, don't you?" Her voice held a stunned, breathless note. "I can't masturbate until I'm with you again?"

"I never said that."

"But wait..."

"You can't come. In fact, I want you to stroke your clit and fuck yourself with a dildo."

At his casual use of the words, she gasped.

After taking a sip, he smiled. "I said you couldn't come. Feel free to play with your beautiful little pussy any time."

"Oh God. That's even worse." Her protest was filled with a plaintive wail.

"Be grateful I'm not making it a requirement."

"Uhm..." Though she inhaled sharply, she didn't protest further.

"I expect you to kneel twenty minutes a day after you return home from work. You'll stay in one place without moving. No getting up, no fidgeting. Consider it a submissive's meditation." He waited for her to argue. When she didn't, he smiled his approval before continuing. "Think about pleasing me, and notice your body, everything about it. Discomfort, arousal. Study your breaths. Try to relax. And while you're doing this, where will your gaze be?"

She didn't answer for so long that he wasn't sure she was going to.

"I'll be looking at the floor, Sir."

"Good. Set an alarm so that you're not tempted to glance at a clock. Any questions about my expectations?"

"No, Sir."

"Repeat them to me."

"I'm not to orgasm between now and when I see you. And I'm to kneel twenty minutes a day while looking at the floor."

"And you'll be naked. As I mentioned, I want you aware of your body, but I also want you to become more comfortable with your nudity."

"Yes, Sir."

"In case you're tempted to push the limits, I want one thing perfectly clear. My rules are not open to negotiation."

"I understand."

"You're still in position, aren't you?"

"Yes, Sir."

"Your legs are spread?"

"Yes, Sir."

"Is your pussy still damp?"

She took a breath. "Definitely, Sir."

"You're still wanting to come?"

"Yes. Yes, Sir. *Please.*"

"You're so perfect when you're begging."

"Thank you, Sir."

Marcus glanced at his sleek Bonds watch. "Set the alarm on your phone, but don't get up until eleven after the hour. Put your hands behind your neck again. Do not touch your cunt. And, Julia?"

"Sir?"

"I'm looking forward to tying you up and spanking you." His cock demanded release. "At eleven after the hour, you may come. One time. But do not do so again. Am I understood?"

"Yes, Sir."

Thoughts of her bringing herself off would torment him for the rest of the week.

Filled with restless energy, he stabbed his phone screen to end the call.

He slammed down his mostly untouched whiskey, then headed to his bedroom to change into workout clothes.

A brutal workout should help rein in his libido.

If it didn't, he was fucked.

* * * *

"He's damnably frustrating." While talking to Lana on the phone, Julia paced her kitchen. "He's got a freaking diabolical streak."

"Most Doms seem to." Lana laughed softly. "And Master Marcus knows exactly what he's doing."

Before she'd met Master Marcus, Julia had rarely thought about sex. Well, except for wondering how to avoid sleeping with certain guys, then, with others, how to get the act over with quickly.

But since their conversation three days prior, she'd been consumed with images and memories of him, of what they'd do, and how she'd behave.

"What's the most difficult part?"

It still wasn't easy talking about her intimate secrets this openly.

"Jules, you can tell me. It won't be anything I haven't heard before. Promise."

Julia was grateful she had someone to confide in who understood. "Orgasm denial."

"That's the worst."

"God." She blew out a breath, and Lana stayed silent, giving Julia time to choose her words. "I'm afraid I'm becoming obsessed with him."

"Are you?" There was no judgment in the question, just curiosity.

"Honestly, I'm not sure of anything anymore. I keep wondering what kind of a person he is, why he isn't involved in a relationship." And if it were possible for her to get involved with him without losing herself.

"As for the relationship, you'll need to talk to Master Marcus about that. If I say anything more than I already have, you won't be the only one suffering from orgasm denial."

Julia grabbed a bottle of water from the fridge. After uncapping it, she took a long drink.

"What were his other instructions? I assume there were some?"

"He actually wants me to…uhm…play with myself."

"Without coming?" Lana laughed. "You're right. He *is* diabolical."

"And he wants me to kneel every day for twenty minutes. Naked. A meditation of sorts, allowing me to think things through."

"How's it been going?"

"It's awful. There are five million things I'd rather do, and all of them seem urgent since I can't get to them."

"Have you tried making a concerted effort to give up the fight, relax a little?"

"That seems like a bit of a contradiction."

"But is it? And isn't all of this a bit of a contradiction? Pleasure and pain."

Freedom through submission.

"Could you see his command as a gift? It's only twenty minutes a day. And he's right. The time is an opportunity to sort through your feelings and think about what you want."

Julia frowned. "I'm not sure what you mean."

"Even in college, I was interested in kinky things. And as soon as I could, I attended munches—"

"Munches?"

"Sorry for the lingo. They're vanilla gatherings of Doms, subs, switches, people who are interested or just exploring the lifestyle. Gatherings are often held at restaurants, or sometimes at the club. But street clothing is worn, and it's very lowkey."

Sounds interesting.

"Anyway, I went regularly so I could soak it all up, and a Dom placed me under his protection. It was a safe way for me to learn and explore."

"That makes sense."

"Your interest is new, and I'm afraid I threw you into the deep end of the pool when I invited you to my wedding. Maybe I shouldn't have."

Julia was quick to respond. "Don't be ridiculous. I'm honored that you did. But like you said, this is all new to me."

"There's no one better to introduce you to the lifestyle than Master Marcus. He might be stern, but he's understanding. Right?"

"I suppose so."

"He talked you through things. Explained safe words. Gave you what you wanted, and maybe pushed you a little, without going too far?"

"He did."

"And he honored your desire for distance after you scened. He could have asked us for your contact information. To be clear, we wouldn't have given it without your permission. But he respected you enough to wait."

Julia leaned her hips against the cabinet.

"If you do as Master Marcus says, then see him on the weekend, you'll get some more exposure to that side of submission. You'll be gathering information about what parts of BDSM you might enjoy."

"That's a good point."

"You may want more of that kind of submission. Maybe you'll find that kneeling calms you, centers you, kind of like the benefits of yoga, when you actually go."

"There is that!"

They both laughed.

"I'm talking to myself as well," Lana admitted. "God knows I need more time to just relax and do nothing, though kneeling is fatiguing—"

"My knees are protesting like mad."

"Try using a pillow or some sort of pad. I found one online. Wait. Unless Master Marcus forbade that?"

"He didn't." Or he didn't think of it. One thing was certain, Julia had no intention of asking for clarification.

"Perhaps you'll come to realize that all you're interested in is a little taste of kink, being tied up, blindfolded, or an occasional spanking. Vanilla could end up being your favorite flavor."

"I'm pretty sure my time with Master Marcus at your wedding showed me that it's not."

"Well, you wouldn't have called him if you weren't at least somewhat interested."

"True."

"So you don't hate following all of his commands?"

"Uhm. No." In fact they gave her an illicit thrill. While she was at work, she was consumed by her memories of her experiences.

"The only way to find out what works for you is if you sample it." Lana paused before rushing on. "As long as it's not on your limits list. You did talk about that, right?"

"He asked. But I'm not sure what to put on it."

"There will be things that he might suggest that don't appeal. You can try them or not. And if you change your mind later, you can always renegotiate."

"This..." Julia opened the fridge again, but this time she reached for the wine. "Maybe I'm crossing a line, but I'm curious about something. You'll probably think I'm being nosy."

"Go for it. I can always refuse to answer."

"Is there anything on your limits list?"

"Of course. And there have been a few things I've changed my mind on. I always had a rule about no permanent markings or breaking the skin. But when we got engaged, I told Ben I was willing to get a tattoo if he wanted. I know he'll have me pierce my nipples or clit at some point."

Julia splashed a large amount of the chardonnay into a glass and took a calming gulp.

"Neither would have been right for me until our relationship was permanent."

"Makes sense."

"But I still refuse a belt."

Since that was a fantasy of Julia's, the information surprised her.

"It's..."

The hesitation in Lana's voice bothered Julia. "You don't have to tell me anything you don't want to."

"It's okay. Let's just say I had a bad experience with a buckle with a Top who went too far. And Ben beat the shit out of him in return—with the same belt."

"Oh God, Lana." Breathless, she put down the glass. "I'm so sorry."

"Always back to the contradiction, right? It was terrible, but it's what brought Ben and I together...his protective nature. He didn't stop there. Ben wasn't satisfied until he got the guy banned from the Den, and he contacted the Retreat in Denver, also."

Julia had had no idea. "Good for Ben."

"Well, his actions earned him a long suspension from the Den. Master Damien and Gregorio have rules. They would have handled the situation differently." Lana exhaled. "But they're not Ben."

"It's hard to fault him."

"Which is why he was suspended, rather than banned. But he also received a stern talking to and was accepted back on a three-month probationary basis. Everyone knew what happened. You know, as an example of when Dominants don't follow the rules, also."

"I get it, but it seems a little unfair."

"Rules are rules, right? Whether we break them or our Masters do."

Masters?

The word sent a shiver down Julia's spine. She generally referred to Master Marcus as Sir. The honorific flowed easier now than it had at first.

But if he were her master…? If she shared the same kind of relationship with him that Lana had with Ben…?

Julia couldn't catch her breath.

The wicked thoughts wouldn't leave her mind, and she shook her head to clear it. There was no way she'd ever wear a Dominant's collar.

Would I?

Julia became aware that her friend was still talking. "Sorry. My imagination was running away with me."

Without showing any impatience, Lana started over. "I was saying that belts are a hard no for me, and Ben would never suggest it."

How had she never known this about her friend? "Thank you for telling me."

"Of course. I trust you. We all have things that have happened in our past, and sometimes BDSM brings them back. For example, I enjoy the way Ben uses a cane on me. But one time, I don't know what happened inside me—maybe the alignment of the sun and moon and the stars was off, or something. I couldn't tolerate the way it seared the way the pain went so deep and radiated, and I felt disconnected from him. I safe worded and added the damn thing to my limits list. It's still there. As far as I am concerned, it can stay indefinitely."

"I'm glad you spoke up."

"Ben immediately threw aside the cane and held me close. My point is, being with the right Dominant matters. Someone who cares for you and protects you, treats you with the respect you deserve. Even if Master Marcus isn't for you, there are plenty of options. We can sponsor you at the Den. Please don't feel as if he is your one and only opportunity to play or scene. There are a lot of Dominants who would be interested in you."

But only one of them appeals to me. "I appreciate that."

"Something else bothering you?"

After everything Lana had admitted, how could Julia hold back on her earlier realization? "I've never been really into sex."

"And now because of Master Marcus's decree, you can't think about anything else? You're desperate enough to hump the bed or your shower massager?"

"*Yes!* You've been there?" With her wine, she sank onto a kitchen chair.

"To the point I thought I might die from frustration? Yes. Ben was overseas for two weeks last year, and he issued the same order. Except he would video call me and make me masturbate until I was ready to come, then he would tell me to place my hands under my back and keep my legs all the way apart and just lie there while he looked at me. When he was satisfied I was no longer close, he'd end the call. Every damn night for fourteen days. Can you imagine?"

"That's awful."

Master Marcus had allowed her to come when they spoke, and he'd never insisted that she play with herself. She couldn't imagine enduring that torture.

"I didn't die from the frustration." She gave a quick, wry laugh. "And neither will you. Even if you think you might."

"I'm not convinced." But at least she'd see him soon.

"What helped me get through my initial training—"

"Training?" Julia blinked.

"All Dominants and Tops are different, as we've discussed. Ben prefers a higher protocol at home—submission and servitude—in addition to impact play."

Are Master Marcus's instructions part of my training? "I don't know how I feel about that."

"You don't have to know. As I said, this is an exploration. Trust the process."

"You make it sound easy."

Lana laughed. "When you know what you want, it is. I wanted to be with Ben, and I wanted him to be as happy as I was. So I concentrated on that. I followed his orders because he wanted me to. Having me suffer pleased him, and..."

Julia waited for Lana to go on.

"I really hadn't thought of it this way until now, but it gave us an intimate connection when we couldn't be together. It was our secret. And when we talked, when he told me what to do and when to stop, it was *so* sexy. You can't imagine how much I looked forward to his calls and how hot I was for him when he got back. I wanted to pounce on him, and that's exactly what I did. My sex drive was through the roof for days. I couldn't get enough." Lana laughed. "Don't tell him, just in case he decides to withhold again to get a similar result."

"I solemnly swear." This—whatever it was with Marcus—was bringing her and Lana closer together, and she loved that.

"As a submissive who is finally getting all her needs met, may I offer a suggestion?"

Though she didn't see herself as a sub, Julia instantly agreed. "Any advice is welcome."

"See how Saturday night goes, then decide what you want. In fact, wait! You love numbers. So think of this as a research project. You're weighing the pros and cons. You can analyze the results later."

That Julia could do. "I appreciate you."

"Call me anytime. Or we can get together whenever you want. And in fact..." She hesitated before going on. "There are a few of us from the Den who meet every Tuesday at a coffee shop right off I-25 and Alameda. It's centrally located. Subs, only. If the weather's nice, we sit outside. But they have a private space where we can talk freely. It might help to meet others who live the lifestyle."

"I'd like that. Thank you."

"I'll send you the information, and really, Julia? Knowing some of the members may reassure you."

After they ended their call, Julia took a drink of water. The wine looked more appealing, but water was a smarter choice.

Then, deciding to follow her friend's advice, Julia went into the living room and tossed a pillow onto the floor near the fireplace. Taking her time, she stripped, to kneel by the fire.

She was barely five minutes into her assignment when the phone rang, shattering the silence. Unable to resist, she glanced at the screen. Seeing Master Marcus's name there for the first time ever jolted her, and she debated what to do. Closing her eyes, she asked herself what he would expect from her.

Her answer was clear.

She continued to concentrate on her task then called him back after her twenty minutes were over. "I apologize for not answering. I had just started kneeling when you called, so I decided to finish what I was doing first."

"You made the right decision."

His compliment made her heart skip a beat. His approval thrilled her.

"And are you naked as you're supposed to be?"

"Yes, Sir."

"I'd like you to shave your pussy for me."

In shock, she blinked. From what she'd read, that wasn't an uncommon request, and the request shouldn't have surprised her as much as it did.

"I want you completely bare, hiding nothing. Will you do that for me, Julia?" His voice held an irresistible purr.

"Anything, Sir." In that moment, she meant it.

"I'll ask about the experience later. Do it tonight?"

"Of course."

"This is the third day you've knelt for me?"

"Yes," she whispered.

"How are you finding the experience?"

Still naked, her body chilled, she walked to the bedroom to grab her robe and shrugged into it. "I chatted with Lana earlier, and she gave me some good advice." After tying the belt around her waist, she started back down the hallway. "So today was easier. I didn't struggle as much."

"I'm glad to hear that."

Tomorrow, she might not dread his order like she had the previous evenings.

"And your day? How was it?"

She missed a step.

Though he was always solicitous, this was a shift, and it caught her off guard. Until now there'd been a formal D/s air between them, and now his voice sounded relaxed, filled with genuine interest.

After recovering her equilibrium, she walked into the kitchen to pick up her barely touched wineglass. "It's been a good week, for the most part." When he waited for her to go on, she did. "To be honest, I've been a little distracted since we spoke."

He chuckled and the sound wrapped around her. "That's two of us."

She opened her mouth, then snapped it closed. "Do you mean that?"

"Yes. You're a beautiful distraction, Julia. And that's something new for me."

His revelation sent her soaring.

They spoke for a few more minutes before he interjected. "I'm looking forward to seeing you."

She responded with her heart, rather than her mind. "Same for me, Sir."

"We'll finalize our plans tomorrow, if that suits you?"

"Of course, Sir."

"Before you go, Julia…?"

"Sir?"

"Think of me this evening."

How can I not?

Without another word, he ended the call.

For a moment, she stared at the blank phone screen. She'd started off her conversation with Lana talking about what a frustrating man he was. And she was ending the evening with the same thought.

Even though she took a warm shower and listened to soothing music, sleep eluded her.

Two hours later, she was convinced Lana was wrong about it not being possible to die from sexual frustration.

Chapter Seven

At work the next day, Julia had difficulty concentrating. Instead, she was obsessing over the lingerie she needed to buy, and the fact that she'd need to change her razor blade before shaving her pubic hair.

Most Fridays, Julia went out with a large group of friends. They drove to the same place and ordered the same drinks and appetizers. They'd done it for so long that the server came over to the table, plonked down coasters and asked, *"The usual?"*

But today Julia was restless. Since she didn't feel like socializing, around three o'clock, she sent an email to the group, excusing herself from the outing. The Friday After-Work Gang gave her a fair amount of hassle, teasing her about a man being more important than friendship. She'd promised that wasn't true and reassured everyone she'd be at the next outing.

In an action completely out of character, she logged off her work computer an hour early and drove to a Cherry Creek lingerie boutique.

Typically, she picked up a few new bras every year at a department store sale. And she replaced her cotton briefs a six-pack at a time.

This place, with its endless displays of naughty-and-nice outfits overwhelmed her. Before tonight, she'd never had a proper fitting, but the determined saleswoman wouldn't accept no for an answer. She whipped out a tape measure, looked at Julia, then opened several drawers and filled Julia's arms with a dozen different types of bras, from demi-cups to ones that added two full cup sizes. There were lace ones and sheer ones. There were several in black, a couple in white, taupe, purple, red, and one that was the color of sherbet.

By the time she was done, she'd spent almost half a paycheck on a new pair of heels, garter belts, stockings, bras, panties, even a couple of thongs that the very helpful—and probably on commission—cashier had suggested.

When she was carrying the bags out to her car, she wondered when her life had become so plain and boring. Without realizing it, she'd become locked in a routine. Each workday morning at six, the alarm blared. She hit the snooze button twice before getting up, to make herself an omelet to go with her two cups of coffee. Then she showered, dressed in plain undergarments, black slacks, one of five blouses or sweaters—depending on the weather— a blazer, and sensible, arch-supporting heels.

It wasn't just the Friday After-Work Gang that defined her routineness, it was everything.

Twice a week she went to the gym. On Tuesdays, she watched her favorite television show. Even though she'd accrued two weeks of vacation time, she hadn't scheduled any time off to take a vacation. How funny that she'd thought of Harvey as boring. She was just as bad, if not worse.

Her cell phone signaled an incoming message.

Master Marcus. The man—the Dominant—who'd shaken up her life.

Once she was inside the privacy of her car, she glanced at the text. It contained his address and a reminder of how much he looked forward to seeing her.

As she drove home, the temperature dropped, and snowflakes drifted from the sky. Though it was pretty, she was suddenly ready for spring and short-sleeve shirts and skirts.

Her life was much different now than it had been even a week ago.

Even after dinner and a small glass of wine, restlessness still churned in her, and she hoped the kneeling time would help her relax. After turning on the fireplace against the chill, she settled in, breathing deeply a few times.

An orgasm would take the edge off and maybe allow her to sleep well. Tonight, she was tempted to give in and please herself. After all, he'd never know.

But I will.

Monday's discussion with Lana had left Julia resolved to follow his orders. As her friend suggested, it was an experiment, enabling Julia to know whether submission was for her.

Right now, she wasn't sure. This neediness was as real as it was uncomfortable—annoyingly so.

As she stared at the floor, the dancing flames teasing her peripheral vision, she stopped fighting the inevitable thoughts about Master Marcus. And when she gave in, the angst dissipated.

She replayed the evening at the Devil's Den, then anticipated what may happen tomorrow night.

Her phone alarm shattered the silence.

The noise jarred her. For twenty minutes, she'd been at peace. Now she understood what he meant about the practice being meditative.

After turning off the alarm, she stood. That, too, was easier than it had been. This time, her muscles weren't quite as cramped.

Feeling somewhat proud of her newfound knowledge, she wrapped herself in the robe again, turned off the fireplace, checked the locks then turned off the lights. All in all, not a bad Friday night.

She climbed into bed with her e-reader. This week, the half of her paycheck that she hadn't spent on lingerie had been allocated books. She hadn't been choosy. She'd downloaded spanking fiction, a domestic discipline anthology, several BDSM novels, a how-to guide for subs, and even one for Doms. She'd read bits and pieces of all of them, and was really engrossed by the one for subs.

As Master Marcus and Lana had both told her, there were as many different types of relationship as there were couples. There were many terms of respect, expectations, punishments, even various types of servitude. She didn't fancy having her back used as a coffee table for her Master's drink, but she had softened on some of her earlier, uneducated beliefs. Wearing a collar might not be right for her, but she understood Lana better.

Now, after scrolling through all her book choices, Julia selected one of her BDSM novels and began to read. Before long, she was turned on. Absently she reached between her legs and stroked her clit. When she realized how close she was to an orgasm, she immediately removed her hand and closed her legs.

But damn it, that made the throbbing worse.

Exasperated, she parted her legs, hoping that would relieve the pressure.

How will I survive until tomorrow night?

Even her dreams were erotic, and the next morning she woke up feeling as if she'd never been to sleep.

Determined to shake the exhaustion, she worked out at the gym, then ruined the positive effects with an extra-large latte and a cranberry and orange scone. Because she realized the whole day would be consumed with preparation for the evening, Julia treated herself to a mani-pedi before stopping in to see her hair stylist.

When she returned home, her phone signaled an incoming message.

Yes. You have to kneel today.

She checked the clock. *Crap.* It was stupid not to have planned that into her day. Now, if she did it, she risked running late.

Drumming her fingers on her thigh, agonizing over what to do. Skip it and risk a punishment? Kneel and run the risk of being late?

Every moment she considered her decision was one less she had to actually accomplish something.

Earlier this week, when he'd issued the order, he'd been serious.

And she needed to treat it that way.

Hastily she stripped and dropped to her knees. Because she had so much to do, doing as he said was more burdensome than it ever had been.

She gritted her teeth and drew in a few shallow breaths.

Realizing she was frustrated rather than compliant, she readjusted, exhaled through pursed lips, then gazed at the floor.

The realization that she'd been on his mind—enough so that he'd messaged her—calmed her and made it possible to endure the last fifteen minutes.

When the alarm signaled that twenty minutes had passed, she all but leaped up.

In the books about BDSM, there was a lot written about moving gracefully. Yesterday, she'd managed it. Today was a different story.

She hurried into the shower, and it took her considerably longer to shave her pussy than she had imagined it would. But the act was ultra-erotic, spiraling her into a different mindset.

When she was dried off, she studied herself in the full-length mirror.

The sight shocked her.

Her sex was prominently displayed.

No wonder he'd made the request.

Aware of time ticking away, she sorted through her lingerie. She wanted to be sexy, but not provocative. Right? Classy. Elegant. And yet, now that she was devoid of pubic hair, some of the more risqué choices appealed to her.

The pile of discards grew in the middle of her bed before she settled on a black demi-cup bra, a silky, skimpy, black thong, stockings, and a lacy garter belt.

That was one of the most frustrating things she'd ever dealt with. Trying to slide the plastic piece through the metal clasp was annoying enough, but having to reach behind her to fasten them, all but sight unseen, was next to impossible.

Why people bothered, she had no idea. And then she caught a glimpse of her reflection.

She had never considered herself to be sexy, but the rich black color against her skin was beautiful. The aggravation had been well-worth the effort.

As the clock continued its relentless march toward five-thirty, the time she needed to leave, Julia slipped into the shoes she'd just purchased. They were ridiculously high, and the slant pitched her forward. The heels were pencil slim, and the arch support nonexistent.

And yet, they, too, were perfect.

In the mirror, she barely recognized herself.

The trim at the salon had revitalized her hair, and it fell in soft curls around her shoulders and down her back.

The shoes made her legs look impossibly long, and, for the first time in her life, she noticed a little definition in her calf muscles. Most surprising was the fact she almost didn't notice the extra pounds she carried, and she felt more confident than she ever had—more confident. A wildly wicked part of her wondered what else was possible.

Following his orders, she hadn't worn regular clothes and instead slipped into a coat. She buttoned the wool garment and tied the belt in a double knot so it couldn't come undone.

Her image shocked and scandalized her. Her entire life, she'd never rebelled. And her parents were proud of her for being a good girl. In college, she'd skipped the parties in favor of studying, and she'd spent her entire work career in a conservative office, routinely earning promotions.

Her behavior right now was beyond her comfort zone.

But it made her ultra-aware of her femininity. Five minutes later, she'd programmed her GPS and was driving toward his place. She'd been to that area of town a few times for dinner, and she loved the energy. Fortunately it wasn't far from her condo.

She followed his meticulous instructions and didn't make a single wrong turn. It was four minutes after the hour when she punched in the code for the underground parking garage.

Once the red and white arm opened, she pulled through. All of a sudden anticipation made it impossible for her to remember his directions.

She followed arrows to the guest parking area, and when she arrived, Master Marcus stood nearby, arms folded, waiting for her.

Her heart rate surged.

Over the past month, she'd managed to convince herself that her imagination had been working overtime when it came to him. There was no way he was as tall, as broad, as ruggedly handsome as she remembered.

But he was. All that and more.

Tonight, he was all in black. Boots, jeans, belt, T-shirt. His short hair emphasized the angular planes of his face and the firm set of his mouth.

He pointed to an empty slot, and she maneuvered the sports utility vehicle into place and gripped the steering wheel tightly for a few moments to regain her equilibrium.

In the comfort and safety of her home, the idea of playing with him tantalized her. But the reality of being here sucked the courage from her limbs.

She pushed the button to shut off the engine. Then, with false bravado, she stiffened her shoulders. After gathering her small purse, she reached for the handle.

Before she could grab it, he opened the door. "Julia. My sweet." He offered his hand. "I'm delighted you're here."

Grateful for his assistance, since she was no longer certain her legs would support her, she slid her palm against his. His touch ignited a flame inside of her. Nerve endings sizzled.

"May I have your remote?"

His old-world manners made her feel as if she'd stepped back in time. She gave him the fob that had the rest of her keys on it. After he'd closed the door, he pushed the button to lock the vehicle.

He took a step back to sweep his gaze over her.

"Those shoes… Thank you for wearing them."

His appreciation thrilled her, making her want to please him more.

"I want to get you somewhere more private." With firm tenderness, he cupped her elbow and navigated them toward the elevator.

Inside the compartment, he pushed the button for the fourth floor, then, as the doors quietly slid shut, he backed her against the side wall.

Her breath whooshed from her lungs as he captured her chin and tilted back her head. "You drive me mad, Julia."

His gruff, demanding tone made her momentarily squeeze her eyes shut. "I've never wanted anyone the way I want you."

"Don't expect the same restraint I showed at the Den."

"A threat, Sir? Or a promise?"

Desire flared in the depths of his shocking green eyes. "You're playing with fire, my sweet."

Emboldened by the new side of her that he'd uncovered, she replied, "I'll take the risk."

"Brave? Or foolish?"

With a ding, the elevator slowed to a stop. After a shocking, quick kiss that left her gulping for air and her insides warm, he released her and indicated she should precede him.

The hallway they entered was well-lit, beautifully tiled, and had abstract paintings on the walls.

He pressed his thumbpad to a button next to his door, and the lock snicked. "Welcome."

As befitting a bachelor, she'd been expecting an unimaginative leather-bound domain, maybe with some wood paneling, maybe with lots of clutter.

This, however, was stunning.

The condo was wide open, but not in an industrial-looking way. Instead, it was a gorgeous contemporary design that could grace the front of an architectural magazine.

A sweeping, curved metal and glass staircase led to a second floor, and a waterfall cascaded down one wall, falling into a shallow pool that contained water plants and koi. "I'm…" She tried to take it all in. "I've never seen anything this gorgeous."

"Thank you. I had a concept, but my creative design team deserve the credit. Would you like to leave your purse here?"

"Thank you." She placed the small bag on a nearby table, and he dropped her keys into a copper bowl.

"Let me show you around. I want you to feel comfortable."

He hadn't asked for her coat. She wondered if he stayed up at night, thinking of ways to keep her guessing what his next move would be.

She followed him into the great room.

A comfortable, white, sectional leather sofa faced a roaring fireplace. A huge flat-screen television was mounted to the wall. Several large rugs strategically covered the wooden floor, adding warmth.

"My suite and the playroom are both upstairs."

Playroom? "You have a place designated for that?"

His grin was quick, feral. Intimidating. "And it's all ready for you." A thousand images swam through her brain, but she realized he was still talking. "My office and a powder room are on this level, but this is the reason I bought it."

How could it possibly get better?

He beckoned her toward the bank of windows. As they neared, she noticed that two of the panels were doors that led to a patio. No curtains or blinds obstructed the view of downtown Denver.

"Privacy windows," he explained. "At night I make them translucent so no one can see in. This controls it." He flipped a switch.

"I didn't know something like that existed."

"A feature suggested by my designer. I like to see out without feeling as if I'm in a fishbowl."

"This is magical. This view is sensational."

He'd arranged another sofa and two chairs to take advantage of the skyscape.

"There's a rooftop garden so you can also see the Rockies."

"And watch the sunset?" She had to drive for miles for an unobstructed view.

"You'll have to join me sometime. A glass of wine, and if it's cool, we'll light the firepit."

The kitchen was off to the left, and as she followed him into the space, she began to relax slightly.

The counters were crafted from marble, and the walls had a complementary backsplash. A pot rack hung from above, with copper-bottomed pans gleaming in the light. The appliances were a name she'd heard on the New Orleans home renovation show she loved, but she'd never seen them in real life. "Do you cook?"

"I do. But I don't need anything this fancy. My chef requested this set up for the parties I host."

"Chef?"

He swept his gaze over her as he grinned. "I have other things I'd rather do with my time than prepare all my own meals."

The way he narrowed his gaze told her all she needed to know.

The island had several stools tucked underneath, great for conversing during a party, or maybe sitting for a quick, informal meal.

A small alcove between the dining area and kitchen contained a large pot that she thought she recognized as being crafted by a famous artist from a New Mexico pueblo. His home was all things modern and sleek, but comfortable at the same time.

"This is a fabulous spot."

"I'm glad you like it."

"You've told me you have a few playmates, but nothing serious." She turned to face him. "I'm curious what you want out of this…from me?"

He scowled, ferociously, intimidatingly. But she refused to back down.

"You want me to tell you all my secrets, yet you don't want to give up much in return. I don't know anything about you, what kind of man I'm giving myself to."

"I collared a woman once. Amber. She became dependent on me for everything, her emotional as well as financial and sexual needs. No matter how much I gave, it wasn't enough. The relationship wasn't healthy. For either of us."

"So random women, hook-ups, scenes, keep your life less complicated?"

He didn't respond.

"Isn't that a little lonely?"

"It can be. But I'm in no hurry to get back into another commitment."

Intrigued, glad he was revealing more than she'd expected, she cocked her head to one side to study him. "Why?"

He frowned. "It's in the past."

"I thought we needed to be honest." Her heart picked up a few extra beats as she challenged him. "That goes both ways, I assume, Sir?"

His scowl deepened. "Dependency."

They were in uncharted territory. Maybe she should be satisfied with his answer, but she wanted to know everything she could about him. "With the way you like to be in charge"—*an understatement*—"I thought you'd like that?"

"Of course, partners should lean on one another. But I can't become someone's entire world ever again."

"Sounds as if it were intense." *And left you hurt?*

Rather than answering, he asked a question of his own. "How about you?"

"You could say I had the opposite issue. Jason tried to control me, choose my friends, insist on me coming home immediately after work." She wrapped her arms around herself. "Now I'm looking for a nice man."

"Ah. Someone undemanding?"

She nodded.

"Something easy? Uncomplicated?"

Exactly.

He smiled, but there was no humor in it. "I don't fit your criteria." With a touch of menace, his words hung in the air. "Yet here you are, Julia."

And she'd been the one to initiate the meeting. Not for the first time, she questioned her sanity.

"Have you discovered that a man who checks your boxes bores you to death?"

Damn you and your perceptions. Thoughts of Harvey taunted her.

"Why else would you be here? Dressed, I assume, in something sexy beneath that coat?"

"I'm okay with being playmates." She brought her chin up. "Let's not complicate things."

"Just spank you and fuck you and send you home?"

With bravado that she didn't really feel, she continued on. "Isn't that what we both want from this arrangement, Sir? A no-strings hook up?"

"Not necessarily."

His words, cold and final, echoed deep inside her head.

"I'm guessing you crave a man who's your equal. Not someone you can push around, but someone who encourages you to explore your full sexual potential."

"In a partnership, I'm looking for a man who treats me with respect, who values my opinion."

"Nothing I said contradicts that." A devastating smile flirted with the corner of his mouth.

And hadn't Lana said something similar?

"And what about sex? I notice you didn't mention that with your preferred type of man."

"Which is why I'm here."

"And when you find this spineless man—someone who is milquetoast—what then? Will you still show up at my door and scream my name when I make you come?" He smiled. "Or had you not thought it through?"

Because his questions unsettled every part of her, she brought up her chin in a show of false bravado. "Can we just have tonight, Marcus?"

"Sounds reminiscent of what you said the evening we met."

"The question still applies." But deep down, in a place she didn't want to look at, she knew the truth. Every part of her hungered for him, his touch, his company. But she wouldn't admit that to either of them.

"Would you like a sparkling water?"

After the way he had dug around in her psyche, what she wanted was wine, but she already knew better than to ask. "That would be nice. Thank you."

He crossed to the bar area. "Lime? Or maybe something sweeter? Grenadine?"

Which would make it a little more like a cocktail. "That sounds perfect."

She slid onto a barstool while he took out two blue goblets and filled them. Then he poured a splash of grenadine into one, then sliced a lime and squeezed a slice into his.

After picking up both drinks, he offered one to her. "Cheers." He touched the rim of his glass to hers. "I'm glad you're here."

A growl vibrated in his voice, sending a ripple of desire through her.

"Now..." He allowed her a couple of sips before pointedly looking at her. "Please open your coat."

Her mouth dried. She'd known that was coming, but here, in the kitchen, it caught her off guard.

Knowing better than to question his order, she reached for the belt. Her fingers shook as she loosened the knot in the belt.

"Keep going."

His steady voice soothed and encouraged.

Fingers shaking, she parted the lapels, then forced herself to remain in place while he swept his gaze over her, taking in every single detail.

"Fuck."

She licked her lower lip as she met his gaze.

"I remembered you being beautiful. But you're breathtaking."

"I..." *Don't know what to say.* No one had ever said those kinds of words to her.

"Take your coat all the way off and place it on the stool. Then slowly turn around for me."

Was it possible to deny him anything?

Fighting back her instinctive self-consciousness, she did as he asked.

"Stop."

With her back to him, her heart slammed into overdrive. "Yes, Sir."

"God, Julia. Your ass is perfect. So spankable. I've been thinking about you."

She couldn't help but glance back over her shoulder at him.

Green fire was stoked in his eyes causing arousal to unfurl inside her.

He made a small circle with his index finger, and she finished her turn.

"No arguments from you this evening?"

"No, Sir." She'd thought of nothing but being his to command.

"Let's see how well you remember my preferences."

With the way he was studying her, she'd be fortunate to string two coherent thoughts together.

"I'd like you to wait for me in the living room." He folded his arms across his chest, waiting for her compliance.

Nerves taut, she glanced outside.

"I promise you, no one can see in."

Despite his assurances, the uncovered windows made her feel exposed, and her skimpy clothing left her vulnerable. At the Den, others had been similarly dressed, but here, with him everything was new.

Her knees wobbled as she walked from the kitchen, making her wish she'd bought pumps with a shorter heel.

He hadn't been specific about where he wanted her. On the rug near the fire? In the middle of the room? Relying on instinct, she opted for a place in the great room, near the fire.

Then, like she'd been practicing, aware of him studying—*and judging?*—her every move, she lowered herself to her knees.

"You're doing well. Just continue to focus on what's important."

Pleasing you.

Taking a breath to center herself and calm her thoughts, she thrust out her chest, spread her legs as wide as she could, then placed her hands behind her head and lowered her gaze to the floor.

In her peripheral vision, flames flickered. Wood crackled and popped. She listened deeply for sounds of him moving, but beyond this room was a void.

"You *have* been practicing. I'm impressed." His boots echoed off the hardwood floor.

Because she was supposed to keep her gaze down, and it was almost impossible to do so, she squeezed her eyes shut.

"Very, very good, Julia."

"Thank you, Sir."

"And such beautiful manners."

She swallowed deeply.

"You may look at me."

He stood mere inches from her, arms folded, towering over her.

Her breath caught. Her submissive position made her aware of his dominance and power.

"Tell me about your experience this week. Did you struggle to be obedient?"

Obedient? Julia scowled. The word chafed. Yet that's what she'd been, and what she was in this moment. The realization vexed her. "Do we need to talk about this?"

"Yes. I want to understand where you're at."

By digging deeper into her thoughts? They were difficult enough for her to deal with. The closer she allowed him in, the more she risked her emotions and maybe even her heart.

Why do you have to be so damn persistent? Since he wouldn't relent, she sighed. "The first day was the worst. I was making mental grocery lists." She shook her head. "Not literally. I mean I was thinking about the dozens of other things I needed to do and considered it a waste of time. I also knew that you would never know whether I had done it or not. But then…"

"But then?"

He hadn't moved, and this close, she breathed in his scent—the outdoors, of leather and spice. "I figured you would ask, and I would end up telling you the truth. Yet it was more than that. I wanted the experience. I thought that kneeling would put me in a different mindset."

"Did it?"

"Yes, Sir." A small cramp made her neck twinge. "It became easier to stay in place. As you suggested, it became meditative in a way. Transformative."

"Oh?"

She shouldn't have revealed that.

"Tell me more."

How to backtrack? "We both know I'm not a true submissive."

"And what is a true sub?"

"Someone who has always wanted to be dominated or has been intrigued by the possibility." *Like Lana.* "It's part of who they are."

"Hmm." His response was noncommittal. "I'm interested in hearing more. Please have a seat on the couch."

She blinked. *"What?"*

"I'm enjoying the conversation."

"Marcus..."

His back was rigid, and his arms implacably folded.

She'd already informed him she only wanted to scene with him. The confounded man exasperated her.

"In case you're confused, that was neither a suggestion nor a request."

If she wanted to play, she'd have to go along with his wishes.

He offered a hand up.

Seconds later, she accepted. Despite her confusion and annoyance, she reveled in the strength of his grip as he brought their bodies within inches of each other. "Thank you."

He moved aside, and she curled up on the far end of the buttery-soft leather sofa.

"From what you said on the phone, you've been researching, and you've talked to Lana."

"She helped me become more comfortable with your kneeling assignment." And to stop her internal fight.

"Is that where you got the idea that certain people are born with the desire to be submissive?" He shrugged. "Or dominant?"

"Maybe."

"Have you ever traveled somewhere new and discovered you liked it?"

Her protest was immediate. "That's hardly the same."

"Or found a new type of cuisine?"

"Your point is, you're not born knowing you love the Amalfi Coast? Or that street tacos in Mexico are the best thing ever?"

"Something like that."

"But still..."

When she hesitated, he encouraged her. "Go on."

"Certain things speak to us, right? At the wedding, I was more shocked than intrigued by what was going on between Lana and Ben. Doesn't that mean something?"

"Does it?" he countered. "You agreed to spend some time with me. I'd call that at least a little bit intrigued."

"That's not it. I just..." She sought out the words she wanted. "It was about understanding."

"Did the multiple orgasms I gave you help with that?"

Heat prickled her skin.

"People come to BDSM in a dozen different ways. Through a partner who is interested, for example. Movies. Books. Online videos. Artwork, whether photography or paintings."

"You made your point." Much as she hated to admit it.

"So what is your struggle really about? What makes you the most uncomfortable about the idea of submission?"

That he homed in on what her real objection was didn't surprise her. "Losing myself."

Rather than objecting and telling her why she was wrong, he asked another question. "And you assume it will. Because of the experience you told me about?"

"That's right."

"You've known Lana a long time. Are you concerned about that for her?"

"Not at all." She shook her head. "But that—what they're doing—isn't for me. I don't want any man to have that much control over me."

"We talked about the various levels of power exchange, if you recall?"

"And I read up on it."

"Tell me what your understanding is of how it works."

She'd never considered what it meant to her or what she wanted. "Basically, the Top or Dominant agrees to the nonnegotiables that the submissive, or bottom has outlined."

"Even in a relationship like Lana and Ben's, where she's collared?"

"According to you and others, there's always a power exchange? Right?"

"There may be some extreme relationships out there, but that's not what we're discussing. I only play safe, sane, and consensual."

"Not even RACK?"

He lifted an eyebrow. "I'm impressed."

She was ridiculously happy by his reaction to her knowledge of the acronym for risk-aware, consensual kink.

"Even then, there's consent." He paused to study her. "Back to your experience of kneeling for me."

Did he ever lose the thread of a conversation?

No doubt he liked to talk, and he seemed to enjoy exploring the complexity of seemingly simple ideas. His questions forced her to laser in on what she knew and on what she believed. In previous relationships, she hadn't discussed sex or her opinions about it or voiced exactly what it was she wanted.

"You used the word transformative."

"It..." How did she confess this to him? "It was. I was different a week ago than I am now. I gave myself over to the experience."

In silence, all of his attention focused on her, he waited.

"That's the reason I knelt when I wasn't in the mood or when you wouldn't have known the difference." Needing something to do with her hands, she grabbed a pillow. "I don't know what your motivation was when you commanded me to kneel. To see if I would? Or because you hoped I'd learn something?" She brushed hair back over her shoulder. "Then those questions lost relevance." Julia glanced at the dancing flames before looking back up at him. "I did it because I wanted to please you."

He moved in a little closer. "Thank you." With his knuckles, he traced her jawbone. "That means a lot to me."

She closed her eyes and savored his tenderness. The cramped muscles, aching knees, and relentless sexual thoughts were suddenly all worth it.

"You're a quick study. Thoughtful. My motivation was everything you suggested, and more. I hoped you'd explore the idea of submission. At any point you could have told me no, to fuck off. Or you could have safe worded. If all you wanted was a bit of kink, I would have still invited you over."

With him this close, breathing the same air that he did, her thoughts tumbled. "Instead, you tested me?"

"You tested yourself." His contradiction came quickly. "Otherwise I might have required you to provide a video each day. Watching you would have filled many voyeuristic fantasies."

The idea made her squirm.

"Is it fair to say you had a submissive experience?"

"I'm not ready to go there."

"Fair enough." He angled his head to one side. "Through power exchange—even as a submissive—you never have to give up who you are."

"A few days is one thing. It was fun, but I don't think I want a steady diet of it." *Or do I?*

Receiving wicked texts had been delicious. During that time, she'd never been more aware of herself as a sexual being. "I was so sore after our first meeting that I don't think I want to be spanked more than once a month."

"There are other parts of your body to torment."

She shivered. "I read about some of them." Including the soles of the feet, labia, and anus.

"In our time apart, what else have you learned?"

"I should have a limits list."

"Agreed."

"But I don't have enough experience to know the things I hate. I might have told you I didn't want to try a tawse, until you used it on me. But there are a few things that scared me enough that I don't want to try. Knife play. Having my nipples pierced."

"I know women who can come just from the idea of that happening."

She shook her head several times. "That is definitely not me."

"Got it. Anything else?"

"I'm not sure about humiliation." Even as she said it, she felt heat flood her body. "That's a real murky area for me, and I was kind of hoping we could discuss it..."

"Of course."

Suddenly she was flailing. "What one person might find humiliating, another wouldn't. I read a blog post about a woman whose Dominant displayed her in a window. But since she was an exhibitionist, she enjoyed the experience. I would find it horrible. I'd be terrified of the police being called. There is no way I could enjoy something like that."

"What if there were extenuating circumstances? For example, what if it were at the Den? The place is secluded, and only other people in the lifestyle are allowed to be there. What if it were totally safe? What if I wanted you in that window because I find you so hot and desirable that I want others to see you?"

Her skin tingled, but no longer from embarrassment. His tone—when he spoke of finding her sexy—was gruff with desire.

"Would that be acceptable? What if I wanted your breasts pressed against the cold glass for the pure sensuality of the experience?"

His words painted a vivid picture in her mind. "I hadn't looked at it that way." She was starting to understand why he wanted to talk so much. It wasn't just to allay her fears—it was to open her mind to what was possible.

"As you said, humiliation play may be nuanced, influenced by attitude and perhaps other external circumstances. Being displayed naked on the top floor of a high-rise hotel in Las Vegas might give you an adrenaline rush."

The evocative image tantalized her.

"This evening, you wore no street clothing beneath your coat. And I had you in front of the window at the Den. Were either of the experiences humiliating?"

"More scandalous than anything."

"You came hard when I finger-fucked you."

"Yes." That night had been like walking a high wire—risky, dangerous, disturbing, but also safe because of the safety net he'd put in place.

"We'll try many different things—knife play and piercing aside. And you can safe word or say yellow as we experiment."

"Thank you."

"When we talked on Monday night, I instructed you not to orgasm."

"I followed your orders. And the restlessness from it has been awful."

"Good."

All of a sudden, she understood power exchange in a different way. He couldn't use denial as a tool unless she agreed. This relationship was more honest than anything else she'd been involved in.

"I assume you're anxious for a little relief?"

"More than you can imagine."

"In that case, sub, stand, please."

Chapter Eight

With the order, Marcus's tone shifted, edging his words with authority. *His Dom voice.* It melted her.

He took the pillow from her. Other than that, he offered no help.

As they'd sat on the couch, she'd been desperate for him to get on with it. But now that he'd taken control, the butterflies assaulted her, full on.

"Over there, where I can see you better." He pointed to a spot about three feet away. "Remove your bra and arch your back, looking straight ahead, your feet shoulder-width apart. Put your hands behind you so that your breasts are more prominently displayed. They'll be even more beautiful when they bear my marks."

Once more, he'd stolen her breath. She hated not being able to look at him and read his expression.

"Turn a full circle again but do it slowly."

Focusing on maintaining her balance, she did as he'd said.

"You're exquisite, Julia."

Her heart hammered. She'd never been with a man so effusive with his praise.

When she faced him again, she remembered to look straight ahead, as difficult as that was.

"Perfect. Now remove your thong but leave on the stockings and garter belt. I like the way they look against your skin." She slipped the material down exposing her shaved pubic region.

"*Fuck.* What a beautiful pussy."

Before him, the comment would have embarrassed her. Instead, it thrilled her.

"Come a little closer."

After she'd stepped out of her underwear, she did.

With a determined gleam in his eye, he captured her left pussy lip between his forefinger and thumb and ran a finger up the inside, exploring the length. "Smooth. Very thorough job." He checked that the other side was clean-shaven as well. "Are you getting wet just from this?"

From everything I've experienced over the last five days… "Yes, Sir," she whispered. She needed his touch, hungered for it.

He lowered his hand. "Now turn away from me and spread your legs as wide as you possibly can and bend over to show me all of your hot little cunt."

He was truly gifted at this. He had barely touched her, yet she was ready to come undone.

"Do it now, my sweet. Unless you want a reprimand?"

The sharpness in his voice galvanized her.

Suddenly grateful that she didn't have to look at him, she did as he'd said. The position made her tremble, and the exposure of her private region felt lewd.

He remained silent for so long that her legs began to shake.

"Run one finger over your clit until I tell you to stop."

Keeping steady was tricky, but she managed to do as he asked. After only three light strokes, she moaned as desire became demand.

No!

Coming without his permission would earn her a punishment.

With determination, she concentrated on her breathing.

A few seconds later, with a climax looming, she dropped her hand.

"I didn't give you permission to stop."

"But… Sir…"

"Finger yourself, girl."

Misery made tears swell in her eyes as she murmured, "Yes, Sir."

"Do you want to come?"

"Please. A thousand times, please." Though she'd once vowed never to beg for anything, she'd learned that relief trumped pride. "I want to come, Sir. I… Oh!!" To stave off the orgasm, she had to move her hand slower. But after being turned on for nearly a week, that was impossible. Without conscious thought, she began to thrust her hips.

"Do you think you deserve an orgasm?"

Do I? What were the criteria? Each day, she'd knelt. She hadn't come, and she'd been honest about that. Then today, she'd arrived all-but naked beneath her coat. "Yes, Sir."

"Stop."

The word barely registered.

"I'll let you climax when I decide you're ready."

She whimpered.

"Place your fingers on the floor as you think about the correct answer to my question."

How could she have forgotten everything she'd read? "I apologize, Sir. It's up to you to decide whether or not I deserve release."

"Much better. Continue playing with yourself."

"I really don't know that I can hold off much—"

He tutted. "So disobedient."

Julia squeezed her eyes shut.

"Take hold of your ankles."

He left her there, breathing ragged, wondering what would happen next.

"What time were you supposed to arrive?"

"Sir?"

"You were given specific instructions."

"Six o'clock, Sir. Prompt."

"And what time did you arrive?"

Damn her inability to lie. She forced the words past a sudden knot in her throat. "It was about four minutes after, Sir."

"Is the definition of prompt open to interpretation?"

The room temperature plummeted several degrees. "No, Sir."

"Did I or did I not ask if it would be a problem for you to arrive on time?"

She could barely breathe. "You did ask. And I promised it wouldn't be."

"Choose a punishment."

His words were so close to what she'd been fantasizing about. She barely stopped her first answer from spilling out. "Whatever you deem reasonable, Sir."

"That's a girl. Kneel, facing me. Look at me."

Damn. She'd told him on the phone that she wanted to be tied and subjected to a flogger. But there were a dozen other things she wanted to try. She bit her lower lip to keep her mouth shut.

"Now, answer my question."

She didn't know how many more times she'd have the opportunity to scene with him, and she wanted this fantasy to remember. "Your belt, Sir."

"Interesting." He studied her. "It can sear."

"I trust you, Sir."

"Jesus."

"Because I was late, will you use your belt on my ass, Sir? This was the first time in her life that she'd so boldly and brazenly asked for what she secretly craved.

"This one?" He reached for the buckle.

She inhaled a sharp breath. "Yes." All of a sudden this was real. Almost too real.

Bravado faltered when he dragged the leather through the loops.

"Tell me your safe word." He'd told her they'd go through this often, but it felt like a confounding waste of time. "Red. Yellow to slow down, Sir."

"And what color are you now?"

"Green, Sir." Nerves unfurled inside her, and she now believed that would be a continuous situation where he was concerned.

"I want you on the guest room bed." He pointed. "It's down the hall."

"Not over your lap?"

"That's the wrong angle. And I want the exact right amount of force."

"I see." She straightened.

"In the absence of any other instructions, when we are sceneing, assume you are to crawl."

Even though she'd done it before, making her way across the floor on all fours made her aware of the gentle sway of her breasts and the side-to-side movement of her hips. And it served as a powerful reinforcement of his dominance.

"Just a moment."

Pausing, she glanced at him.

"Carry the belt for me."

She reached for it, but instead, he crouched in front of her.

"Open your mouth."

Marcus was masterful at compounding his orders. Her mouth dry, she accepted the leather.

"No teeth marks. It's one of my favorites."

The wooden floors were horribly uncomfortable on her knees, and the other room seemed to be a mile away.

He followed closely behind her, not urging her on, footfall heavy, increasing her tension.

When they arrived in the room, he turned on the lights. "Stay where you are for a moment."

While she waited, he rearranged the pillows.

He took the belt from her and doubled it over, holding the buckle tight. Then he took a few practice swings, striping the pillow.

With each forceful thump, she winced. *Is this a good idea?* After all, Lana hated the belt for a reason.

"Up you go. Facedown." He offered her the belt. "Now place it on your back."

Somehow, she managed that.

He allowed time to drag. She shook, both from the memory of the sound of the belt blasting the pillow and from the extra serving of nerves.

"How many minutes late were you?"

"Four, Sir."

"And how many spanks do you deserve?"

It depends how hard they are. "As many as you see fit, Sir."

"Since I'm in a generous mood, I'll settle for twelve."

She froze. "Isn't that excessive? I mean most people wouldn't have even noticed four minutes."

"You seem to have me confused with a nicer man."

"I..." *Don't know what to say.*

"I'd generally administer twenty. You may want to consider yourself lucky, my sweet."

Remembering his training, she responded quickly. "Thank you, Sir."

He laughed. "You were close to me changing my mind and making a point."

"In that case, I'm very grateful, Sir." Julia hazarded a glance over her shoulder.

"I'm going to rub your ass a bit."

His touch was so vigorous that she dug her fingers into the bedding in a vain attempt to remain in place.

"After every swat, arch your back and then offer your ass for the next one. Unnecessary delays will cost you. Any questions?"

She shook her head. "I mean no, Sir." Hoping to please him, she lifted her pelvis.

He picked up the belt. "There will be no more than twelve."

"Does knowing that help?"

"My subs tell me that information helps to manage expectations and compartmentalize what's happening."

"Another kindness, Sir?"

"You're smart to recognize that. Ready?"

Though she tried not to, she clenched her muscles.

"Breathe." He landed the first across both buttocks, scalding her.

She yelped. That was much worse than she had expected, but the sound told her he hadn't used the same force as he had with the pillow.

Instantly he pressed his fingertips against the heat, and the pain dissipated.

"The first is always the biggest shock."

Good to know. Slowly she offered herself for his next stripe.

Marcus caught her left thigh, and she jerked. He was right—it didn't sear as bad as the last, and also, the realization that she was already part way finished helped her tremendously.

"I'm waiting. Take as much time as you need."

She turned her head to the side and drew in a breath. It was only then that she realized she'd been holding it.

"You may want to try uncurling your fists."

At his prompting, she splayed her fingers.

"That's it."

His third stripe was much, much easier to take.

The fourth, fifth, and sixth fell in a comfortable rhythm.

Shocking her, the seventh turned her on. How was that possible? Maybe it was from the way he soothed her, or the heat that burned her skin.

She imagined him behind her, wielding the leather he'd worn, wanting to please her.

After the eighth, she was whimpering, ravenous. She stuck her ass back up in a blatant invitation. "Sir!"

"I smell your arousal, Julia."

In the past she might have been ashamed by that observation. Now it was as if everything she'd been holding back for years had been unleashed."

"I'd like to see for myself. Spread your legs. And position your rear as high as you can."

His voice, the heat where his belt had impacted, all melded.

Then he stroked her pussy, arcing electricity through her. "So hot. So wet. Drenched for me."

"Yes, Sir." She rocked back and forth.

"Moroccan leather was made for you."

He inserted a finger deep inside of her and fucked her with it, finding her G-spot. Within moments, she was ready to come. Like a shameless hussy, she angled her body toward him, seeking more.

Her entire being vibrated with tension.

Before she could steal an orgasm, something she was willing to do at this point, he stepped away.

She remained where she was for long moments, silently pleading with him to finish what he'd started. When he didn't, she drew a ragged breath, lifted her head, arched her spine and waited.

He continued, catching the top of her buttocks.

She'd found that stalling between each stroke didn't really help. She wanted it over with. Curling her hands into fists, she waited for the next.

"Surrender."

At his prompting, she exhaled and opened her hands, no longer fighting—absorbing it, breathing with it.

"That's a girl." He matched the pace that she set.

He delivered the last with a beautiful fury that made her scream.

The belt fell to the floor, the buckle clattering against the hardwood, and he pulled her toward him, then flipped her onto her back.

She was barely aware of him kneeling. Then he lifted her legs and held them apart to lick her pussy. She cried out his name in blissful protest.

"Put your knees over my shoulders."

He pulled back her clitoral hood and ate her out. She thrashed and whimpered, trying to rein in her response. She had never been more desperate to come in her entire life. "Please. Please!" She shuddered. "Oh, Sir."

Inserting two fingers into her feminine heat, he thrust hard and fast, over and over.

Her thighs quivered from the effort of restraining herself. She couldn't last much longer…

He continued to lick, to suck, to finger her. She was unraveling from the inside out. "Master Marcus! Master, Master, Master… Oh…" She grabbed hold of the edge of the mattress and dug in her fingers. She bit her lip to distract herself.

"Come *now.*"

He shoved a third finger in her, stretching her mercilessly.

She reached for him as she orgasmed in a slick rush that left her panting, replete, unable to think or move.

Nothing in her life had prepared her for the experience of hanging on the precipice for so long, only to have him shove her over the edge.

"That will do for a warm-up." He studied her intently as he captured her wrists.

Chapter Nine

Marcus had been determined to deny her for much longer, but her use of the word *Master* for the first time undid him. In return, he wanted to give her the stars and the moon, all wrapped in a silver bow.

He lowered her legs from his shoulders and helped her to sit up before joining her on the bed.

"I..."

She leaned into him, letting him take her weight. He kissed the top of her head and held her tight, not wanting to let her go.

"Thank you, Sir. That orgasm was..."

Was he so arrogant that he wanted to hear her say it?

"Spectacular."

He'd settle for that.

"The most intense I've ever had."

Those were the words he'd wanted to hear. He didn't normally lick and finger-fuck a woman's cunt until she'd climaxed. But then, no other submissive had screamed out the word Master for the first time and begged for release like Julia had.

When he scened, he endeavored to remain objective, stay in control and gauge his sub's reactions so he could draw out every possible nuance of her experience.

While she'd begged, she'd ground her pussy demandingly into his face.

Maybe he could have made her wait just a little longer, but the way she'd grabbed his hair and tightened her legs around his neck had sealed the deal.

Julia, with her sweet sass and curiosity could get a lot from him that he'd never given anyone else.

He picked her up and carried her back to the great room where he placed her on the couch. "I'll be right back."

"But—"

He placed a finger against her lips. "No arguing."

"Sorry, Sir."

He grabbed a blanket and covered her. She looked perfect snuggled there, her hair an untamed mess, her lips slightly parted, her eyes bright blue as she looked at him unblinkingly.

He left her, returning less than two minutes later, with water, a hand towel, a warm washcloth. After making sure she drank half the bottle, he moved part of the blanket aside to wipe between her legs.

"Sir! I can do that myself."

He loved the way she blushed. After everything they'd done together, she still experienced embarrassment. "One day, my sweet, you'll stop arguing. And it will be glorious. Your keeping quiet when things are not open for negotiation will save us both a lot of aggravation. Or there's always a gag so I don't have to listen."

Wisely she pressed her lips together.

"Excellent call." He dried the sweat from her body. "Now let me see your buttocks."

After a short hesitation, she threw back the blanket and turned over.

"How did it feel?" Marcus traced his marks and those from the garter belt's straps. There were several spots that might bruise later if he didn't take care of them.

"Amazing." She exhaled. "But I'm not sure I learned my lesson. If that's what happens when I'm late…"

Glad she was facedown, he grinned. "You may not want to test my good humor again. I went easy on you because you're still new. I promise you, you do not want to be on the receiving end of my wrath."

She shuddered. "In that case, Sir, thank you."

"In addition to spankings, there are other ways to punish you, Julia. And that may involve me withholding my attentions or giving you a prolonged period of time to consider my wishes. Perhaps on your knees in the corner."

She struggled to look over her shoulder. "You're serious?"

"Oh yes."

"I wouldn't like that." Her words were muffled by the cushion.

"Precisely the point."

"In that case, I'm extra grateful."

"As you should be. I would rather give you a sensual experience. Through your behavior, the choice is always yours." He draped the blanket back over her. "Remain where you are."

He jogged up the stairs to grab a bottle of arnica, then returned to rub some of the cream into the tiny red marks.

"That feels good, Sir."

"You're welcome, my sweet. When you're ready, the playroom is prepared for you. Unless you've had enough?"

She turned back over. "No. I've waited so long."

He stood and offered his hand, drawing her against him. With a gentle, contented sigh, she leaned her head on his chest, and he wrapped his arms around her.

Not since early in his relationship with Amber had Marcus held a woman this tenderly. And he liked the intimacy.

Eventually—long before he was ready—she pulled back. Then, as if needing something to do, she smoothed her hair over her shoulders.

"After you." He indicated the stairs.

"Uhm, you don't want me to crawl." She crossed her arms across her chest. "Do you?"

"Not necessary." He grinned. "But I do want you to walk in front of me so I can watch your hips sway." *And admire my marks on your ass.*

The sight was everything he'd hoped for.

When she reached the second level, she paused.

"First room on your left."

He'd left the door open so that she'd immediately see the Saint Andrew's cross he'd had constructed for her.

Once she'd entered, she stood, riveted in place, as she looked around.

In addition to the cross, he had a spanking horse, an overhead hook on a pully, a wheeled stainless-steel tray, a counter, a dresser, and a small cuddle couch where he could hold her. Something he looked forward to.

His spanking implements were neatly arranged and displayed on the far wall. "Feel free to explore."

"I..." She looked back at him. "It's a little overwhelming."

"Think of it as a candy store meant for your pleasure."

She shivered. "Pleasure might be a stretch, Sir."

"Is it?"

It took her a few seconds to answer. "Maybe not. Until I met you, I never craved a man's belt."

And he wanted her only tasting his.

Her heels struck a soft staccato as she moved deeper into the room. "This seems better equipped than the Den."

It might be.

"Am I allowed to touch?"

"They are all yours. I've never used them with anyone else."

She turned to face him. "You mean that?"

"Some of them are handcrafted." Enjoying this more than he'd imagined possible, he watched her, drinking in the play of emotions in her eyes—apprehension, uncertainty. "Select anything you want."

She trailed her fingers down the suede of one of his floggers, then traced the outline of a coiled single-tail whip.

Next, she lifted a crop from its hook and grinned as she glanced back at him. "It has a heart on the end."

"Delivers a nice smack. But not a lot of pain."

"Really? Even with you wielding it?"

"Is that a comment on my strength?"

"Well" —she blushed—"I have seen your arms. You, Sir are no weakling. And definitely not an ogre."

Though she turned away, it wasn't quick enough to hide her saucy grin.

Julia quickly bypassed the canes but touched the logo he'd burned into a tawse. "Go ahead and look in the dresser."

Curious, she moved to the piece of furniture. "Holy... Wow." His restraints and clamps were arranged in velvet-lined drawers.

"There's a gift for you. If you choose to accept it."

She turned toward him, her eyebrows furrowed. "Sir—?"

"In the box." He pointed toward the top of the dresser.

"I'm not sure..."

"Open it, then decide."

When she did, she gasped. "This is..." Julia picked up the thin strip of leather with his logo stamped on it. "A collar?"

"Of sorts. Nothing permanent."

"But doesn't it represent...?" Stiffening her spine, she quickly dropped it back in place. "I mean you don't own me, and you're not thinking—?"

He held up a hand. "As with most things in BDSM, it signifies only what we decide it does." Remaining in place, giving her the space she suddenly seemed to need, was one of the most difficult things he'd done. "I'd like you to wear it while we scene—either here or at the Den." As he'd crafted the piece yesterday, he'd made that decision.

In front of him, she looked tiny and uncertain, and she was silent for so long he wondered if she was going to use a safe word.

"So what does it mean to you?"

"That when we're together you acknowledge me as your Dominant."

She quickly sucked in a breath. Still, despite her hesitation, her nipples had hardened, and she'd put no more distance between them.

Positive steps.

"Nothing more?"

Marcus countered with a question of his own. "Is there something you want it to mean?"

"I'm fine with what you said." She tipped her head to one side. "As long as you don't think it's more significant than that?"

"We are in agreement."

Her breath caught.

"In that case, Julia, I'd like you to wear my collar."

Her lips alluringly parted for a moment before she whispered, "If it pleases you, Sir."

Fuck. *Fuck.* His already-hard cock throbbed. Were there any sweeter words?

With deliberate strides, he crossed the room to capture her shoulders. Small tremors shook her body, and he pressed his fingers into her flesh to reassure her. "Thank you. And it does please me."

Their gazes connected for a few moments, and she seemed to draw in courage.

Movements precise, she lowered herself to her knees in his preferred position. Then she lowered her gaze as she scooped the hair from her neck.

"Your grace is exquisite." Such growth in the time they'd been apart.

After picking up the thin strip of leather, he crouched in front of her. "I made this for you with the hope this moment would happen."

"It wasn't an expectation?"

"Not at all." Marcus shook his head. "This moment isn't one I was sure you'd honor me with."

"What do you mean? An honor, Sir?"

"Indeed. As agreed, it has no meaning that we don't give it. But if you didn't trust me, I doubt you would have agreed to even a temporary collaring."

"You're right."

He secured the ends behind her neck, then slid a finger beneath it to be sure it wasn't too tight.

Seeing her there punched him in the gut.

All day, he'd visualized how it might look, but the reality—the black leather against her creamy skin—knocked him in the solar plexus.

Now that he'd had a taste, he wanted more, imagining her locked in a handcrafted steel one.

Slowly she lowered her hair.

Marcus forced himself to focus. "How's that?"

"It's..."

He waited.

"Fine."

The response was probably honest, but disappointing. But what the fuck had he expected? Her to fall at his feet in gratitude for something that obviously was a challenge for her?

Getting a mental grip on himself, he stood. "I'd like to begin with the Saint Andrew's cross. I had it built for you." The structure was stained with a light pine gloss that would easily wipe clean. "You did say you wanted to be flogged."

She shivered.

"If it's your preference, there are also hooks attached to the walls and ceilings. Basically, I can tie you or suspend you virtually anywhere. For our purposes, the spanking bench is for a different use."

"I see."

"Please select the flogger you prefer." He folded his arms. "I recommend you select a short one with thick strands for your introduction. We can move on to others later."

While she did as he'd instructed, he turned on a small space heater to ensure she didn't get cold.

After studying all of them, she selected one with mauve-colored falls.

"How would you like me to give this to you?"

"Do you really need an answer to your question?" He lifted a skeptical eyebrow. "Or are you stalling?"

Rather than answering, she looked away, then lowered herself to her knees and crawled toward him, then, when they were scant inches apart, she knelt up and extended it across her upturned palms.

She couldn't have been more poised if she'd done this dozens of times.

He accepted the implement and flicked it several times to test its weight and responsiveness. As he did, she silently tracked each movement.

After attaching the flogger to the side of the metal tray, he beckoned her toward the cross. "Facing me, please."

"Yes, Sir."

"I'm looking forward to this. Your backside is already red. Now your front will match."

In under two minutes, she was secured in place, at his mercy. "You look every bit as wonderful as I imagined you might."

Her chest rose and fell, showing her state of nerves as she tested the bonds and discovered the leather cuffs had no give.

"This is all about your pleasure. If it's too much, not what you want or expect, use your safe word. There are many other things we can do." Having her here, in his collar, had satisfied him completely. "Have you ever played with nipple clamps?"

"No." She gulped. "I'm willing to try."

"That's my good girl."

At the approval in his tone, her eyes took on a glazed, faraway look.

"We'll start with a tweezer style. They're not my favorite because they come off too easily. But they'll be a good introduction for you." He opened a drawer, selected a pair, then draped the chain over his index finger.

She stared at them. "On second thought…"

"Dare to experiment." He cupped her left breast then sucked her nipple into his mouth, laving the bud, tantalizing her until he breathed in the heady scent of her arousal.

"I like that." She moved her shoulder, offering him more.

"You're sensitive. I like that." He compressed the nipple until her eyes drifted shut, then he placed the clamp, tightening it just enough for it to stay in place.

"I expected something much worse," she admitted. "I'm wondering what I was nervous about."

"Other types can be worse. But we can work you up to them if you want to try."

"I might."

He repeated the process with her right breast. When both tweezers were properly adjusted, he tugged on the chain.

She winced slightly.

"Still okay?

"It hurts a little, Sir."

"Let's see if this helps." He stroked between her legs.

"Oh. *Yes*! That's… The pain in my nipples makes your hand feel more intense."

"Now tell me how this is." He tightened the clamps.

She cried out and strained against her bonds. "I understand why I was nervous." She whimpered.

He played with her pussy until she was panting and moving her chest in a sensual dance.

The tips of her nipples were distended beautifully. He moved two fingers rapidly through her slick folds. He liked how aroused she became, and how quickly it happened. "Don't come yet."

"There's no chance."

Want to bet? "Such a pretty pussy." As he spoke, he continued to fondle her.

Her thighs began to quiver. *"Oh!"*

"Are you on the verge?"

"Yes…" She drew out the s into a soft purr.

"Good. I like the way you look. Helpless. Bound. At my mercy."

Her eyes were closed, and she was panting with desire.

He grabbed the flogger and shook out the dozen thick strands. "Are you still with me? Green?"

"This is amazing."

"I need a yes or no answer."

She blinked her eyes open. "Yes. I'm green, Sir."

"We're starting with three strokes."

"I understand."

He landed them gently where he wanted them, her torso, then her belly, then a little lower so that strands licked her inner thighs.

"Oh. My." She met his eyes. "May I have more, please?"

He smiled. "Anything for you, my sweet. Harder? Or the same?"

"Harder. And…everywhere."

With a gentle rhythm, he flogged her body, her breasts, thighs, ribs.

She sighed. "I like this."

As he continued, he took a small step back to give him more leverage and freedom of movement.

Her head fell forward a little.

Watching her carefully, he went on, slightly increasing the amount of force as her breathing pattern deepened and she surrendered to her bondage.

And then, she was gone… "Can you hear me, Julia?"

She didn't respond, letting him know she'd reached a blissful state inside her own mind, where she floated on an endorphin high.

He shook out the falls and placed the flogger down. "Come back to me, sweet Julia."

"Shh."

He placed a gentle kiss on her forehead. "Look at me."

"Uh-uh." Her head lolled to one side.

With infinite patience, thrilled with her perfection, he stroked his knuckles down the column of her throat.

"More, Sir."

"You've had enough for now."

"But—" Blowing out a breath, she finally opened her eyes.

Marcus recognized the glaze of arousal mixed with a layer of annoyance. "You are lovely in your submission."

"I wasn't done."

"Another time."

She ground her toes into the hardwood flooring.

"Please, Sir, I really want to come. I've never felt like this before."

"My pleasure." As he fingered her, he loosened each of the clamps, sucking on each nipple to lessen the pain as the blood rushed back into them.

"That's…" She began to jerk against him.

"You've earned it." Her body was hot, her breaths were labored, and she was pulling restlessly against her bonds.

"My whole body is on fire. From the inside out."

"Come when you're ready." He slipped two fingers deep inside her.

With a long moan, she cried out his name. A feeling of possession pulsed through him. Now that he'd seen her in his collar, he never wanted to let her go. He wanted her in his life, wearing his ring.

Where the hell had that thought come from? Even though it wasn't in their agreement, he never wanted to let her go.

He'd proceed with caution so as not to frighten her. But this woman was *his*.

He continued to stimulate her as sobs racked her body. "Give me everything, your screams, your raw emotion."

"Thank you." Minutes later, gasping, sobbing, she came again. "God. Oh God. Thank you, Sir."

He kissed her and muttered soothing words against her ear. "You did well.". Using his thumbs, he traced the lovely tracks of her tears. "Let me get you off the cross." Kneeling, he released her ankles and rubbed circulation back into her lower legs before standing once more to repeat the process with her wrists. "Slowly."

She offered a half-smile. "I'm not sure I can stand up."

In a single move, he scooped her up and carried her into his bedroom. Still surrendered, she nestled into his body. The way it was supposed to be.

When he placed her on the bed, she rolled onto her side to study him. "Will you make love to me?"

Not fuck. Make love. The words made his already-hard cock throb. But her needs came first. "You just had quite an experience."

"As I also said at the Den, I know my mind." She pulled a pillow closer to her. "Please."

"There's nothing I want more. But first, I want to get you warmed up and make sure you're feeling okay."

"Honestly I'm—"

"Fine, right? Save your breath." He went into the bathroom, turned on the shower, then grabbed a bottle of orange juice from the bar-sized refrigerator he kept stocked near the wall-mounted television in the bedroom. "Drink." He unscrewed the lid.

With a small, adorable frown, she accepted the beverage. When she'd taken a few sips and her cheeks were once again bright, he offered his hand.

She hesitated for only a moment before following him into the steamy bathroom where she took off her stockings and garter belt. There were two showerheads, one on either side of the oversized unit, and he adjusted one to cascade over her shoulders.

"Have you thought of everything in this house?"

"Upgrades are a constant. As soon as I finish one thing, I move on to another."

"It's fabulous."

Until this moment, it hadn't mattered that he had no one to share it with.

"May I?" She reached for his cock and stroked several times before kneeling.

"Julia..."

Warm water cascaded over her head as she looked up at him. This was supposed to be about her, but as she lowered her mouth toward him, his abdominal muscles contracted.

Without waiting for his permission, she closed her lips around his cockhead and sucked him deep into her mouth.

He gave himself over to her enthusiastic service. When a sub did something like this, he generally gave continuous and detailed instructions, controlling how deep she took him. He couldn't recall the last time a woman had asked permission, of her own volition, to pleasure him.

Shocking him, in only a few minutes he was ready to spill. Watching her, so genuine in her desire to please, heightened his ardor. "Stop."

While continuing, she looked up. It wasn't defiance he saw in her expression—she was enjoying herself.

He took hold of her head and pulled her back. *"Julia."*

Instantly she stopped.

"You asked me to make love to you, and if you continue, that won't be happening."

"Oh?" She grinned impishly, and he dug his hand into her hair. A whole new level of teasing and intimacy had just unfolded between them. He turned off the faucets before sliding open the shower door to grab a towel and wrapping it around her.

"It's warm."

"The rack is heated."

"My house could use some of your upgrades."

Something he could certainly manage.

As he shucked water from his body, he watched her move about his bathroom.

She used his brush, and she washed away the remaining tracks left behind from her tears.

It surprised him how natural it seemed to have her in his house, his life.

He stepped out of the shower to see her studying his reflection in the mirror.

"Everything okay?"

How had she noticed he was lost in thought? Not since Amber had been angling for a proposal had he been subject to this much consideration. The trouble here was, Julia wanted nothing but a part-time Dom. "Thinking about filling your hot little pussy. Get your ass in the bed."

"Yes, Sir!"

He ripped the towel from around her, and she squealed, attempting to dodge past him. Responding in kind, he stalked her, something primeval flaring in him.

It took only three steps to catch her, and he swooped her from the floor and tossed her on the mattress.

She scrambled toward the headboard and wrapped her arms protectively around her knees.

"Think that will save you?" He grabbed her ankles and yanked her toward him.

"Do me." She spread her legs wide. "Fuck me, Sir."

He left her long enough to get a condom from the nightstand. Since he lacked the patience to have her put it on him, he rolled it down his cock and returned to her. "Are you wet?"

"Find out for yourself." She shot him another sassy grin. *"Sir."*

With his cockhead, he stroked her clit, then pressed against the entrance to her pussy. Their teasing foreplay obviously aroused her as much as it had him. "You are ready for me."

In silent response, she dug her heels into the mattress and lifted her hips to meet his first thrust.

He drove inside in one rapid, powerful stroke.

She cried out as he seated himself, balls deep. He gritted his teeth, then reached for her arms and pinned her wrists above her head. He fucked her hard, determined to wring a climax from her sexy, submissive body.

"Sir! May I come?"

"So quick?"

"Now!"

He pulled out, then thrust several times quickly. "Yes. *Now.*"

She arched her back, offering her pelvis, taking more of him. She turned her head to the side, eyes closed, as she called out his name.

It took all his determination not to come as her internal muscles contracted around him.

When she let out a shaky breath and opened her eyes, he turned her face toward him and kissed her, slowly, gently.

She smiled, and raw masculine pride filled him. He'd made his woman happy.

"Thank you."

He took hold of her and reversed their positions so that she was on top of him. "I want to look at your breasts and play with your nipples. Arch your back for me."

She didn't hesitate. "That position makes you so much deeper in me, Sir."

He took hold of her hips and moved her up and down in time with his movements. "Keep your hands behind you."

Julia grabbed his legs for balance while he filled her hot pussy with his hard cock.

Before finding his own release, he gave her another orgasm, causing her to collapse forward onto him.

"You're pretty good at that, Sir."

"Pretty good?" He held her tight while their breathing returned to normal.

Neither of them seemed inclined to end the moment, and he stroked her spine, enjoying the sensation of having her close in his arms. "It's time you were introduced to the pleasures of a forced orgasm."

Julia wasn't sure how many more new experiences he could give her.

"I use orgasm denial as a training tool, as you know."

She opened her mouth to speak, but he held up a hand, forestalling her.

"One you dislike. A forced orgasm can be just as brutal, or it can be simply something that overwhelms you. I want you to come again and again for me, Julia. Into the playroom. Lie flat on the top of the spanking bench."

Her spanking bench. She loved that he'd created this space for her. That no other woman had ever been here thrilled her.

He approached, totally naked. Seeing his sexy, powerful body gave her an erotic thrill.

"Scoot down a bit."

After she had, he tied her legs to the bottom of the bench, spreading her wide and exposing her bare pussy. Her ass was over from the edge slightly, meaning she couldn't really move away from him. He secured her arms loosely. It didn't hurt, but it prevented her from pulling away.

He showed her a massive vibrator, one that plugged into the wall. She'd seen something like it on one of the videos she'd downloaded. The woman in the clip had screamed unbelievably when the Dom had held it against her clit. "That looks a little scary, Sir." So far, she'd only used small, battery-operated bullets.

"I've denied you orgasms plenty of times. Now I'm going to make you come. But first…"

She stared, mesmerized, as he put the vibrator down, building the fear and expectation.

He returned with a different set of nipple clamps. These looked a bit vicious.

"They're clover, and they won't pull off. They're some of my favorites."

This time, he didn't ask for her safe words before sucking her left nipple into his mouth.

At the rough sensation, her pussy became slick. She'd had no idea how much she liked nipple play.

When he secured the first one in place, she winced. "That, Sir, is a son of a bitch."

"If you can endure the first minute or so, I think you'll enjoy it."

"That seems unlikely."

Rather than responding, he tugged on the chain, increasing the pressure.

"Yellow!"

He dropped the chain and smoothed back her hair. "Talk to me."

"It damn well burns."

"I will remove it if you request, but recall the tweezers?"

"They were nothing like this."

"And your orgasm was intense."

The best of her life.

Even as he spoke, the pain receded.

"If you want to continue, breathe into the pain, through it."

Sometimes she felt as if he crawled into her mind and read it before she had even finished forming her thoughts. "Green, Sir." *For now.*

"Brave little sub." After sucking her right nipple until it was hard, he quickly clamped it.

She thrashed about. If her hands weren't fastened, she would have ripped the nasty little things off.

"Well done." He ran a finger across each of her eyebrows, calming her in a way words couldn't. "Hang in there another two minutes." He picked up the vibrator and a hum filled the air. Then he placed the toy between her legs.

"You're already wet."

The pulsing, relentless head tormented her. He moved the gigantic thing across her clit, her pussy, down toward her anus.

She no longer registered the pressure on her nipples as pain. In fact, it eased into pleasure, driving her libido.

"That's my sweet sub. Come. Come hard for your Dominant."

The sensations were too much. She tossed her head from side to side, trying to escape the frustrating, demanding vibrator.

A climax crashed through her.

"Let's go for another." Instead of stopping, he increased the vibrator's speed. The little beast was simultaneously too much and not enough.

He tugged on her nipples, and she came again. *How is this possible?*

"Good girl. Let's go for three."

She couldn't. It wasn't possible. But he mouthed her pussy, then shoved a couple of fingers in her before putting the vibe back on her swollen clit.

But he didn't stop. Time after time, he made her climax.

Finally, he placed the toy on his wheeled tray and donned a condom.

"Yes."

He towered over her and slid his hard dick into her. Despite being emotionally and physically wrung out, she wanted him.

The angle allowed him to thrust in and hit her G-spot. Although it shouldn't be possible, she was mere seconds away from shattering again.

"Oh my sweet you're going to come for me, aren't you?" He reached for the vibrator again.

Frantically she shook her head. The thing was an instrument of torture.

With the toy on low speed, he leaned back slightly to place the head on her clit. Then with his free hand, he fisted the clamp's chain between her breasts.

She fractured—pain obliterated by consuming pleasure.

Julia had no idea how much time had passed, but when she could string two thoughts together, they were on the dungeon's couch, and she was in his arms, comforted and protected.

"I've got you."

She allowed her head to loll against his chest.

If Master Marcus was a drug, she'd gotten her fix.

He smoothed back her hair and gently kissed the top of her head.

There was no place she'd rather be.

Until he said one word that terrified her.

Chapter Ten

"Stay."

At Master Marcus's tone, Julia froze. It was more command than invitation. And it wasn't what she expected. The evening had surpassed any of her expectations, leaving her more vulnerable than she'd ever been.

To protect herself from falling for a man who was nowhere close to being someone she wanted to marry, Julia had to stay within the boundaries of the agreement they'd made.

When she'd gathered her wits, she pressed a hand to his strong chest and pushed herself away from him. "Thank you. But I need to be going."

"It's late."

And you're far too persuasive. "I have yoga class in the morning." Not that she couldn't skip it like she did most Sundays, but she seized on the first excuse that came to mind.

"I see."

His scowl told her he didn't.

She offered a small grin that he didn't return.

Shaking from a sudden, ridiculous onset of nerves, she wiggled off his lap. "Thank you." She hesitated, then opted not to add an honorific. Earlier, she'd slipped, calling him Master. In the moment, it had been as natural as breathing. But now, feeling a little uncertain, afraid that she wanted him more than she should, she needed to escape. "I…" *What should I say?* "The evening was everything I dreamed."

Part of her desperately wanted to change her mind and stay, maybe for as long as he'd have her. Before she could give in to temptation, she scrambled off his lap.

They returned to the bedroom. While he dressed in casual clothes and slipped into a pair of shoes, she gathered her stockings and garter belt but opted not to put them back on. Then, with him close behind, she headed back downstairs and gathered her belongings.

She slipped on her thong and fastened her bra. And once she'd shrugged into the coat that he held for her, she stuffed her remaining garments into the pockets.

"I'll walk you to your car."

The set of his jaw told her any argument would be futile.

In silence they rode the elevator. She wanted to converse but had no idea what to say. Small talk didn't seem appropriate. Nor did a discussion of what they'd shared. Truthfully, she wasn't even sure she could put the experience into words—at least not yet.

After opening her car door and helping her inside, he offered her the key fob. Then he leaned into the driver's compartment, his face mere inches from hers.

Don't kiss me. I might not be able to resist you if you do.

But he didn't.

Instead, he lifted her hair and untied the collar, leaving her skin chilled where the leather had warmed it.

"Call me when you need an orgasm." He rapped knuckles on the roof, then closed the door.

That's it?

For long moments she stayed in place, fingers curled around the steering wheel in a death grip. He hadn't kissed her. Hadn't even tried.

The blasted man had honored her wishes, and disappointment careened through her.

Finally, she was able to start the engine, back out, then drive for the exit.

She was unable to resist looking in the rearview mirror at the man—the Dominant—she was leaving behind.

Hands tucked in his pockets, he stood in the spot she'd just left, watching her go.

* * * *

Almost a week later, she was in her kitchen, a glass of wine on the counter, staring at her blank phone screen.

Marcus hadn't contacted her. Which made her wonder if he wanted to see her again.

With a frustrated sigh, she dug a hand into her hair and scooped it back from her forehead.

God.

She wanted space, insisted on having it. And when he gave it to her, she was lonely—annoyingly so.

Talking to Lana hadn't helped because her suggestion was to call Marcus.

Chardonnay untouched, she paced the small confines of her home. Thoughts of him filled her every waking hour, just like they had the week he'd had her kneel for him.

Being apart hadn't protected her from that. In fact, not knowing if they'd see each other again made it worse. Eventually, she had to face the truth. Even if it wasn't smart, she needed him.

Before she could change her mind, she returned to the kitchen, snatched up her phone and then scrolled to his contact information.

Drawing a steadying breath, she pushed the Send button.

Right before she expected to receive his voicemail, he answered. "Cavendish."

Which was much more formal than he'd been the last few times they'd spoken. "It's Julia." Which he already knew.

"Nice to hear from you."

"I'd, ah…" While he waited, she took a fortifying sip of her wine, then tried again. "I'd like to see you."

"Next Saturday?"

More than a week from now? "That's fine." Since he'd been a bit standoffish, and his voice had shockingly not been tinged with a dominant tone, she responded in kind. "What time would you like me?"

"I'd like to take you on a date."

"A…" She blinked. That wasn't part of their agreement. "I thought I could maybe come over tomorrow night and we could—"

"Dinner at seven? I'll pick you up at six."

Her mouth fell open. When she thought she had him figured out, he changed the rules of the game.

"Text me your address."

Without another word, he ended the call.

Stunned, she once again stared at a blank screen. *What just happened?* She'd expected him to make a steamy request or issue an order.

Seconds later, her phone chimed. Thrilled, she checked the notification.

Send me your address.

That was it.

Exhaling, she typed her response. And for the next long, agonizing three days, she heard nothing else from him.

Tuesday evening, she arrived home from work to find a package waiting outside her door, labeled with the name of a designer store.

Stunned, and more energetic than she'd been all day, she hurried inside to open the box. When she parted the tissue paper, she gasped. A gorgeous gown in a pastel pink color lay there, shimmering in the overhead light.

Gently she pulled it out. The front was low-cut, but not scandalously so. The form-fitting material would hug her curves, ones she'd been embarrassed by until he'd banished her self-doubts.

She hurried into her room to try the garment on.

Both the fit and the feel were perfect, and she couldn't wait to wear it for him.

Then realization plowed into her.

He had been thinking of her. Not just thinking, but planning. The dress couldn't be more perfect, which meant he'd considered her hair color, and he knew her measurements. Not only that, but she had no doubt, it was the most expensive piece of clothing she'd ever owned.

The doorbell rang, and she hurried to answer it.

A delivery driver stood there, carrying two more boxes, both from boutiques in Cherry Creek.

Matching shoes and a purse.

He'd thought of everything.

Since a thank you by text wouldn't suffice, she called him.

"Julia."

So much better than Cavendish, like last time. "Thank you. I don't know what to say. Other than your taste is exquisite, and…well, thank you."

"I'm glad you're pleased. You'll be ready on time?"

He left her breathless. When she was convinced he'd stepped back from dominance, he reasserted himself.

"Of course…" *Sir.*

"See you then."

Once again, he ended the call without any formal goodbye.

Unable to emotionally comprehend what was happening, she called Lana, but received voice mail.

Belatedly she realized Lana was at the meeting with other subs that she'd mentioned. Julia scowled, annoyed with herself for skipping the invitation. Tonight, of all nights, she could have used the support of others in the lifestyle. Maybe they could help her understand Master Marcus better.

But honestly, she didn't consider herself a submissive. Rather, she was a woman who enjoyed occasional kink.

Right?

Even as she dressed for their date on Saturday, she was no closer to an answer.

Ten minutes before he was expected, she was swiping on her lipstick. So when the doorbell rang at precisely six-thirty, she drew a steadying breath, then smoothed the front of her dress and answered the summons.

Breath vanished from her lungs.

In leather or casual clothing, he was as sexy as sin. In a suit, he was devastating.

He pulled a bouquet of flowers from behind his back. "I've missed you."

"Marcus…" What did she say to a man who treated her as if she were a princess?

"Are you going to invite me in?" A smile curved his lips and lightened the color of his eyes.

Finally, she recovered enough to remember her manners. "I'm sorry. Yes, of course." She took a step back.

With the door closed, the size of him overwhelmed the space and her.

He extended the flowers toward her. "For you."

The bouquet was beautiful, filled with massive, colorful blooms and beautiful pink rosebuds. After inhaling the fragrance, she smiled at him. "They're beautiful." The way he was behaving truly was like a man intent on a relationship. Which she didn't want. "Thank you."

"It's what you do when you're taking a beautiful lady to dinner." He leaned forward and placed his index finger beneath her chin.

Slowly he tipped back her head, then captured her gaze. "May I kiss you?"

You're asking? The request caught her off guard.

In a breathless whisper, she replied, "Yes. *Please.*"

Instead of consuming her as she expected he gently brushed his lips across hers, leaving her yearning for more. *That* was also not what she'd expected.

To cover her confusion, she turned toward the kitchen. "Let me just put these in some water."

He followed her. "I like your condo. Great area."

"It is." Grateful for a safe topic, she found a vase under the sink. "I love people watching. And it's a great place to walk or run." She glanced over her shoulder as she filled the vase. "Not that I ever do."

But Marcus definitely might.

"May I offer you something to drink?"

He glanced at his expensive, gadgety Bonds watch. "We have reservations."

As she already knew, he preferred punctuality. "Of course." She turned off the water, then placed the vase on the countertop. "Let me just grab my purse then we can go."

"I have another present for you."

"Sir?" The honorific fell easily from her lips.

"First I want to see you in the dress."

"Honestly, I never wear this color. I'm surprised how fabulous it is."

"My shopper helped me pick it out."

She blinked, both from the fact he had a personal shopper and that he'd hired her to help with her dress.

"We found your picture on social media. She considered your hair color and complexion."

"That was a lot of work."

"My sweet, you are worth every second."

As usual, the way he looked at her caused heat to simmer inside her.

"Will you turn around for me?"

Slowly she did so.

When she faced him again, he was leaning forward. "My imagination has been painting a vivid picture. But the reality leaves me breathless."

Because she recognized his sincerity, pleasure cascaded through her.

"Now for your gift."

"You've already done so much."

"Indulge me."

The implacable demand in his voice made her apprehensive.

"Raise your dress up to your waist, please."

This is what she had been expecting since she'd called him last week. The order put them back in welcome, familiar territory.

"Beautiful panties."

She'd selected a dusty rose color to match her bra and complement the outfit he'd given her.

He extended his hand. "Give them to me."

Since it wasn't the first time he had pocketed her undergarments, it didn't shock her like it might have.

But his next request did.

"I'd like you on your back on the kitchen island."

"The…?"

"You'll pay a penalty if I repeat myself."

She glanced from him to the long piece of granite. "I'm not sure how I'd get up there."

"Leave that to me." He swept her off the floor and placed where he wanted her. "Raise your legs, then spread them as far apart as you can."

His dominance made her reel.

He ran his fingers on the inside of her labia, checking that she'd done a good job of shaving. "That pleases me."

Then he reached into his jacket pocket and pulled out a bright purple piece of fabricated silicone in the shape of a U.

"It's a vibrator. With a remote control that I'll be holding on to." His grin was wicked, as he showed her that one side was slightly longer than the other. "This part goes against your G-spot."

Her eyes widened.

"The other end with the curve to it will be pressed against your clitoris."

"You expect me to wear this thing to dinner?"

Naturally he did not respond.

Jaw set in a determined line, he slid a finger inside her already-slick pussy, then he teased her, stopping short of allowing her to come. When she was writhing, he replaced his finger with the toy and ensured it was pressed where it should be, making her gasp. Then he bent the flexible material so that the other part was seated against that tender nub of nerves.

"It feels bigger than I expected."

"Let's give it a try. Shall we?"

She knew that really wasn't a question.

He reached inside his pants pocket and suddenly a gentle sensation rocked through her, making her press her fingertips against the granite. Then the toy began to vibrate with more intensity.

"Oh, Sir."

He left the vibrator running. Then, when she lifted her hips from the granite, he wickedly increased its speed.

Julia gasped. It had been so long since she'd seen him, and the intensity was so perfect she wanted to come right away.

Abruptly he shut off the vibrator. Denied, she closed her eyes to tamp down her annoyance.

Which was worse? Orgasm denial or forced orgasms?

"This will suit my requirements." He offered his hand and helped her to sit up. "Another delight for you, my sweet. Edging."

"I've read about that." Definitely something that had intrigued her more on the page than it did right now. "Then you realize in advance that I intend to keep you on the verge of an orgasm for hours, bringing you to the precipice while withholding the ultimate pleasure."

Already the toy made her uncomfortable. "That's diabolical."

"It is, isn't it?" With his usual skilled competence, he lifted her from the island and placed her on her feet, holding her waist until she was steady on the heels.

"May I have my panties back, please?"

"No. No underwear, Julia."

"But..." *Do you mean that?* "That's..."

"Shall we go?"

She shook her head. "The toy will fall out."

"Embarrassing for you."

Unable to comprehend that he really meant it, she stared at him.

"You'll want to concentrate on squeezing your internal muscles to keep it in place."

Which would make the entire experience even worse.

"We have reservations."

Julia took a step and the thing shifted. "Sir! I don't think I can do this."

"It might take you a moment to figure it out. But I trust you will." He cupped her elbow and slowly walked with her from the kitchen.

Her steps were a tiny shuffle as the little thing jiggled around.

"Your purse?"

"It's on that table." She pointed to the spot near the door.

He left her long enough to fetch it, then rejoined her. To his credit, he didn't encourage her to move any faster.

She thanked her lucky stars that there were no stairs to descend because getting into his luxurious SUV was difficult enough.

"Not so bad, was it?" He glanced at her as he exited the parking lot.

"It's awful."

"Perhaps this will be an evening you won't forget."

Every moment with him was memorable.

He drove with skill and competence—the way he did everything.

Then he headed west on the highway, leaving the city behind.

She angled herself to look at him. "Where are we going?"

"A place I hope meets with your approval."

With a frown, she guessed the names of a couple of restaurants in the area.

"You won't have heard of it."

"Oh?" Now she was intrigued.

"It's a private club on Lookout Mountain."

"You're right. I didn't even know something like that existed."

"I thought you might enjoy the drive, and there's a view of the city that's really beautiful."

Marcus took a left turn from the steep, winding road, onto an unmarked tree-lined street that she'd never noticed before.

"You're full of surprises, Sir."

The building that came into view took her breath away. The log-cabin type of structure was nestled among pines and had soaring plate-glass windows.

The moment he parked in the circular driveway, her door was opened, and a handsome young man offered his assistance.

Because she was trying to keep the toy in place, she was more than happy to accept.

Marcus rounded the hood of the car and possessively placed his fingers at the small of her back and guided her toward the massive door that was opened for them.

"This is amazing."

He smiled at her. "I hope you enjoy the rest of the experience as much."

When they entered, the maître d' greeted him by name, and the two men shook hands. He then smiled at her. "Welcome to Lookout Pointe."

No doubt playing on the name of the mountain.

"It's…" She glanced around at the stone fireplace. Tables were spread far apart, and thick etched-glass partitions divided the space to make each place into a private nook. Candles flickered on the tables, next to bud vases with columbines in them. The attention to detail was awe-inspiring. "Magnificent."

"If you'll follow me? As requested, sir, you have a window seat that's also near the fireplace."

As Marcus had suggested, the view of Denver's distant twinkling lights was exquisite. She wondered what it would be like in the daylight.

At the table, Marcus held her chair for her. Then, against her ear, he murmured, "Sit leaning forward slightly so the vibrator is on the seat."

Mouth dry at his scandalous request, she did as he said.

"May I start you with a glass of wine this evening, sir? Or would you like me to send over the sommelier?"

Marcus glanced at her. "Does red suit you?"

His question confused her. He'd made it clear he didn't scene if he'd been drinking. Or perhaps he was thinking that they'd be clear-headed by the time they arrived home? "Whatever you think."

"Ask Daniela to bring over a bottle she thinks we will enjoy."

"Certainly, sir." The maître d' nodded. "Please let me know if there's anything I can do to make your visit memorable."

"Thank you, Jean-Paul."

Once they were alone, she studied him. As usual, she'd uncovered another side of the man who dominated her, body and mind. "You're well-known here."

"It's convenient to my cabin and a good place to stop on the way to the Den."

"You have a cabin?"

"Nearby. Between here and Evergreen. Nothing special. Just a place to get away."

Someplace I might never be invited. Why did the thought bother her?

Before the conversation could continue, their server appeared to introduce himself and go over the evening's specials in great, mouth-watering detail. While he was speaking, someone else brought over a basket filled with bread and two choices of butter—regular and with sea salt—and a plate of olive oil drizzled with balsamic vinegar.

"May I start you with an appetizer? I recommend our lobster ravioli."

That was something she'd always wanted to try and had never splurged on because her budget didn't allow for that kind of extravagance.

"Julia?"

Though she was tempted to defer to him, she went for it. "Sounds wonderful."

As he moved away, Daniela joined them with a bottle of wine bearing a label Julia had never heard of.

"Evening, Mr. Cavendish." She presented the bottle to him, label side up.

"That will do nicely."

After uncorking the bottle, she poured a sample.

He went through the complicated tasting ritual that Julia had never seen anyone actually do before. "More than satisfactory. Excellent choice."

"I'm glad it meets your approval."

Daniela filled Julia's glass before topping off Marcus's.

When they were finally alone, flames licking at logs in the hearth, he proposed a toast. "To you, my sweet."

Since she had no idea how to respond, she touched her rim with his then tried to make herself comfortable.

After her first sip, she placed the stemware back on the table, then traced tiny circles on the base. "I'm already blown away. Thank you for bringing me." She looked across the table at her handsome date. "But I'm wondering if you have nefarious intentions toward me this evening?"

Instantly the vibrator hummed against her clit and her G-spot. With tiny inhalations, trying not to cry out, she sat up straighter.

"Of course I do, Ms. Lyle. Ones you can't begin to imagine."

When he finally relented, she relaxed her shoulders, unsure how she would make it through the evening.

Several more times and—always when she'd let her guard down—he would give her either a momentary pulse or sustained ripples of pleasure.

By the time their server had cleared the dishes and asked if they wanted dessert, Julia was a wreck, nervous and aroused, ready to leap out of her skin.

"The chocolate melting cake with a scoop of hand-churned vanilla ice cream is our most popular."

Somehow, without her ever noticing, the server had continued to list the options.

"Darling?" Marcus prompted.

Darling? Where had that come from?

"I'm thinking the chocolate cake or crème brûlée. Do you have a preference?"

A dizzying array of appetizers and massive entrees had more than filled her up. "Everything sounds good." Or everything she'd heard sounded good. "But I think I'll just go for a cup of coffee, please."

"Certainly, ma'am. Cream?"

"Thank you, yes."

"Same," Marcus ordered.

They lingered over the rich, hot beverage, and Marcus told her more about his construction business, including the fact his firm had built this restaurant. "They hired the architect I suggested."

"So you know everything about the place."

"No detail was overlooked."

"I'd say." She again wondered about his cabin. Had he also built that? "It's impressive."

"The architect deserves the credit, along with the interior designers."

"But you have to be proud."

"It's one of my favorite projects."

She almost asked about others but pressed her lips together. The deeper their connection, the harder it would be to remember she preferred nice men.

Before they left, Jean-Paul once again stopped by to wish them a good evening. "I hope to see you both again soon."

Marcus stood then offered his hand.

"Wait," she said as they neared the exit. "We didn't pay the bill."

"I have an account."

How had she not known that places like this existed?

Unbelievably their car was waiting for them with both the driver and passenger doors open. Had Jean-Paul notified the valet that they were on their way?

Less than a minute later, Marcus was driving back down the mountain, headed back toward Denver. But instead of taking her to his home, he drove straight to her condo.

"I'll see you inside."

Was he planning to scene with her in her condo? That would be unique. But not at all unwelcome.

In her condo, she placed her purse on the small table, and he dropped her panties nearby before capturing her shoulders in a gentle grip. "Think of me." He leaned forward to give her a searing, toe-curling kiss.

Slowly he released her and brushed hair back.

"Are you leaving, Sir?"

"I wouldn't want to keep you from your yoga class tomorrow morning."

With that he wished her goodnight, leaving her staring at the closed door.

What hell had just happened?

Julia wrapped her arms around herself, but the action didn't comfort her.

She'd never been more confused.

When it hit her, she leaned her shoulders against the wall.

The last time they'd been together, he'd been clear that he wanted something more from her. She'd resisted, and he was now showing her what she was missing.

Then, electrifying her, a ripple passed through the vibrator to her clit and G-spot. Gasping, she tightened her internal muscles so the toy remained in place.

The exasperating Dominant was still exerting his will, even though he was nowhere around.

What am I going to do about it?

* * * *

The next Tuesday, she'd joined Lana and others from the Den at the weekly coffee shop meeting.

Though the women were extraordinarily welcoming, Julia kept to herself to observe and figure out if she actually belonged there.

Within an hour, she was as comfortable as she'd ever been with a group of friends. Lana seemed to be loved by all.

Sara—who was in a relationship with a Dom—listened attentively to everyone and offered wise advice. Sydney arrived late, having just arrived from a trek in South America. She was a world-traveling adventurer who didn't attend the Den or the coffee meet-ups very often, and she seemed to be a bit like Julia in that she didn't want to be pinned down by a permanent relationship. But, unlike Julia, Sydney sought out BDSM experiences.

Then there was Maggie, a high-profile businesswoman who occasionally attended the Den, mostly for the stress-relief of impact play. Her best friend, Vanessa, was also there. In her bubbly way, she said the most outrageous things, keeping everyone in stitches.

Finally, after grabbing a second hot chocolate to soothe and fortify herself, Julia opened up. Though she tended to be reserved, she was eager to get input from others.

In a way that was cathartic, she opened her heart and spilled her doubts and fears.

Vanessa and Sydney insisted it was okay for her to want what she wanted. But everyone agreed that if she wanted to scene with Marcus again, she might have to be willing to also be flexible in making sure the arrangement also suited him.

"As long as you're honest with yourself and with Master Marcus," Vanessa had added. "The man knows what he wants."

Julia had appreciated the input, and after considering their advice for several days, she again contacted Marcus.

He'd invited her over, but added he'd like her to choose when she'd be willing to stay overnight.

She'd opted for Saturday night, even if it meant skipping yoga class. He promised to ensure she received plenty of exercise, and he'd meant it, taking her for a short hike on Lookout Mountain.

The next weekend, he'd invited her to his cabin.

That had been a month ago.

Since then, they'd fallen into a routine she loved, and she spent part of most weekends with him.

Now, in preparation for seeing Marcus in less than an hour, she pulled out a matching bra and panty set, along with fishnet stockings and a garter belt from one of her dresser drawers. Accumulating new lingerie had become a passion. And several times he'd had deliveries sent to her office and home.

He was always effusive in his praise when she arrived at his condo, and her confidence had grown. Maybe she couldn't do it in public, but when she was alone with him, she pushed aside her embarrassment and flaunted her assets.

As always, she fumbled with the cursed fasteners on the garter belts, but it took her far less time than it used to.

Finally, she wiggled into a short skirt then pulled on a pair of fur-lined boots, an outfit she would have never even considered a few months ago.

As she was driving to his place he telephoned.

Automatically she checked the time, making sure she wasn't in trouble for running late before answering. "Hello, Sir."

"I apologize. My meeting is taking longer than planned. I'll arrive a few minutes after you get there. Let yourself in and get ready for me."

She shivered in anticipation.

"I assume you know what to do, girl?"

Though he didn't often call her that, a thrill chased up her spine when he did. He always made the word part purr, part growl, and full-on sexy. "Yes, Sir."

Early on, he'd programmed his locks with her fingerprint. She had the same access to his house that he did.

"I look forward to seeing you." With that, he ended the call. She kept a firm grip on the steering wheel, needing to concentrate rather than think about him. Flakes were falling again. At times she forgot that March and April were Colorado's snowiest months. She let herself be convinced that seeing the first crocus meant spring had arrived and that summer wasn't far behind.

At his condo, she let herself in, and laid down her purse and overnight bag, then placed her keys in the small copper bowl, hung up her coat and changed from her boots into the high-heeled pumps she kept in the foyer closet.

All the while, she marveled at how comfortable she was and how much she enjoyed their routine.

He often cooked for her, and he sometimes involved her in his business, showing her architectural plans and soliciting her feedback. They'd binge an entire series in a weekend with a pizza or laugh through a comedy show.

At night, in bed after a hot scene in the dungeon, she'd snuggle into his arms and ask him probing questions. He told her she was nosy, but that didn't stop her from pushing to understand him.

He was an only child and his father had taught him about leatherworking while his mother had taught him to bake. They lived in Sedona, Arizona, in a home he'd built for them.

Knowing what he expected, she knelt on a rug in the foyer, facing the front door.

When the door lock *snicked,* she adjusted herself to ensure her posture was perfect.

Around her, each sound echoed in the stillness, ratcheting her tension. When his keys clattered on top of hers, she jolted. Then…there was nothing except nerve-wracking silence. But instead of looking up, she remained where she was.

Even though she resisted the temptation to look up, every part of her vibrated with the awareness of his proximity. She inhaled his crisp, mountain-swept scent. And his power was a palpable, exciting aura.

A small squeak reached her. The closet door? Then… The echo of his boots.

Moments later, they were in front of her, the focus of her gaze.

"You've learned well, my sweet."

She glowed beneath his approval. "Thank you, Sir."

"Lift your hair."

Once she had, he fastened the now-familiar thin, leather collar around her neck. As always, he checked the fit.

"Welcome me home, Julia."

All week, she'd wanted to touch him. "My pleasure, Sir." She stood, the motion much more graceful than it had been a couple months ago, and she knew he appreciated the transformation.

With a genuine smile, she lifted onto her tiptoes and placed her hands on her Dominant's shoulders. "I've missed you." The time between their visits had stretched interminably long.

She instigated the kiss, capturing his chin in her hand and teasing his lips with her tongue.

He groaned.

Then, as she'd known he would, he took control, flattening one palm on her rear, fisting his other into her hair to imprison her. He kissed her hard, using his tongue, silently communicating his desire.

More than once over the last month, he'd suggested she move in. Every time, she'd demurred. She needed her space, she insisted. If she didn't keep her distance, the force of his determination would consume her.

"I've got to have you."

"Yes, Sir." Her whisper was sweet, sweet surrender.

He swept her into his arms. Desperately she reached around his neck, holding on as he strode up the stairs toward the playroom.

"Undress then lean your body over the spanking bench." He lowered her to the floor. "Would you like to be secured?"

"Whatever you prefer, Sir."

He nodded. "Then you're bound by my will."

Her mouth dried. That meant she wouldn't be physically restrained, but his command served the same purpose. This was the first time he'd asked that of her.

"Remove your bra and panties, but you may wear the stockings and garter belt. I like the look of the red marks against the black straps."

"Is it permissible to hold on to the straps, Sir?"

"Since it's your first time being tied by my will, yes."

She turned her head so she could watch as he selected his favorite tawse, the same one he'd used on her the first night at the Den.

"This is an erotic spanking because you've pleased me." Rejoining her, he slapped the leather against his open palm. "You're allowed to come. And I want you to enjoy."

"Thank you, Sir." This was a treat she intended to savor.

"That is..."

No doubt he had a condition.

"Unless you can't keep yourself in position, in which case this will become a punishment, and your orgasms will be denied."

"I understand."

He moved behind her to massage her buttocks. She closed her eyes. Even though some pain was inevitable, she loved receiving his attention.

He rubbed more and more vigorously, until her entire body was moving from the force. He dipped his hand between her legs and teased her clit.

"Oh, Sir, you've already turned me on!"

"A small reward for your excellent behavior when I arrived."

She smiled.

The first strike from his tawse stole her breath. It took all her concentration not to release her grip and reach back to soothe her reddened rear. *This is supposed to be pleasurable?*

"Relax into it."

"How do you do that?"

"Hmm?" He rubbed her pussy.

"Read my mind like that."

"I see your flinches, your tension. I listen to your breaths, your whimpers."

She moved against his hand.

"That's my good girl." He used the tawse again several times, but then he fingered between her slick folds.

As he'd encouraged, she released her mental fight and allowed the bench to take her whole weight.

"Perfect."

Somewhere along the way, she got lost in the moment. He blurred the line between pleasure and pain, and she could no longer tell where one ended and the other began. He fingered her pussy and inserted one finger in her rear.

Frantically she shoved her hips back, meeting his fingers, his tawse, and orgasm after orgasm crashed through her.

"I want to fuck you."

"Yes."

"Release the bonds."

She let go, and he placed her on top of the bench, leaving her only long enough to grab protection.

He returned to her, instructed her to place her knees over his shoulders, and drove in hard.

She cried out at the depth of his penetration. When he squeezed her nipples, she thrashed.

"Wait until I give permission."

"I'll try." Panting, she fought to obey.

"That's it. Now squeeze my cock with your pussy. Come for me my sweet. And do it *now.*"

He pulsed in her, prolonging the extraordinary orgasm.

The longer they were together, the better this was, and the more she needed him. And that scared the hell out of her.

* * * *

Marcus held her on the cuddle couch while she dozed against his chest, then they shared the shower.

Since he had a conference call with someplace on the opposite side of the planet, she curled up on the living room couch to watch a documentary.

Later, while he prepared dinner, she filled glasses with the red wine that Daniela had suggested at the Lookout Pointe. "I need you to fulfill a fantasy," he told her.

"Sir?" She glanced over at him.

He turned the grill on high and turned to face her. "I want you as the centerpiece on the dining room table."

Just when she thought she was unshockable… She gulped. "I'm listening."

"When I bring the plates in, I want to see you on the table, your knees upraised, your legs parted. You don't have to stay there, but it's an image I can't get out of my head."

Not knowing what to say, she settled for something noncommittal. "You, Sir, are most definitely kinky."

"More than you know."

She had her safe word, and her attitude toward his request would make all the difference. The experience was what she made it. "I'll be in the dining room, Sir."

"Come here."

She walked over, her hips swaying in the high heels.

"You're an absolutely wonderful sub."

Before she could even consider a protest, he ensnared her chin and gave her the gentlest of kisses, wordlessly expressing his appreciation. As she left the kitchen, she was aware of his heated gaze on her still-sore rear.

If anyone had told her three months ago that she would actually do something like this, she wouldn't have believed them. But she found it shockingly exciting. It wasn't as if he hadn't seen her looking obscene before. In fact, the more she revealed herself, the more he seemed to like it.

In the dining room, she moved the candles to the sideboard, then lit them for the ambience. She dimmed the overhead light. After a moment's consideration, she followed his directives.

Concentrating on her breathing, she waited.

When he entered the room, he whistled low and long. "So much more beautiful than I imagined. Your nipples are hard, your pussy deliciously pink."

Despite a flush of embarrassment, she kept her legs spread as he set down the plates and returned with the wineglasses.

"Thank you."

She shivered as he skimmed a finger between her pussy folds.

He then traced her collar. "I'm not going to be able to eat now that all I can think about is fucking you. Dominating you. Proving you're mine. *Mine.*" He grasped her nipples and twisted them then licked her.

Grinding her bare heels into the polished wood, she screamed out an orgasm.

"Oh, yes. You're perfect, girl."

He left her there for several minutes, and she breathed, relaxing into the aftershocks of her orgasm.

Eventually he helped her from the table, and, as if nothing untoward had happened, pulled back her chair and invited her to sit on his left.

Since it wasn't all that unusual to dine while he was clothed and she was naked, she cut into her steak.

After dinner, he advised her to take a warm bath to soothe her tired muscles while he cleaned the kitchen.

"I'm going to use you again." He fisted her hair. "My sweet sub."

She offered a cheeky grin. "I'll be in the tub with the rest of my wine while you're cleaning the kitchen. And that's how it should be." Glad she was on bare feet, she dashed toward the stairs.

But not fast enough.

He flicked the edge of the dish towel and caught one of her thighs. "I'll teach you to sass me, girl."

"Please do!" With a giggle, she hurried to his en suite.

It was only when she was up to her neck in bubbles that she realized she'd left her wine behind.

Thoughtfully though, he brought it to her.

When she was warm, snuggled into one of his thick robes, she walked into the bedroom.

"Drop it." With his index finger, he indicated the garment. "And bring your naked self here." Once she'd complied, he bound her to the bed and used a feather to torment her before fucking her into a deep sleep.

When she awoke the next morning, she was tucked against his body. Rather than feeling constricted, it struck her as nurturing. Part of her wanted to remain in place forever.

It had snowed all night, and many roads were impassable. So they dressed and walked down to a local coffee shop for a latte. She eyed a chocolate croissant, and he bought it for her, promising he'd help her burn off the calories.

She enjoyed every bite, as well as his promise.

"There's a party next week at the Den. I thought we might attend."

"That sounds interesting."

"We can talk about it more this week."

When they were almost back to his condo, a playful urge overtook her. With a grin, she scooped up a handful of snow and tossed a wet, sloppy snowball at him, hitting him square in the back.

"That's it." With a menacing growl, he stalked toward her, picked her up, then slung her over his shoulder, knocking the breath from her. She giggled and kicked as he carried her into the building.

"Hold the elevator," he called to one of his neighbors. "Someone's earned a spanking for throwing snowballs."

"Oh my *God*!" This time she truly was afraid of dying from embarrassment.

"Think before you act, my sweet." He swatted her upturned ass.

The neighbor laughed.

Inside, after he'd soundly spanked her, he fucked her long and deep, as if they had all the time in the world.

It would be easy to succumb to his charms. Too easy. She loved laughing with him, teasing him, earning a sensational spanking.

The temptation to give herself to him became stronger each visit.

And now, not wanting to leave, the realization terrified her.

Suddenly she couldn't breathe. Needing space and distance, she climbed from the bed and started to dress.

He encircled her wrist. "Where are you going?"

"I have things to do."

"Only a fool would leave."

"Didn't we have a similar discussion that first night at the Den?" They'd come full circle.

"We need to talk."

He threw back the covers and pulled on a pair of slacks as he stood next to her, towering over her.

Hating the determination in his tone—that damn Dom voice—she took a step back. "Can it wait?"

"It's time you moved in."

Moved in?

Give up her home, her life?

With a shaky hand, she drew her hair back. "I…can't." It wouldn't take much for him to completely consume her. "Let's discuss this another time." *When I can think straight.*

"I could tie you to the bed again."

"Thanks for the nice weekend."

He raised an eyebrow. *"Nice?"*

Threat laced the single word. He was strong, handsome, seductive. The way he continued to stroke her skin banked her desire.

"Very nice," she amended.

She pulled away to gather her lingerie, then grabbed a pair of yoga pants from the closet. When she reached for one of his T-shirts, she looked up to see him lazing against the doorjamb, still wearing just that pair of pants that were unfastened at the waist. He filled the entrance. King of his domain. He made her weak, aware of her femininity. She had to leave before she never could.

Determinedly she squared her shoulders, reached up and unfastened the collar, then reverently folded it and put it on the shelf in the exact spot he'd instructed her to leave it each week.

"I'm waiting for you to admit the truth to yourself." The calm inflection in his words stood in calm contrast to the fire in his green eyes. "You like wearing my collar."

"You're presuming a lot."

"Am I?"

"Look, Marcus. Let's not confuse this." She fought to keep her emotional distance. "I like playing with you." Liked? *Loved.* "You're a good Dom. We both agreed that we weren't looking for anything more."

Marcus scrubbed his hand down his face. For the first time since she'd met him, he appeared to be at a loss, maybe even holding his temper by a thread.

"I can see myself out."

"Damn it, Julia. You can run from me, but not from yourself."

"It's late." Her false smile teetered on shattering.

"I'll walk you to your car."

"That's not necessary."

He just stood there, regarding her. "Argue one more second, little lady, and I'll spank your fucking ass."

Wordlessly she followed him downstairs.

She took her coat and boots from the closet and pulled them on, aware of his heated gaze.

He pulled on a leather jacket and a pair of casual shoes. The attire made him look impossibly more badass. A man who could be dressed so casually and still wear an air of command was a force to be reckoned with.

Thank God she was going home while she still could.

He palmed her keys, and she swallowed her protest. No matter what, he was always a gentleman. *Or a considerate Dominant.*

Even the parking garage was cold. Standing on ceremony was going to get her a case of frostbite.

Marcus opened the door to her SUV door and helped her inside. "You know my number." He leaned in, overwhelming her with his scent and the small pulse ticking in his temple. "When you need what I give you and you're willing to crawl to me and beg for it, call me. It won't be as easy as you want it to be. I will demand and expect you to own who you are. I want you on your knees while you're admitting the truth to yourself as well as me. That you're a sub—*my* sub—and you belong to me, with me. Don't come back until you're ready to wear my collar. Permanently."

Chapter Eleven

Permanently? Julia started to shake. "Marcus… Don't. Don't issue an ultimatum. I'm begging you. *Please.*"

"You've known it was coming."

"No." She'd had no idea. Frantically she shook her head. This couldn't be happening. "We both want the same thing."

"Bullshit won't work for me anymore. You're wrong about me, Julia, and I'm willing to admit the truth to both of us. I want a relationship based on honesty with a sub who doesn't have to turn her life over to me. But that doesn't mean I want someone who shows up on her schedule and then blithely forgets what we shared until she's horny and can't take it anymore."

She recoiled at his hurtful and crude words. "That's not how it is."

"Isn't it?" His challenge hung on the frosty air. "The right woman, one with the courage to look in the mirror and be honest with herself, is worth taking a risk for."

The cold seeped around her, through her.

"*You* are worth the risk." Without waiting for a reply, he closed the car door, turned his back, and walked off.

Trembling, she pulled out of the spot. When she hazarded a glance over her shoulder, he was gone.

The drive home felt interminable. *What have I done?* His words seared her, a contrast to the night's chill.

She went through her bedtime ritual on automatic since she was unable to think clearly. Even though she'd added an extra blanket to her bed, put on long, thick, fuzzy pajamas, she slept fitfully.

When she woke Monday morning, her body ached. Her shoulders were sore. Her nipples tingled. Her ass hurt. Even her pussy throbbed. Everything reminded her of the day before.

Anxiously, hoping against hope that Marcus had tried to contact her, she grabbed her phone from the nightstand. There were no missed calls, zero text messages and half a dozen junk emails. She tossed her phone in frustration and dropped her head back on the pillow.

What did I expect?

She'd repeatedly told Marcus she wanted to be his playmate. At every turn, she'd asserted her independence. Of course he wouldn't contact her, and she should be grateful he was respecting her wishes.

So why did she feel more alone than she ever had?

After work, she went to the gym.

When she was back at home, she was at a loss. She didn't know what to do with a vast chunk of time now that her life was her own again and she had no demands on her weekends and the collar was where it belonged—no longer around her neck.

Suddenly she couldn't breathe.

At times, she felt freer when she wore the piece of handcrafted leather. Having it in place did change her mindset. The rules were clear, the understanding was concrete.

Absently she reached up and traced the path where his collar had lain.

Damn it. Damn, damn, and double damn.

She paced, bored and restless, slightly confused, angry that he'd changed the rules and issued an ultimatum.

With determination, she repeatedly told herself it was better that she knew this now rather than falling for him even deeper.

Falling for him?

The thought made her freeze in place.

That wasn't possible.

So why was she obsessing? Unable to stop thinking of him.

The next few days dragged by, and by Thursday the weekend loomed like a horrible, empty specter.

Needing support, she called Lana to talk things out.

"I'm so sorry, Julia. If I could, I'd meet you right now, but we're getting ready to go out of town."

She shouldn't ask… "Are you going to the Den?"

Lana hesitated before answering. "Yes. It's Master Alexander's birthday party, and we haven't seen him for a long time. It's going to be a huge celebration. Everyone will be there, and there will even be a rock star, I'm told."

Julia squeezed her eyes shut. Was this the event Master Marcus had mentioned? If things were different, would she also be going to the party?

Then a much worse thought hit her, and she squeezed her eyes shut. Was he planning to go alone?

Or, worse, with someone else?

"Ben suggested we make a weekend of it, so we're staying at the hot springs resort near Winter Park. He even booked a facial and a massage for me."

"Sounds wonderful." Though her own heart was shattering, Julia was happy for her friend.

"How about Monday after work at the coffee shop?"

Could she hold on that long? "That sounds great."

"Are you okay?"

"I will be." She attempted a smile. "Just…go and have fun."

"Breakups stink."

Is that what this was? A breakup? How was that possible when there'd never been a real relationship?

"At least you'll have a chance to go to yoga."

"Yes. There's that." And maybe she should attend. God knew she needed some Zen in her life.

Since her place was already spotless, she headed down to the condominium complex's hot tub for a soak. It certainly wasn't a hot springs resort, and because there were a lot of other people in there, laughing and splashing, she was more alone than she could remember being.

Not knowing what to do with herself, she walked back to her cold, empty condo and opted for a shower.

Now that she was alone—and lonely—thoughts of Marcus returned.

Master Marcus.

Sometime over the last month, without her realizing it, that thought had become so natural.

The first night at the Den, even the idea chafed, and she couldn't force herself to say the word.

But now…?

As the water cascaded over her, heavy tears fell. His ultimatum settled in, hurting her heart.

If he didn't matter so much, the fact they were no longer together wouldn't matter. Emotion overcoming her, Julia detached the showerhead from its holder and turned the setting to the pulse mode. She parted her still-smooth labia, closed her eyes, then directed the warm spray toward her pussy.

Even though she held the water there for a few minutes, she couldn't quite get off. She leaned her forehead against the tile and imagined Marcus lashing her breasts. She was glad to be on the cross, facing him.

As he lashed her in her mind's eye, his eyes darkened. When she cried out, he furrowed his eyebrows and concentrated on her. His cock grew harder with every flick of his wrist, each intentional, deliberately placed stroke.

Despite the vivid pictures, she couldn't orgasm. *Damn you.*

Giving up, she toweled off then dressed in her nightclothes, went into the living room, and turned on the television. When her phone finally chimed with an incoming message, she lunged for the device.

It was Lana.

We didn't confirm a time. How about five thirty?

That was the last message Julia received all weekend.

She was in a miserable pit, of her own making.

* * * *

"You're scowling as if you'd like to take somebody's head off."

Marcus glanced up from where he was standing at the makeshift bar in the Den's living room and reluctantly acknowledged Damien, who was interrupting his morose musings.

"Should I ask?"

"No." Around them, annoying excitement filled the air.

Tonight's gathering was in honor of his friend's birthday. It had been a year or more since the scandal that made Alexander take a step back from public life, and this was the first public outing that Marcus knew about. It was damn good to see Alexander.

Yet seeing everyone else celebrating only increased his bitterness. Even the expensive Bonds whiskey wasn't lifting his mood.

"Haven't seen you look this bad since you released Amber."

Jaw tight, he looked at his friend. The man knew how to pick at wounds. "I told you not to ask."

Damien shrugged. "What are friends for?"

"Drinking," he suggested. "And shutting the fuck up when input isn't wanted."

"If you want a drunk fest, come over to my house tomorrow night. I'll indulge you there."

Was that what he wanted? Another damn drunk fest?

"Looks like you've had enough of those."

"Fuck off, Damien." It was one thing to acknowledge facts to himself, another to have them pointed out by someone else. And his friend's remarks were too damn close to the truth.

Since she'd walked out, with a stricken, devastated look in her eyes, Marcus hadn't slept. He'd called himself a dozen kinds of fool and wished he'd handled the situation differently.

But in that moment, he'd been incapable of it.

The way she'd kept distance between them had pissed him off and allowed frustration to dictate his action.

He wasn't proud of his behavior. In fact, there was nothing remotely Dominant about it. He deserved to reap the consequences of his shitty decision.

"There are plenty of subs and bottoms in the dungeon."

Plenty of whom were wearing wristbands indicating they were available to play. "Not interested."

"That's how it is."

Not answering, Marcus swirled the untouched whiskey in his glass.

"Have you even said hello to anyone since you got here?"

He scowled. "Who the fuck are you? The Etiquette Police?"

"Misery loves company. But company does not love misery."

"Suddenly you're a damn philosopher as well?"

Damien considered his friend. "Guessing it's about a woman…"

Gregorio joined them. "Julia."

How the hell did he always seem to know?

"Ah yes. Julia," Damien said. "From the wedding."

"It's serious?" Gregorio asked.

"Didn't sign up to be double-teamed." He'd rather wallow alone.

Both men ignored his not-so-subtle hints that they should move along. Instead, Gregorio folded his arms. "I don't want to let her go."

"So you asked her nicely to stay? Or were you your regular jackass self by issuing demands?"

Marcus raked a hand into his hair. The question was far too close for comfort.

"Did you ever paint a picture of a compelling future you two might share?"

He faced Damien. "A compelling what?"

"That's a no." With a shrug, Gregorio supplied the unnecessary commentary.

"Did you propose to her? Get down on one knee and tell her how much you love her…?"

Love?

Marcus shook his head.

What the hell?

Damien continued to speak, the words droning around Marcus.

"…or discuss what being your submissive might look like, from your perspective? How you'll care for her?"

The two men shared another glance.

"Also no," Gregorio guessed.

"You've been patient, giving her all the time she needed?"

He remained silent. *No.* He'd forced an issue that he shouldn't have.

"Look…" Damien spoke a little softer, and the friendly teasing was gone from his voice. "Don't look to me for relationship advice. God knows I'm not one to speak. Talk to Ben. He navigated some tricky waters with Lana."

Julia was much more fiercely independent than her friend and insisted she wasn't a sub. Marcus knew differently. Her actions were exquisite, and when she wore his collar and stayed out of her own head, she found joy.

The trouble was, she wouldn't admit the truth to either of them.

Damien excused himself. "I have a party to host. Some of us want to celebrate instead of staring at the bottom of a glass."

Marcus exhaled, and Gregorio clapped him on the shoulder.

"I talked to her that first night."

He remembered.

"She's independent."

"That might be an understatement."

"You may want to try a different approach. Submission is earned, not taken."

Fuck. Marcus winced as the stinging words found their mark.

"Women like to feel cherished and nurtured."

He'd tried to do both—and utterly failed.

"And move at their own pace."

"You calling me a bull in a china shop?"

"How would you like to be rushed? If she demanded a ring, and you weren't ready for a lifetime commitment." Then, like a true friend, Gregorio shrugged. "I wasn't there. Only you can decide if the commentary fits."

Unfortunately, it did.

"Anything worth having is worth fighting for." Gregorio folded his arms. "Even if you have to swallow your pride."

Without a word, he too walked away, leaving Marcus alone, navigating uncharted territory.

He fucking missed Julia. The distance between them hadn't made it better. In fact, time intensified his anguish.

The advice from his friends made him regret his stubbornness, and he realized he couldn't have handled the situation any worse.

For the first time, however, a woman had refused him, and now that he'd screwed up, as a Dominant, as a man, he had no clue what to do next.

Good move, Cavendish.

Just then, Master Damien called for everyone's attention.

When the crowd fell silent, he spoke again. "We're celebrating Master Alexander's birthday tonight."

He beckoned Brandy, who pushed a rolling cart into the living room. A half-sheet cake was ablaze with dozens of candles.

Damien led the group in singing happy birthday.

Then, when the awful rendition ended and everyone had applauded, Alexander blew out the candles.

"Thank you all! Being back is the best gift of all."

The crowd cheered enthusiastically.

"Chelsea here will be helping to serve the cake."

The woman—sub?—that Marcus had never seen before frowned at Alexander. He whispered something to Chelsea as Brandy offered her a knife.

Interesting.

Seemed he wasn't the only one with a perplexing dilemma.

While Brandy discarded candles, Chelsea cut the dessert, her lines a little jagged from an obvious lack of practice.

After Brandy whispered something, Chelsea took a slice to Alexander who sent her back to the table.

A moment later, she was involved in a conversation with Gregorio. The man missed nothing that happened at the club.

While Alexander was alone, Marcus decided to say hello.

He picked up his whiskey to drink the shot, then changed his mind and slammed the glass back down.

The bartender looked across at him. "Sir?"

"I'm done for the night."

With a nod, the man scooped up the drink.

As he walked over to greet his old friend and wish him a happy birthday, Gregorio's words rolled around in Marcus's mind. *"Anything worth having is worth fighting for."*

Julia was worth fighting for.

He just needed a plan.

Chapter Twelve

When Julia entered the funky coffee shop after work on Monday, Lana stood up, joined her, and gave her a hug. "How are you doing?"

"Hanging in there." She offered a half-smile. "Taken a lot of yoga classes in search of some peace."

"Let's grab coffee and talk about it."

Together, they went to the counter.

Since she hadn't been sleeping, Julia skipped coffee in favor of a green-tea lemonade. And because she didn't want to go home and cook, she ordered a panini sandwich with potato chips.

Her friend, however, opted for a caramel frappe with extra whipping cream.

"I think I'm having food envy," Julia admitted when they found a table outside. Though the early evening was still chilly, the sun was shining, and they had privacy.

After popping the lid off her frozen concoction, Lana licked the cream off her straw. "Which is exactly why I ordered this. I'd regret it if I didn't."

Lana was quiet while Julia took her first bite, then she leaned forward. "Okay. I've given you long enough, Jules. Now tell me everything."

"I mostly did on the phone." Since her appetite was still not what it had been, she pushed her plate aside. "We wanted different things."

"Meaning…?" Lana frowned. "Wait! Did he dump you?"

"No!" Julia brushed her hands together and took a sip of her sweet, refreshing beverage. "Kind of the opposite."

"I'm listening."

"He's…" Julia paused, debating what to say. Of everyone she knew, Lana would understand. "Complicated."

"Oh, Jules, I think you're making it complicated. Men? They're fairly straightforward. They know what they want and they're considerably less shy than we are about asking for it. So, break it down for me."

"He wants me to move in."

Slowly Lana nodded. "And it's too soon for you?"

"We had conflict about that. And when I started to leave…"

"Go on."

"He told me not to come back until I agreed to wear his collar permanently."

"You're serious? He gave you an ultimatum?"

She nodded.

"He must have been frustrated."

"Probably."

"But still, for a Dom to handle a problem like that is pretty crappy."

In the subtle overhead light, Lana's metal collar winked. Maybe even more than her wedding ring, the collar spoke of obligations and expectations.

"You two have been playing together for a while now. And if he wants to make it more permanent, he is serious about you. Frankly, none of us thought…" She trailed off, as if searching for words. "Let's just say I was pleasantly surprised when you hit it off at my wedding."

"Are you referring to his relationship with Amber?"

"What are you afraid of?"

Lana's intuition shouldn't have surprised Julia. Since the night she'd driven away from him, Julia had asked herself the same question. "Of losing myself."

"Like you did with Jason."

It was more of a statement than a question. After all, Lana had been the first one to point out how Julia had slowly lost herself in that relationship.

"I'm uncomfortable with the idea of being his submissive."

Lana sighed. "Submission is not synonymous with being a doormat. You're the math expert. Apply the same logic here. On what planet does asking for what you want make you subservient to someone else?"

Intellectually Julia conceded Lana's point. Emotionally was another story.

"Do you believe human beings are capable of learning?" Lana asked. "Or are they doomed to repeat the same mistake until they die?"

"Were you a psych major?"

Grinning, Lana shrugged. "I took a few classes. Now answer my question."

"Yes. We change and evolve."

"And when you saw what was happening with Jason the Jackass, you ended it."

Julia picked up her cup, but then placed it back down.

"You and Master Marcus have discussed a power exchange, yes?"

"We have."

"Do you have safe words?"

"From the very beginning, he insisted on it." Julia nodded.

"And does he honor your wishes?"

"He's been a Dom—a beast—but he's never crossed a line."

"Do you love him?"

"I..." Julia's hand shook, and she lowered it to her lap to cover her nervousness. "I hadn't thought about it."

"Because you're approaching all of this from logic, like you do your job."

After breaking up with Jason, she'd retreated into her work, finding comfort in things that had reliable answers.

"Do you love him?" Lana repeated.

Do I? "Is that why this hurts so damn much?"

"I think there's a bigger question at play here. Can you trust yourself?"

Julia frowned. "I'm not sure what you mean by that."

"Are you going to repeat the past?"

"Never."

"Then what are you worried about?" Lana took a gulp of her frappe. "Look, I didn't hesitate to let you know when I thought Jason was using you and that you were a shadow of yourself."

"And?"

"When you were with Master Marcus, I wasn't worried about you. In fact, when you were at that Tuesday meeting, you were glowing, totally confident. New experiences, new joy. I hadn't seen you happier in years."

She took in the information, and wondered if it was true. Had she blossomed while playing with him?

Lana finished off her beverage. "Are you making Master Marcus pay for what Jason did to you?"

Julia's breath rushed out. "That hurt."

"I'm sorry." She placed her hand on Julia's. "But you're not the only one hurting. I've never seen Master Marcus more melancholy."

"You ran into him?"

"You know I'm not supposed to say."

But she was going to, Julia hoped.

"At the Den."

She shouldn't ask. Shouldn't… But she had to know. "Was he…?"

"He was alone. He wouldn't answer any questions about you." Lana looked at Julia. "I'm your friend and I'll love and support you no matter what. The only thing I want is for you to be happy. Which means you have some decisions to make. But if you want to be with Master Marcus, you may have to contact him. Maybe you can't wear his collar right now and maybe you can't move in, but you could give him a chance to reconsider."

"I don't think he would."

"The man at that party was hurting."

And that caused tears to spring to Julia's eyes.

"Plenty of other women would be happy to have him..."

Oh hell no.

But the fact that Julia's reaction was instant and visceral told her a lot.

"Just one last piece of advice?"

Julia attempted a smile. "You might as well."

"As long as you're sure you can trust yourself, don't let fear ruin your life."

She nodded. "Thank you."

They talked and enjoyed each other's company until Lana needed to get home, then they hugged goodbye and promised to see each other soon.

Still confused, needing to sort through her thoughts now more than ever, Julia cranked up her music and started driving, heading out of town, west on I-70.

Without conscious thought, she drove into the foothills and turned off the highway at the Lookout Mountain exit.

It was no accident, she was sure, that she'd ended up at a place she'd been to with Marcus, one memorable, happy evening.

She continued past the turn for Lookout Pointe to a parking lot near the summit.

After grabbing a jacket, she got out of the car and wandered a little way down a hiking trail to sit on a park bench.

Lana's probing questions had been astute.

To keep warm against the sunset chill, she sat back, pulled her knees up to her chest, then wrapped her arms around her legs.

Of all the questions Lana had asked, one rocked Julia the most.

"Do you love him?"

That was the crux of the turmoil, and now she had to face it. She did love him, and she wanted to be with him.

But as Lana had helped her to realize, Julia could trust herself. She was no longer the same woman who'd been with Jason the Jackass. But had she made her emotional walls too high, impenetrable?

If she were honest enough with herself, she'd admit her objection really wasn't about submission. It was about losing herself.

But Marcus had never once tried to control her outside of an agreed-upon scene, hadn't expected her to do things for him. He did most of the cooking, even sent her to take a bath while he cleaned the kitchen. He didn't try to control her free time or curtail outings with friends. He even encouraged her to go to yoga classes.

While his ultimatum had terrified her and she wished he hadn't done it, she'd reacted badly. She hadn't asked if they could sit down and reasonably discuss things.

Now she wanted nothing more.

Her biggest fear was that it might be too late.

* * * *

She returned home to see a vehicle that looked like Marcus's SUV parked in a visitor spot. A streetlamp reflected off his license plate. EGLBLD.

Shorthand for the name of his construction company?

But why would he be here?

Her door was ajar. If it was Marcus, that wasn't a surprise. He wouldn't let a pesky lock stop him. With a frown, she entered the apartment, then shock froze her in place.

In jeans, boots, a black T-shirt, and a sexy toolbelt slung low on his hip, Marcus stood there, in a semicircle with several other men.

Her furniture was gone, and her carpet had been torn out.

One of the guys saw her and cleared his throat. "Hey, boss."

With a huge grin, Marcus looked at her.

She frowned. *What in the hell is going on here?*

After excusing himself to his guys, he joined her, hands on her shoulders and moving her back outside. "Welcome home."

Frantically she shook her head, not able to formulate the millions of questions tumbling through her mind.

"You asked about a rack to warm your towels."

She blinked. "Are you serious right now?"

"And several other upgrades." He shrugged.

Against the cold and shock, she wrapped her arms around herself. "Where's my stuff?"

"Safe."

She nodded. *Whatever that means.* "And my...*carpet*?"

"You've mentioned wanting hardwood flooring."

It would take her years to save for all the upgrades she'd dreamed of. "Anything else?"

"A soaker tub. Air conditioner in the bedroom."

Speechless, she gaped at him. All that was going on behind the closed door?

"I hope you're pleased."

That was an understatement. "But... Why?"

"I'm not good at apologies. And, it turns out, a few other things. So I'm sticking with what I know."

"Construction?"

"Yeah. Tearing shit down."

Was he admitting fault for what had happened between them? "Is that a metaphor?"

"It is."

"Marcus—"

"Julia—"

They spoke simultaneously, then he extended his hand to indicate she should go first.

She shook her head. "You're here. I want to know why."

"I've missed you. And it took losing you to realize what a jackass I'd been. Well, that and Damien pointing it out." He winced.

That made her smile.

"I want to be with you, under whatever circumstances are comfortable for you. I had no right to issue an ultimatum. I ran out of patience. As a man, a Dom, that's unacceptable. And I wanted to ask for your forgiveness."

"By tearing apart my house?"

He shook his head. "By creating the home you said you wanted, even if it's not with me."

Her heart shattered.

"Wanting to live together, to collar you, none of that's changed. I want you more today than I did when you left that day. But I want you to know I respect your wishes, and your need to protect yourself from hurt. If you never move in, wear my collar or my wedding ring, I'll still love you and..."

Her ears buzzed, drowning out everything else he was saying. Finally, she lifted her hand. "What...? You...?" Had she misheard?

"I pushed you too hard, too fast. Ultimatums have no place in our relationship. I fucked up, Julia. Hard. And I'll keep working to regain your trust in me, even if it takes a lifetime. When you left, I realized I love you. I want you to be my partner, my wife, my sub, my equal."

It was as if all the emotion she'd held in check for years was suddenly unleashed. Sobbing, with joy, with relief, she leaned into him, and he wrapped his arms around her.

"Shall we try again?"

"Yes." She put a hand on his chest and pushed herself back to look at him. "Yes, Sir."

He claimed her mouth in a kiss that tasted of both promise and forever.

Then one of his guys popped open the door. "Hate to interrupt, but we're bringing out the old bathroom tile."

The reality of the situation hit her. Her entire home was a construction site.

With a smile, Marcus shrugged. "I'll put you up at a hotel for a few days if you'd like. Or..." He moved her aside so the team could haul out the debris. "There's room in my bed for you."

"I'll pack a bag."

"Since you can't get in the bathroom, I already loaded up your toiletries."

"Oh."

He went back inside with her, and she had to step over tools and buckets.

In her bedroom, her place of sanctuary, she pulled out a suitcase and put it on her bed next to the duffel bag he'd packed. "You took a gamble that I wouldn't be pissed to find my home upside down."

"A calculated risk. I haven't done anything you haven't asked for. Even if you hadn't been able to forgive what happened between us, you could have just accepted what I'm doing as a gift. Anything you don't like can be changed. All of my decisions are about making you happy."

She pressed a hand to her heart.

"I would have put you up at a hotel or resort of your choice for the time you're out of your place, which will only be a week at the most."

"You've thought of everything."

"Probably not. But it's a start on the future I want to create with you."

* * * *

Later that evening, Marcus escaped the construction site at Julia's home and entered his condo to find her on her knees in front of the fireplace, the sound of her breathing— nervous little gulps—hanging on the sensually charged air.

He dropped his keys on top of hers. Seeing them together in the same bowl restored the natural order of things.

Her absence had created a void in his life that he'd been unable to fill. Coming home to her made his life complete.

From the moment she'd arrived at her condo, the evening had been a whirlwind. After gathering her belongings, he'd walked her to the car, told her to go back to his place and make herself comfortable while he wrapped up. Unfortunately, it had taken him an hour longer than expected.

In this moment, though, he forgot everything except his desire for her.

He hadn't asked or ordered her to prepare herself for him—she'd done that all on her own. They might not have settled anything regarding their future—yet—but this was a step in the direction he hoped to go.

After joining her in the great room, he offered his hand. "Stand up, my sweet. And look at me."

Her eyes were wide, her lips slightly parted. She'd never looked more beautiful.

"It's late. Wine?"

"I'd rather skip it."

Hot lust raced through him. *You want to scene?*

"While we were apart, I realized some things, as well."

"Go on."

"I could have talked to you instead of giving in to my fear."

"You have a right to protect yourself."

"You're nothing like my ex. We truly do have a power exchange, and…well, I still may want some space, but even if I get nervous, I won't run. I guess what I'm trying to say is…I love you. And I want us to talk and take steps toward making our relationship more permanent."

That word had terrified her once before. And now she was using it.

"I'd like to scene, then make love, for the connection."

"We don't have to do either for me to love and cherish you. If you just want to talk or watch a movie—"

"Are you still talking, Sir?"

He quirked an eyebrow.

"When you could be spanking me?"

"You know what happens to brats, my sweet?"

"I'm hoping I do." With a soft smile, and love in her eyes, she lifted onto her tiptoes to kiss him.

He grabbed her shoulders and pulled her to him. "I love you, Julia."

"Welcome me back, Master Marcus?"

The words were an aphrodisiac.

"Remove your skirt and blouse." He loved the sight of her beaded nipples, then her shaved pussy. And he especially enjoyed the fact she now dressed the way he liked without having to be prompted. "Leave the rest." The garter belt and stockings and shoes just simply aroused him. Scraps of black lace and silk…? And she'd tied her collar around her neck. *Fuck.* He was done for. "What's your pleasure, little sub?"

"As many over-the-knee spanks as Sir decides is appropriate."

"Twelve of my best, sub. Get upstairs, get my favorite tawse"—to give her a taste of the leather they'd started their journey with—"then kneel and wait for me."

She started toward the stairs, hesitated, then walked back over to him to reach for his cock and give it a hard squeeze.

He grabbed her hand, stopping her determined up and down motion. "You have a thing or two to learn about being a good submissive." And he'd have let her do it another minute or so if he hadn't been afraid of ejaculating in his jeans.

"I saw you in a toolbelt, Sir. It's not my fault if I can't control my ardor."

He grinned as she saucily made her way to the stairs.

A few minutes later, he joined her in the playroom and sat in his chair. "Over my lap, girl."

She extended her palms and offered him the tawse.

He warmed up her ass with a few vigorous rubs. "You haven't been spanked in a long time," he observed. "Your skin is unblemished."

"I presume Sir intends to change that."

He did, indeed. He blazed the first kiss of the tawse above her knees. She cried out, but she reached for the chair leg to keep herself in place.

"One, Sir."

"No need to count. Just surrender."

"Thank you, Sir."

He systematically landed the blows with precise execution, one on top of the other until he reached her buttocks. Then, as she gasped and sighed, he finished her off and pulled her into his arms.

She sobbed into his shoulder, wetting his T-shirt. "Thank you, Sir. Thank you."

"Thank you. I need you, Julia, as much as you needed that." He carried her to the bed. In under thirty seconds, he returned to her wearing a condom.

She spread her legs, and her slickness proved how ready she was for him. He entered her, sliding in, feeling as if he were being welcomed home.

When he was balls deep, she sighed, a deep, satisfied sound, one that reverberated through him.

She had one arm around him, and the other on her collar.

He fucked her hard, dragging an orgasm out of her. "Mine." He growled it to the heavens.

"Yours, Master."

Then he did her slow and deep. "Forever."

"Forever, Sir." Her voice was dreamy as she came again.

Her shudder rocked him, and her muscles tightened around him.

"May I be on top?"

She didn't ask for that often, and he loved it when she did.

He reversed their positions. He liked seeing her breasts with the tight little nipples, and her blissed-out expression.

His Julia caught his face possessively between her palms. Oh, yeah, he loved this woman.

This time she fucked him, and she captured his gaze. "You're *mine.*"

And had been from the moment he'd first touched her. "Forever, my sweet."

Want to see more from this author? Here's a taster for you to enjoy!

Mastered: On His Terms

Sierra Cartwright

Excerpt

"There he is."

"Where?" Chelsea Barton craned her head to get a look at Master Alexander Monahan.

"Near the fireplace," her friend Sara said.

Chelsea glanced in that direction. Dressed in blue jeans, a long-sleeved, western-style shirt, a black leather vest, a silver bolo tie, and a cowboy hat, he didn't fit her image of a BDSM trainer. His height, though—over six feet tall—was definitely what she'd expected. The billionaire Dominant was as gorgeous as he was unapproachable.

"Quit staring!" Sara cautioned. "Good submissives don't behave that way."

That didn't stop Chelsea. Rules were helpful for other people. As for her, she ruthlessly pursued what she wanted. And she'd decided that Master Alexander would help her become the perfect sub—or at least passable enough that no one noticed if she wasn't really all that into it. That was step one in Project Snag Evan C.

Master Evan C was a rocker whose band was climbing the charts. With the right PR firm—*hers*—he could become a megastar. As a double bonus, her company would gain real credibility by signing the celebrity, which would in turn bring her the success she dreamed of…the success that proved she was worthwhile, despite what she'd been told her entire life.

So far, her efforts to ensnare his attention had been a dismal failure.

Six months ago, she'd met him at a party and had developed a certifiable fangirl crush on him. She fantasized about him tying her up and fucking her hard.

Chelsea wanted him. And not just as a client, but also as a Dominant and lover. What could be more fabulous than career success and having a sexy man to boot?

Sara, always the unwelcome pragmatist, had advised Chelsea to forget her ideas. Master Evan C liked well-trained submissives, women who subjugated their needs to suit his. Which, as Sara pointed out, really wasn't Chelsea. Chelsea was headstrong and determined, a driven achiever who chewed antacid for breakfast, suffered from rampant insomnia, and hadn't taken a vacation in over two years. That Master Evan C discarded women like the scarves he wore while performing made her even more resolved to succeed.

That was where Master Alexander came in.

According to Sara, he used to be a trainer, and he was still well respected in the community. He didn't get emotionally involved with subs, and he was one of the best.

"He's looking this way," Sara whispered.

"And he's alone, finally." When Chelsea had learned that Sara and Lyle—her Dom—had been invited to

Master Alexander's birthday party at the Den, Master Damien's luxury Colorado mountain retreat, Chelsea had begged, pleaded, and cajoled for an invitation.

At first, Sara had refused. She hadn't wanted to be part of any more of Chelsea's shenanigans. While Chelsea didn't blame her friend—after all, their last escapade had earned Sara a punishment from Lyle—Chelsea refused to be deterred. "If you'll excuse me…"

"Remember, you don't know me."

She gave her friend a false smile. "Have we met?" After setting her shoulders, Chelsea headed straight for Master Alexander.

A couple stopped to talk to him. Foiled, she paused to grab a glass of sparkling water from a passing server. She was woman enough to appreciate the hottie. He wore a bow tie, but no shirt, and it looked as if he could have been poured into his dress slacks. The material revealed his muscular thighs as well as his hot rear. And she supposed it was possible he had oil rubbed on his bare chest.

With a nod, he said, "Enjoy your evening, ma'am."

Maybe she'd hire this crew for her next event. It would certainly be a shocker, earn her some much-appreciated publicity.

Rather than taking a drink, she rolled the glass between her palms and waited for her chance to approach Master Alexander. Finally, the couple moved off.

After putting down her drink she walked toward him. Damn, his cowboy hat made him look like an outlaw.

He rested his forearm on the mantelpiece and studied her intently as she approached. Even from several feet away, he exuded power.

Calling on the bravado that she suddenly needed, she continued on.

When she stopped near him, he swept his gaze over her, from the toes of her pumps to the top of the shiny clips she'd placed in her short hair.

He didn't greet her. Instead, he waited. That didn't surprise her. She'd done plenty of research on him and learned he was inflexible, a formidable foe in the business arena despite his recent setbacks. "Mr. Monahan, I'm Chelsea Barton." She extended her hand and gave him her most dazzling smile. The look was practiced. She could charm anyone with it. "I wanted to wish you a very happy birthday."

"Did you?" Finally, he dropped his arm to accept her hand.

His grip was warm, firm, reassuring. Electricity shimmied up her spine. This close, he was even more gorgeous. Small lines were etched next to his captivating green eyes, and his lips were firm and full. The crazy notion of kissing him skipped through her mind before she ruthlessly shoved it away. She had a business proposition for him, nothing more.

When he released her, she was strangely bereft. "Who are you here with, Ms. Barton?"

"Uh…a friend," she hedged.

"Are you always evasive?"

"Are you always so direct?"

He folded his arms across his magnificent chest. "Save us both some time and cut through the bullshit. It's my birthday, my party, and I approved the guest list. I saw you speaking with Sara. As she is pretending not to look at us, I assume you wanted to meet me for a specific reason. Because I'm feeling generous, I'll give you thirty seconds. Start talking."

Suddenly she wished she'd taken a drink of that water. "You're right," she confessed. Because he was direct, she responded in kind. "I came here specifically to meet you." Quickly she added, "But not for the reason you might think." She hoped that comment was intriguing enough to buy her an extra minute of his time. "I own a company named You're The Star. We do PR."

"Monahan Capital has a PR firm."

"Who should have done a better job of spinning the Bartholomew deal initially, but they've been passable since then." When all he did was arch an eyebrow, she pushed on. "However, if you did a couple of events in the community, such as a fundraiser, your positive press would shove the other headlines from the first page of the search engines. But that's not my point." Since he was still listening, she kept talking. "I sought you out because I want you to train me as a submissive, and I understand that you're the best."

"At one time that was true."

From his mouth, his flat statement didn't sound arrogant.

"But I'm quite sure you've heard I don't train anymore."

She pushed back the trepidation that had started doing the backstroke in her veins. The years had taught her a valuable lesson—when she wasn't getting what she wanted, she needed to turn up the charm.

Gently, she placed her hand on his arm. When he didn't react, she continued, "I'm sure a man as discerning as you has high expectations and demands excellence. I understand that it comes at a cost. Name your price, and I'll write you a check."

He didn't respond to her tactics. In fact, his jawline could have been chiseled from granite. "I'm not for sale, Ms. Barton."

She gave up on charm and dropped her hand.

From the corner of her eye, she noticed Evan C and a woman were heading toward the stairs. Although she hadn't seen it, she understood Master Damien had a dungeon with some private playrooms. Seeing Evan C with someone who should have been her only increased her resolve. "You're a businessman. Better than anyone, you understand that everyone has a price."

"What's yours?" Master Alexander countered. "Selling your soul for success?"

"That's harsh." Chelsea blinked. "You don't know anything about me."

"On the contrary. I know you will use manipulation in order to get what you want."

She pulled back.

"If you want this conversation to continue, be honest." His tone was as icy as a cold front that raged down from the Arctic.

Chelsea had not expected this to be so difficult. She'd figured most Doms would love to have a sub begging for their attention. Her offer of money should have sealed the deal. "I want Evan C to hire my company and accept me as his submissive."

"And you think some training will intrigue him?"

"It will."

"You sound convinced."

She recalled the party they'd been at. "He snubbed me once because I was too new." Seeing him toss his scarf over his shoulder as he'd walked away had stung.

"What kind of experience do you have?" Master Alexander asked.

"Not much," she admitted reluctantly.

"Be specific."

"How much information do you want?"

He captured her chin, ignoring the way she'd tipped it stubbornly.

She was tall, especially in her spiked 'fuck-me' heels, but he still towered over her by several inches. Since she was accustomed to looking men in the eye as they spoke, having to look up was a little disconcerting. For one of the first times in her life, she felt small, overpowered.

His fingers were strong and firm, as unrelenting as the glint of steel in his eyes. "I'll tell you when I've heard enough."

She tried, and failed, to hide her shiver. For the first time in her life, she wondered if she'd set her sights too high. He'd seen her subterfuge and cut through it—despite the fact she'd become a master at it.

Once she exhaled, he released his grip.

When one of the servers came near, she signaled for a glass of wine, needing the fortification. She had no problem at all promoting others or her firm. But exposing her secrets? That required courage.

She took a long drink of her wine, then held on to the stem as if it were a lifeline. "I didn't know I liked kink until one of my boyfriends blindfolded me."

"What did you like about the experience?"

Several Doms and subs moved into the living room, and she looked around nervously.

"Eyes on me," he instructed.

You're relentless. She caught a glimpse of what he might be like as a trainer, and it terrified her as much as it intrigued her.

"Or excuse yourself now."

She looked up from where she'd been staring into the depths of her wine.

He missed nothing.

"I liked that I had no idea what would happen next. My hearing seemed heightened. And when he touched me, the sensation was magnified."

"Go on."

"One guy would sometimes swat my bottom when I passed him." She had no idea this would be so embarrassing. There was nothing sexual about the conversation, rather, the facts were somewhat clinical. But that didn't stop her from blushing. "Last Halloween, I attended a BDSM party. Compared to this…" She swept her hand around. The gathering at Master Damien's house was for people who lived the lifestyle. "It's clear now that most of us were just dabbling. We wore outfits we bought at the costume store, but afterward my date tied me up for the first time. It was just to his bed, and he used a light whip on my ass. I liked it. Well, enough to explore more, but he said it really hadn't worked for him all that well. He didn't like hurting me. Even though I promised him he hadn't."

"You're telling me most vanilla guys aren't interested in spanking an ass like that?"

She blinked.

"I noticed you when you first came in, and you wore that skirt hoping I would."

"Yes," she admitted. "I did." It was one size smaller than she bought for business meetings, and she'd never wear it out in public. The material hugged her rear so tight she was nervous about sitting down.

"So show me."

"I beg your pardon?"

"Lift your skirt to your waist, turn around, spread your legs as far as you can, then bend over and grab your ankles."

For a moment she could hardly breathe. He said nothing further and he looked unconcerned, as if it didn't matter to him one way or another whether she did as he said. She recognized the order as his first test.

He extended his hand to take her glass. That was probably for the best—she was suddenly afraid of dropping it. He slid the stemware onto the mantel, then used his thumb to tip back his cowboy hat.

She pulled up her skirt and she was grateful she'd worn a thong. Exposing herself to a stranger was far different than playing with a man she'd been dating.

Master Alexander continued to say nothing. She realized then that he was a man of few words, and he didn't repeat himself. There was no cajoling from him, no teasing, no 'Oh, come on, Chelsea, have a little fun'. This man was a Dominant all the way to his core.

Mouth dry, she turned away from him and followed the rest of his instructions. For at least sixty interminable seconds, he said nothing. Her heart thundered. The tops of her shoes dug into her ankles, and blood rushed to her head.

"This is the ass you've had a difficult time convincing men to spank?"

"Yes," she said. Then she wondered what the protocol was for addressing him. Sir? Mr. Monahan? Master? Alex? Alexander?

He caressed both her bare butt cheeks.

Slowly she began to relax.

Other people continued to move through the rooms, and a man stopped to talk to him. He removed one hand and continued to rub her with the other.

This was awful, humiliating. She wasn't accustomed to being exposed, unseen, completely ignored.

Horrified, she started to stand, but, saying nothing, he pinched her upper thigh.

Though she yelped, she forced herself to stay in position, fighting off her instinct to stand, drop her skirt and get the hell away from him.

Instead, she drew on the determination that had seen her work two jobs through college. Now, like then, she kept her eyes on the goal.

Eventually, the man moved off. Although he kept one hand on her, Master Alexander still didn't speak, leaving her with no idea what to do.

Right then, he slapped her left buttock, hard. She cried out, more from shock than because it had hurt.

"You did well for a beginner. Stand, pull your skirt down, then face me."

As she followed his instructions, her legs quivered. In the last three minutes, she'd had a bigger taste of BDSM than she'd had in the last six months. She wasn't sure she liked it.

"Tell me about your thoughts while you were bent over."

"I felt nervous and exposed."

"And how did you feel when I smacked you?"

"I was startled, I suppose. And I didn't like how impersonal your touch was. I could have been anyone."

"Was it difficult for you to remain in position?"

She reached for her glass of wine and took a deep drink. "Yes."

"Why?"

The question vexed her, and she snapped her answer. "This isn't supposed to be an exploration into my psyche."

"Anyone who engages in BDSM with me opens every part of themselves. It's your choice." He shrugged. "Leave at any time."

Chelsea had spent years shielding herself from criticism, so much so that she rarely shared her innermost thoughts with anyone, even close friends. But this man was demanding access to her emotions, requiring vulnerability that made her shake. Since she had no other option, she opened up a little. "I don't like to be left out. When you ignored me like that? Frankly it pissed me off."

"Yet you stayed in position. Why?"

"Because I want you to train me. And I wanted to show you I can do it."

"Very good. By the way, you have a very spankable ass. It turned bright red with my handprint."

No doubt the color matched her face.

"Being a submissive is very different from being tied up, wearing a blindfold, or even getting a spanking. What you just experienced is a sample of what my submissives endure."

Wildly she wondered if she had any idea what she was asking for.

"Doms typically adore and cherish their subs. Some couples, as you may have ascertained, indulge like you and your previous boyfriends, just with a few more rules and a bit more regularity. They may even use the words Dominant and submissive. To me, submission comes with strict protocols, with service, along with delicate body movements."

"What you just showed me… I didn't know it would be that hard core."

"Go on."

"The whole being submissive thing…" She worried her lower lip. Once she realized she was doing it, she stopped immediately. Her mother had spent years reinforcing what an awful habit that was. How would Chelsea ever capture a husband if she couldn't be more elegant? "I guess I thought it was mostly about getting spankings and being tied up."

"It's more a state of mind," he informed her. "What you're talking about falls under the broad umbrella of bondage and discipline. And it could just be added kink in an otherwise vanilla relationship. But submission is about putting someone else's needs before your own. And you do it from a genuine desire to serve, not because you see it as a means to an end. Most of all, it's about mutual trust."

His words landed like a chastisement.

"I appreciate your honesty," he said. "I'm sure you will be able to find a man to spank you."

Realizing he was dismissing her, she made a desperate offer. "Are you interested? I mean, it is your birthday, and someone should get a spanking, and I'm guessing you won't be baring your butt."

"Quite correct."

She wished he'd tip his sexy cowboy hat back once more so she could read his expression better. "You could consider it a birthday present."

"I'm not interested in giving you a spanking. And it has nothing to do with your delectable derrière. As I mentioned, my subs have a desire to serve. Which you do not."

While she hadn't liked being ignored, or the nasty little pinch, she had liked his firm command and the way he'd so masterfully swatted her. It had stung. But it had also warmed her skin, leaving her turned on. "Please, I implore you to reconsider." After all, she could do anything she set her mind to. "You won't be disappointed in me. I promise you that."

Just then, Master Damien called for everyone's attention.

Standing next to each other, she and Alexander turned.

Sara had told Chelsea that the Den's owner could have been a movie star. He had long, dark hair that was secured at his nape. Leather pants highlighted his strong muscles, and a short-sleeved black T-shirt revealed a tattoo she couldn't quite make out.

Some Doms and Dommes urged their subs to their knees for the announcement. Those instructed verbally or through hand commands knelt without complaint.

Now she understood Master Alexander's point. No one else appeared to rebel against the indignity the way she instinctively had.

When the crowd fell silent, Master Damien went on. "We're celebrating Master Alexander's birthday tonight." He beckoned to a woman who pushed a rolling cart into the living room. A half-sheet cake was ablaze with dozens of candles.

He began to sing the happy birthday song—too bad Master Evan C wasn't in the room—and others joined in.

When the terrible rendition ended and the guests applauded, Master Alexander blew out the candles. And because she figured he wouldn't make a wish, she made one of her own.

"Thank you all! Being back is the best gift of all."

Once more, everyone cheered enthusiastically.

"Chelsea here will be helping to serve the cake," Master Alexander announced.

What? Furiously, stomach plunging, she scowled at him.

He leaned down to whisper in her ear. "Let's see how much you really want to be a sub."

No way could she do this. Cake cutting wasn't one of her skills. She could never get the pieces to stand up, and she always ended up with frosting all over her hands.

"You're going to help Brandy."

Be a server, as if she were his submissive?

"Follow her instructions." The command in his tone left no room for arguing. "And Chelsea? You're going to do it with a smile."

To get her going, he placed his fingers against the small of her back and gave her a gentle nudge.

Having no other choice other than to flat out refuse, Chelsea accepted the pearlescent handle from Brandy.

"You do that while I remove the candles," Brandy suggested.

The same man who'd brought her wine earlier carried over a stack of plates.

After cutting a bunch of jagged lines, she picked up the cake spatula and transferred the corner piece onto a plate.

"Since it's his birthday, go ahead and take the first slice to Master Alexander," Brandy said kindly.

"Me?"

"I get the idea that would be his preference. I'll take care of Master Damien, then the hired staff will help us with everyone else."

Chelsea took the plate to him, hiding her internal snarl behind a smile.

"Not good enough. Try again," he said.

Are you serious right now? "Excuse me?"

"Watch Brandy."

As she moved toward Master Damien, she kept her head tipped. She extended the plate and, when he accepted, she offered the fork and napkin as one package.

Chelsea scowled. Considering the ridiculous number of etiquette classes her mother had made her take, she should have noticed. Of course, Mother anticipated Chelsea would go on to be an executive's wife. As such, she'd need to be able to be his hostess. Never in a million years would Marjorie have expected her only daughter to bare her rear in front of a roomful of people.

"Watch what I do." Brandy gave a brief, perfectly executed curtsy.

Chelsea's mouth opened as she rounded on him. "You expect me to do *that?*"

"You would receive this kind of instruction as part of your training." He studied her. "If you'd like to proceed, return to the cart and try again. This time with much more decorum."

Cheeks burning with frustration, she carried the plate back.

A tall, good-looking man with the air of a pirate was standing near the tray, arms folded across his chest. His shoulders and chest were massive, and she wouldn't have been surprised to learn he played professional football. Or maybe he made a living as a bouncer.

"No one is looking at you."

"I beg your pardon?"

"Almost everyone here is with a sub, or they've been around the lifestyle for years. All subs have their behavior corrected from time to time. It's totally natural." He smiled and set her at ease. "I'm Gregorio," he explained. "I work with Master Damien here and I take care of the Den."

"And that includes reassuring wannabe subs?"

His silver earring winked in the overhead light. "My jobs are many and varied."

"I'm not even his sub. I just want him to train me."

"So, he's seeing if you're worth the effort?"

"He turned me down."

"Has he?" his voice was edged with skepticism. "I'd say he's intrigued. You found a way to get an invite to a private party to meet him. So don't give up yet, unless you've decided it's not for you. In that case, move on and find someone who shares your kink."

She nodded.

"Are you planning to take the cake back to him?"

After thinking about it for a few seconds, she softly sighed. "Yes."

"Are you right-handed?"

"I am."

"In that case, I recommend you carry the plate in your left hand. Wrap the napkin around the fork and carry those in your right hand. Keep your head down, gaze lowered. At this point, he won't be expecting you to kneel. Concentrate on the pleasure he will receive from your actions. Offer the fork and napkin first, and then seamlessly transfer the plate to your right hand so you have no awkwardness. The most important thing with service is to think about things ahead of time, plan them out, but have the room to be flexible if your Dom desires it."

No doubt Gregorio was correct. Master Alexander had already said that, service was part of submission. "What about that little curtsy thing?"

"You can manage something, I'm sure. Bonus points if you use the term Sir or Master Alexander when you address him."

"Right now, I'm not sure I can remember my own name."

"That's why you need to concentrate on him, not yourself. Don't overthink," he added. "Try to be natural. You will screw up. Everyone does. Just accept the correction without taking it personally. As I'm sure Master Alexander has already advised, give yourself over to the experience of pleasing your Dom. Get out of your own way, allow someone else be the center of your universe. If you're a submissive, you'll be fulfilled from pleasing him. It's not for everyone. In fact, it's not for most people."

Before she could thank him, he had moved off. Surreptitiously she watched another server. Cake was offered one way to Doms, and a little less formally to subs. Some Doms accepted a piece for themselves but refused one for their submissives. A male sub was hand-fed.

One server was directed to place a plate on the floor. The blonde didn't hesitate before lowering herself to all fours and starting to eat. Her Domme placed the spiked heel of her boot on the girl's shoulder while tasting her own dessert and conversing with another Domme.

As Gregorio had observed, no one seemed to notice.

But the more she saw, the more she questioned the path she'd set for herself.

At that moment Master Evan C entered the room, electrifying the atmosphere with his energy. The woman he'd been to the dungeon with looked beautiful with her smile and tracks from tears staining her cheeks. She walked over to the tray and carefully selected a plate for him, and she looked happy to do so. If others could find pleasure in this, so could Chelsea.

Doubly resolved, she straightened her spine, picked up Master Alexander's plate, along with the utensils. As she moved toward him once more, she focused on the act of serving him, ignoring the little voice protesting what she was doing. "Happy birthday, Sir."

"Thank you," he replied. "But I've changed my mind about having cake."

Aggravation flared. Just in time, she bit back her instinctive curse. "Of course, Sir."

"I've decided I'd rather give you a birthday spanking after all."

About the Author

Sierra Cartwright was born in Manchester, England and raised in Colorado. Moving to the United States was nothing like her young imagination had concocted. She expected to see cowboys everywhere, and a covered wagon or two would have been really nice!

Now she writes novels as untamed as the Rockies, while spending a fair amount of time in Texas…where, it turns out, the Texas Rangers law officers don't ride horses to roundup the bad guys, or have six-shooters strapped to their sexy thighs as she expected. And she's yet to see a poster that says Wanted: Dead or Alive. (Can you tell she has a vivid imagination?)

Sierra wrote her first book at age nine, a fanfic episode of Star Trek when she was fifteen, and she completed her first romance novel at nineteen. She actually kissed William Shatner (Captain Kirk) on the cheek once, and she says that's her biggest claim to fame. Her adventure through the turmoil of trust has taught her that love is the greatest gift. Like her image of the Old West, her writing is untamed, and nothing is off-limits.

She invites you to take a walk on the wild side…but only if you dare.

Sierra loves to hear from readers. You can find her contact information, website details and author profile page at https://www.totallybound.com

TOTALLY
BOUND
Home of Erotic Romance

www.ingramcontent.com/pod-product-compliance
Lightning Source LLC
LaVergne TN
LVHW091032080826
845145LV00002B/455

* 9 7 8 1 8 0 2 5 0 5 5 7 3 *